# DETACHMENT
## BLAKE BRIER BOOK SIX

## L.T. RYAN

### WITH
### GREGORY SCOTT

Copyright © 2022 by L.T. Ryan, Gregory Scott, and Liquid Mind Media, LLC. All rights reserved. No part of this publication may be copied, reproduced in any format, by any means, electronic or otherwise, without prior consent from the copyright owner and publisher of this book. This is a work of fiction. All characters, names, places and events are the product of the author's imagination or used fictitiously.

For information contact:

Contact@ltryan.com

https://LTRyan.com

https://www.facebook.com/JackNobleBooks

# THE BLAKE BRIER SERIES

### Blake Brier Series

*Unmasked*
*Unleashed*
*Uncharted*
*Drawpoint*
*Contrail*
*Detachment*
*Untitled (coming soon)*

# PROLOGUE

ROBBIE NOVAK PATTED HIS POCKETS. Front and back. He didn't need instructions, but he got them anyway.

"Phone, keys, wallet. All electronic devices. Anything on your person goes in the tray." The kid's muscular arm wobbled as he held out the gray plastic busboy bin like a beggar at the end of an I-95 exit ramp.

Robbie wiped an emerging band of sweat from his hairline, gave an unnecessary scan of the empty lobby, then glanced at the canvas name tag sewn to the puffed-up chest of the nineteen-year-old MP.

*Private First Class Carson.*

Carson's combat uniform carried an 82nd Airborne Division patch and, like most everyone else at Fort Bragg, a set of embroidered jump wings. Despite the connotation, he wore a black beret, instead of the division's typical maroon headgear. Young Carson was likely what paratroopers liked to call a "five jump chump."

Five jumps were what the Army required to graduate from jump school. But it wasn't uncommon for a guy to get his wings and take up an assignment with a "leg unit," never to jump again. Sure, the patch said Airborne, but Carson's real MOS appeared to be babysitting a glorified mailroom. And boy, did he take the job seriously.

"This is all I got." Robbie held his phone in one hand and his overstuffed carbon fiber credit card clip in the other. He twisted his wrists in a flourish before dropping the two items into the bin.

"Step through, Staff Sergeant."

Aside from a click and a green LED, the magnetometer had no complaints.

"Stop there. Spread your legs." Carson unsheathed a metal-detecting wand and began waving it around Robbie's body, starting at his ankles and working his way upward. As Carson reached his shoulder, Robbie noticed a change in the kid's expression. A glimmer of hesitation.

Robbie could guess why the kid paused. Carson had noticed the three tabs accompanying his unit patch, one positioned below the other: Special Forces, Ranger, Airborne.

The "Special Forces" tab, also called the "long tab," was only worn by current or former Green Berets. It wasn't what the tabs said that Carson had keyed in on. It was what they implied.

Nowhere on Robbie's uniform did it say, "1st Special Forces Operational Detachment-Delta," and it didn't have to. Robbie knew that Carson knew who he was. Or rather, who he was with. Task Force Green, or Delta Force as it's more commonly known.

Carson shouldn't have counted it as an amazing feat of deduction. After all, they were standing inside the Special Operations Command Records Annex. Then again, Carson didn't seem to be the sharpest tool in the shed.

Peculiar, Robbie thought, how rank seemed to mean little to the younger generation. But every bright-eyed, protein-guzzling lunk looked up to the guys in the Unit. Feared them, even.

"You have a good day, Sergeant," Carson handed Robbie his wallet with an awkward smile. "I'll secure your phone. You can grab it on the way out." His voice wavered. A forced swallow followed.

It eased Robbie's mind. Just a bit. As if Carson's nervousness were a shield against the danger of slipping up and revealing his own. In the past, he had thought he was good at suppressing anxiety in stressful situations, but it occurred to him now that it was only because he had never felt any. *There's a first for everything*, he thought. "Thank you Private. Don't work too hard."

Robbie moved to the inner glass doors. A buzz and a clicking sound rang out before he even reached out to pull the vertical handle. He gave an appreciative hand gesture and passed into the secure part of the building.

For as long as he'd known First Lieutenant Darrell Graham—about two days fewer than he had been dating Darrell's sister Nicole—Robbie had never been to visit the man at work.

The facility was as unimpressive inside as it looked from the outside. Small compared to the expansive Special Operations Command Headquarters building, this annex was one of several allocated to Special Ops.

Manned by the "Dweebs," the short brick structure was nothing more than a big, ugly filing cabinet, tucked away in a cluster of other nondescript government bungalows, about a half mile from the main building. But to hear Darrell talk about it, it was the heart and soul of special operations.

Robbie felt for his stack of credit cards through the fabric of his fatigues.

*You can do this.*

He took a deep breath and walked through the empty corridor.

"Can I help you?" A female voice came from behind him.

Robbie turned to find the voice attached to a floating head popping out from one of the doorways. The woman's blonde hair was tied back tight. So tight that it appeared to tug at the corners of her eyes.

"Darrell Graham, ma'am."

"Last door on the left," she said. Her head retreated.

Before carrying on, he took another moment. Another deep breath. Another affirmation. This was the right thing to do. He was sure of it. But that didn't make this any easier. Of all he had been through, how could this turn out to be the hardest?

The answer was obvious. It was his pride. Not in himself, but in his country.

For all practical purposes, today would be the day he threw it all away.

*It must be done. Someone has to do it.*

Robbie knocked. The door swung open.

"Robbie! Brother." Darrell leaned back and spread his arms as if welcoming an estranged child back into the fold.

"Hey Darrell." Robbie's lack of enthusiasm wasn't a product of his current predicament, or his apprehension. He had just never liked Darrell all that much.

Darrell, on the other hand, made a point to refer to Robbie as "brother" or "family" anytime they spoke.

These were terms that might well become true, but Robbie wasn't a hundred percent sure. He had no doubt that Nicole was getting antsy, but marriage was a big commitment and it had only been five years.

By military standards, Robbie was an old bachelor at twenty-seven. Most of his friends had been married before turning twenty-one. But it was much worse for Nicole. At twenty-four, she was an old maid. And her friends never let her forget it.

"You want anything? A Coke or something? We've got a machine."

"No, I'm good." Robbie put his hands in his pockets and looked around the small eight-by-eight cell of an office. "I know I keep saying I'll stop by, and I never get the chance, but today I was around and I figured—"

"Of course, brother. Glad ya did. I can give you a little tour if you want. This here's my humble abode, as you can see."

"It's great." Robbie pointed at a picture of himself and Nicole, which Darrell had printed on a piece of copy paper and scotch-taped to the wall next to his desk. "I remember that. The Military Ball. Fun night. Except for the thing with Jack and his girl."

"Yeah. They're back together, you know. She moved back in with him about two months ago. Guess she had gone out to California for a couple years. I saw him at Costco. He told me all about it."

Aside from Darrell's desk chair, there was another equally ratty looking seat stashed in the corner. With his palm, Robbie brushed what looked like crumbs from the brown upholstery but none of the spots budged. He sat anyway. "Do you mind if I–"

"Make yourself at home. You picked a good day. We got a lot of exciting stuff goin' on. There's this dedication for some memorial in

Nebraska. We've been tasked with digging through the paper files to find the original copies of commendations for the 134th Guard from World War II. They could be here. I mean, not in this building, we're only digital. But somewhere. Could also be Rucker, Pike, Dawson, no one's sure. NARA in St. Louis don't have them, as far as they say. Pretty interesting stuff."

"No doubt." Robbie glanced at his watch.

*Any minute now.*

"So you want me to show you around? I've just got to clear it first. But yeah, I can show you the server room and we've got a pretty cool break room with an almost full kitchen."

Robbie was in the middle of formulating an excuse when Darrell's desk phone rang.

"Hold that thought." Darrell picked up the phone. His dumb smile fell away and he spoke in a matter-of-fact tone. "Be right there." He hung up.

"What is it?"

"I've got to take an important call," Darrell answered.

"Do you want me to step out in the hall?"

"No. I can't take it here. These lines are only internal. We have a special room. Soundproof. Secure line."

Robbie nodded with feigned interest. Of course, he already knew all of this. It was for these very reasons that he had arranged for the call to be made. Darrell would be away from his office for only a few minutes. He only hoped it would be enough.

"Hang here for a couple of minutes. You're not in a rush are ya? I'll show you around when I get back. I'll show you the SCIF too. Just hang tight."

Darrell scurried off.

Robbie shook his head.

*Dweeb.*

Something about the familiarity of seeing Darrell had calmed his nerves. He no longer felt the stress of the act, only the pressure of time.

From his pocket, Robbie whipped out the stack of credit cards, sandwiched by two thin carbon fiber plates and two strips of elastic. He withdrew the entire stack and shook free the small thumb drive he had hidden inside.

As if a sort of divine sanction, Robbie recalled he had a stack of expired credit cards, hidden away toward the back of the top drawer in his bedroom bureau. Every time he added one to the stack, he'd remind himself to take them to the office to be shredded. And every time he'd forget they were there. This time, he'd remembered.

Pleased with his ingenious plan, he spent a half hour cutting the centers out of each card with an exacto knife until he could stack the cards together to create a mini-safe. Big enough to hide a single USB thumb drive.

Getting caught trying to smuggle a thumb drive into the facility was enough for a court martial. He'd have been better off leaving it in his pocket and saying he'd forgotten it was there.

But he was sure his plan was foolproof. The one thing they never checked was the one thing you handed over to them.

Even Carson.

Robbie didn't waste any time. He inserted the drive into the back of the black computer tower, sitting at the edge of the desk, and clicked the icon on the screen to open the Windows file explorer.

Computers weren't his specialty. Not by a longshot, but he knew his way around the system well enough. More importantly, he knew what he was looking for.

Incidents. Operations. They were all referenced by an alphanumeric code. Every document associated with a particular operation was named accordingly. It would only take a simple search, a wildcard operator, and a copy command to get it done. He had practiced the sequence on his own PC enough times over the past twenty-four hours.

Robbie punched at the keys, hit enter, and waited. An indicator moved from left to right. Slower than he'd hoped.

Much, much slower.

Seconds ticked by. One minute. Two.

Eighty percent. Eighty-two percent.

*Come on. Hurry up.*

Footsteps approached.

# DETACHMENT

*Damn it. Darrell.*

With a frantic quadruple click, Robbie opened the Internet Explorer web browser and maximized the screen.

A man appeared in the doorway. It wasn't Darrell.

"Where's Graham? Who are you?"

"I'm–" Robbie decided it would be best to leave his name out of the conversation. "–just visiting."

"Why are you on Lieutenant Graham's computer? Are you authorized? Let me see some identification."

"Hold on friend." Robbie raised his hands in the international sign for "calm down and slow your roll."

The man wearing the Captain's bars wasn't having it.

"Carson," he hollered. "Someone get Carson."

Robbie's mind spun. He was getting caught. No, he *was* caught. His career, his relationship, his future, down the tubes in the blink of an eye.

Why did he think he could pull this off? Why had he been so intent on doing this? These thoughts crept into his brain for a fleeting moment. They didn't linger. He knew why he was there. This was bigger than him. It was about truth. It was about blood.

*It had to be done. Someone had to try.*

Carson's boots clumped down the hallway.

"Hold on. Hold on Frank," the approaching man said with a voice a couple registers higher than Carson's. "He's my brother-in-law. It's alright, I just had to take a call."

"He's accessing your computer," the captain said.

Darrell pushed by his superior and stepped into the office.

"Robbie?"

"Sorry Darrell, I was just going to look something up on Google." Robbie stood and leaned over the tower as if diagnosing its hardware. "The internet's not working, maybe it's disconnected or something."

"We aren't connected to the Internet, Robbie. I told you this already. Many times. No connection to the outside world. Remember?"

Robbie withdrew his hand from behind the tower, taking care to keep the thumb drive tucked into his palm. He rotated his wrist to avoid flashing it to the two onlookers. "Of course! I remember that now. I'm a dumbass. Didn't mean to cause a shitstorm."

The captain scowled. "Visiting hours are over, Graham."

"Yes, sir."

As the captain walked away, Darrell also began moving into the hallway.

Robbie reached behind and pressed the power button on the front of the tower until the screen went black, then stepped into the hallway after his possible-future-brother-in-law.

"We'll have to do the tour another time," Darrell said.

"Sorry about that. Seems like I might have gotten you into some hot water."

"What, him? He's fine. He's always like that. It's all right, I've got a lot of work to do, anyway. We'll catch up soon. I'll have you and Nicole over the house. All right?" Darrell opened the glass door.

"Oh, Hey. Your phone call? Anything good?"

Darrell hissed. "There was no one on the line."

Robbie smiled and shrugged. "That's good. One less headache, right?"

"Sure." Darrell shrugged back at him. "Robbie?"

"Yeah?"

"Thanks for stopping in. I mean it."

"Had to be done, Darrell. I mean, someone had to do it."

# CHAPTER 1

RON PHILLIPS STARED at the images flickering across the large LCD screen at the far end of the table. The feed from the aging U-2 high altitude reconnaissance aircraft was crisp and clear, giving a perfect view of the unrest unfolding far beneath it.

President William Moore, sitting tall at the end of the table, rested his palms on a leather dossier. It was emblazoned with the seal of the President of the United States, like the chairs, the walls, and even the Windows 10 backgrounds of the various computer screens flanking the room.

The purpose of this pageantry was a mystery to Phillips. In the White House situation room, there was little risk of someone needing the reminder.

Moore cracked the binder. "Not everybody at once."

Based on Moore's stern expression, Phillips decided that the comment was intended less as a joke and more as an admonishment.

As a retired Vice Admiral with the United States Navy, Phillips' extensive combat experience usually made him the hardest man in the room. Especially when the room was full of politicians.

But Moore was a different kind of animal. He had been an investment banker most of his life but made his fortune more recently by running a large hedge fund that touted a sixty-three percent return. Whatever it took to accomplish that feat, Phillips could only assume it was akin to war.

Moore knew how to get what he wanted. And he was unshakeable. Phillips, more than anyone on the cabinet, found the quality admirable.

"Anyone?" Moore barked. "I've got a meeting with the Prime Minister in twenty-seven minutes."

"Of course, sir," David Butler started. "Things are degrading fast on the ground in Venezuela. As you can see."

Butler motioned to the glowing LCD panel over Moore's shoulder. Moore kept his gaze trained on the man.

Butler continued. "Langley's saying Maduro is already on the move. We've got an asset embedded in the Presidential Guard reporting Maduro's extrication from the palace. They're transporting him to a secure location near the Columbian border. We've already got eyes on a faction of soldiers who've amassed near a compound there. Just waiting for confirmation the President is present. We'll know more in the next couple of hours. I'll report to you directly, sir, as soon as we know."

David Butler, Director of National Intelligence, was a bona fide kiss-ass. At least in Phillips' estimation. He was a shyster. As unqualified as they come. Even if Moore didn't see it that way.

It wasn't the same for the others in the room.

The Secretary of State, Laurel Conway, was an example. A touch too meek for Phillips' liking, she was otherwise qualified and had repeatedly proven her acumen. Her competence was put to the test early on when tasked with negotiating the United States out of a precarious situation in the far east. Not only was crisis averted, but the U.S. came out ahead.

Then there was Irving Oakley. Vice President of the United States. What else needed to be said?

Oakley was a hell of a nice guy. A complete 'yes' man, granted, but Phillips didn't hold it against him. It came with the territory. Oakley was a man with no power, no purpose, no voice. Not as long as Moore was still breathing. And there was less than zero chance of that changing anytime soon.

Moore snapped the binder closed. "Tell me now. Is this our doing?"

# DETACHMENT

"No," Butler said. "It appears to be organic. We've seen no intelligence pointing to outside influence. It looks like the people just got fed up."

Phillips could buy it. He'd seen it the world over. Frustrations of an oppressed population boiling over. *Good for them*, he wanted to think. The truth was, he knew what everyone else in the room knew. It never ended well for the little guy.

"Do we have someone in place?" Moore asked. "As a contingency."

"We like Hernandez," Conway said. "He's risen to the top of the opposition. Emerged as the de facto leader. The people like him, and he's been very cooperative with us. It's the State Department's position that Hernandez is the best-case scenario."

"Good." Moore glanced over his shoulder at the screen. A large group of protesters pulsated against the gate as a collective battering ram. On the other side, a smaller group of soldiers waited with small arms at the ready. The resolution of the images was so great, Phillips could identify the make and model of their rifles.

Conway cleared her throat. "Sir, I must say I don't see it playing out. Even if they breach the grounds, even if they take over the palace, President Maduro's reach is wide. He won't miss a beat. Eventually, he'll have these protesters and their associates killed. Maduro will be back in the Palacio de Miraflores within the week."

Phillips had to agree. This was a flash in the pan. Yesterday, there were two dozen activists outside the Palacio de Miraflores. One leaked video goes viral on social media, a few hundred more people join the party, and it looks to the world like another Arab Spring. But it was all smoke and mirrors.

Sure, it was enough to send Nicolás Maduro into temporary Alamo mode, but he wasn't going anywhere. And, as far as Phillips was concerned, that was the way it should be.

Anyway, as Secretary of Defense, he needn't concern himself with local political matters outside of a war zone. At least that's the case he made to himself. And would make to the President. Of course, he had his own reasons for staying in the background on this one. Reasons he wouldn't be sharing. He'd hold his tongue for as long as Moore would let him.

"Never underestimate the downtrodden," Oakley said with an air of buoyancy.

"Thank you, Irving, for your assessment."

Moore's frosty tone hit its mark.

"I'm just saying–"

"Sir," Butler blurted. "I have a suggestion. May I speak freely?"

"Go, Dave."

"Mister President, this could be an excellent opportunity. Laurel's right, this probably won't amount to much, on its own. But most of the world is behind these kids. People *want* to see them win."

"I hope you're not saying what I think you're saying, David." Conway's face carried her disgust.

"Laurel, hold on." Moore leaned in. "What do you have in mind, Dave?"

"We know that Maduro's on the move, but no one else does. What if they breached the gates? What if it looked like they killed Maduro?"

"You're proposing we assassinate Maduro and make it look like a coup?" Oakley squinted, as if trying hard to see an alternative interpretation of Butler's suggestion. "Really?"

"That's ridiculous," Phillips said, breaking his self-imposed vow of silence. "You'll cause an international incident. If Putin hears whispers we've intervened against Russia's interests in Venezuela—and he will—we risk starting World War III. Anyway, do you have people on the ground, Dave? I hope there's a lot of them, because that compound will be swarming with highly trained guerilla fighters."

"We can't go through Martin on this one," Butler said. "Trust me. This isn't one for the CIA. It'll get out. It's got to stay off the Hill. Completely dark. It has to be you, Ron."

"Not happening." Phillips crossed his arms and leaned back in his chair.

"Can you put it together, Ron?" Moore asked.

"It's not a military matter," Phillips said. "Not by a long shot."

Moore slammed his fist onto the thick tabletop with a thud. "That's not what I asked. Can you put this in place? Off the record. Top tier. SEAL

Team 6, Echelon, whoever. Can you give me a team without the Joint Chiefs getting wind of it?"

Phillips felt the low ceilings and wooden paneling of the bunker squeeze in on him. Moore wasn't asking if Phillips could do it. Moore was asking if he needed to put someone else in Phillips' position who could. Phillips had seen the President replace others for less. And with everything he had going on, in Venezuela and elsewhere, Phillips couldn't afford to take the chance.

"Of course, Mister President. If that's the course of action you want to take, I will make it happen."

The truth was, Phillips wasn't sure it could be done. He had access to a team so far off the radar that the Pentagon wasn't even aware of them. But these were his own men. Cultivated over years for his protection and for the furtherance of his own ventures.

Moore would want answers. Details. Phillips couldn't risk exposing his men. Besides, he was sure they would succeed. In this case, success was not the desired outcome.

No, this would have to go through legitimate channels. They'd tip off the Joint Chiefs, that was certain. By that point, it'd be too late.

Moore was known for making quick decisions with little information. No matter how reckless the decision seemed later, he had never once reversed one. If Moore was set on going through with this, Phillips would have no choice but to pull the strings.

"I can't believe we're even talking about this," Conway said.

"Laurel." Moore's voice took on a soothing timbre. The kind of half-baked empathy that won him the election in the first place. "Throughout history, a lot of tough decisions have been made in this very room. Horrible acts for the good of all. It's a dirty job, Laurel. Don't lose your spine on me now."

Conway laughed. "You think I care about Maduro? I just don't think this is the smart play. There's too much at stake if something goes wrong. We're pressuring him with the embargo. The sanctions. And Maduro's leaky government is giving us an inside track on Russia. Hernandez is promising, but we need to bide our time."

"Come on, Bill," Oakley stood up and rested his palms on the table.

"This would break every international law and treaty known to man. Not to mention the havoc it will wreak on the crude oil markets."

Moore stood to meet him. He was Oakley's superior in every sense of the word. "If I wanted an economic advisor, I would have called Jack in. Tell me, Irving, is this the hill you want to die on?"

Phillips chuckled. That was something he would have said.

"No," Oakley said. "It's your decision."

"Damn right it is. Dave, I want every bit of intel you have. Laurel, have your people sure things up with Hernandez. Ron, I want that team ASAP."

As Moore moved to leave, Butler sprung to his feet. The rest of the group followed suit.

"I want an update this evening. Set it up with Cathy. I'm off to have a spot of tea and pretend it doesn't taste like dirt. Let's get this done, people." Moore hurried out.

With POTUS absent, the room took a sign of relief.

Except for Phillips.

For him, things had just gotten complicated.

# CHAPTER 2

BLAKE KICKED his feet onto the massive coffee table and leaned back into the plush chenille cushions.

It had only been two weeks since the sectional arrived. Up until then, the area had been more of a staging area for tools and equipment. At that point, the room was cold. Cavernous. Now, even though the new furniture did little to fill the space, it was beginning to feel like a home.

Blake took a moment to breathe it all in. The "great room" they called it. Thirty-foot ceilings, a large stone fireplace that Ian could almost stand up inside, and enough floor space to park a dump truck.

Despite its size, it was the most comfortable and inviting room in the house. Everyone said it. Blake figured it was due to the floor-to-ceiling windows that wrapped the perimeter on two sides. At least, that was what he liked most about it. It was like being outdoors. And as the great room was open to the kitchen, it was a perfect place to commune.

Fezz, Griff, Khat, Kook, Ima and Ian, Blake and Haeli. They all had their own suites upstairs, complete with a sitting area, workspace, and bathroom, customized to their own specs. Still, everyone seemed to prefer spending most of their time in the common areas.

And today was no different.

"Care for some company?" Haeli kicked her shoes off and hopped on Blake's lap. He shifted to avoid the bony part of her butt jabbing his groin.

"How do you know I wasn't going to say no?"

Haeli answered by leaning in and pressing her lips to his. She lingered for a moment, then pulled away, but not before giving Blake's bottom lip a playful tug with her teeth.

As if by magnetic force, Blake's mouth tried to follow hers. She pulled back further.

"That's how." She grinned.

"Get a room," Fezz called out from the kitchen.

Fezz had been standing at the kitchen island for the past ten minutes, some thirty feet behind them, building a sandwich. Blake hadn't checked on his progress, but he could imagine the skyscraper of meat, cheese, and condiments that must have been coming together.

"Hope you're sharing, pal." Blake smiled and waited for Fezz's snide reply.

It didn't come.

"Sure, I'll make you one."

Blake grabbed Haeli by the hips and moved her onto a cushion next to him. He twisted around on his knee to see Fezz. "You okay Fezz? I mean, you feelin' all right?"

Fezz chuckled. "Do you want a sandwich or not?"

"I'll take his if he doesn't want it," Haeli said.

"I'll make you one, too. How 'bout that?"

"Did you sneak a girl in here last night?" Blake leaned over the back of the couch. "You're like a new man today."

"I'm in a good mood. What can I say?" Fezz slammed the bread knife into the foot-long grinder and sawed through it with two strokes. "What do you two have planned today?"

Blake shrugged. "Griff and I are going to finish that wiring in the bunker. That's about it."

"So much for going to dinner tonight," Haeli said. She picked up the remote, flicked on the ninety-inch television screen hanging above the mantle, and sank back into her seat.

"We're still going," Blake said. "Griff and I only need a couple more hours down there. The day is young."

"Did I hear my name?" Griff asked before bounding down the stairs. "Whoa, Fezz, three grinders. Working up an appetite?"

"They're not for me. They're for these ungrateful slugs."

"Wait," Griff held out his hand. "You're making sandwiches for everyone?"

"Not for everyone." Fezz slapped a piece of roast beef on the pile.

"Everyone but you," Blake jabbed.

"Okay. I see how it is." Griff circled around the arm of the sectional and plopped down in the first seat. "I didn't want one, anyway."

"Oh, stop your cryin'," Fezz said. "I'll make you one."

Blake grabbed Griff's attention, flicked his thumb in Fezz's direction, and feigned a whisper. "He snuck in a girl last night."

Griff gave an exaggerated nod. "That explains it."

Blake sat back down next to Haeli and pulled her in close. "Griff, I was just saying that we're going to shoot to finish that wiring today. We might even be able to set up some of the equipment."

"I hope so."

"We're definitely not making it to dinner," Haeli scoffed.

"Hey party-people," Khat grumbled from the top of the stairs. "What y'all doing?"

"Holy crap, it's Justin Bieber!" Griff patted his chest and then fanned himself with his hand. "I love you, Justin."

Haeli giggled.

For the past few weeks, Khat had been growing out his facial hair. It wasn't horrible. Just a little spotty. But everyone knew they could get a rise out of him. So, of course, they did. Day and night. Even little Ian had gotten in on the action.

"Funny." Khat moseyed down the steps and wandered toward the kitchen.

"Just woke up, did ya?" Fezz asked.

"No." Khat paused, pursing his lips. "Well, kind of, yeah."

"I figured. The five o'clock shadow gave it away."

"Don't be jealous that I look like John Wick, and you don't."

Blake laughed out loud. "You look more like John Wick's dog."

"Yeah," Fezz said, "if John Wick's dog was a prepubescent cancer patient."

"Screw y'all, I'm goin' back upstairs." Khat took three steps, then stopped. He scurried to the kitchen counter, and grabbed one of Fezz's grinders with two hands before stomping back up the steps.

"Hey, that better not have been my sandwich," Blake called after him.

"Relax," Fezz said. "It was Griff's."

"Oh, come on." Griff hopped up and bolted up the stairs after Khat.

Fezz walked over and, as if conducting a ceremony, bestowed a plate holding two delicious-looking hoagies on Blake and Haeli. Blake took the plate and placed it on the coffee table.

"Thanks, brother. Looks fantastic."

Fezz sat and began stuffing his face. He spoke with his mouth full. "Are the roofers coming today?"

After it had rained two days prior, Fezz noticed a wet spot on the ceiling inside the guest house. The guys who installed the roof were experts, but as with any new construction, sometimes little tweaks were needed after the fact. It wasn't a problem. Terrance, the owner, guaranteed the work and promised to send a couple of workers back out as soon as they had a minute.

"No. Looks like tomorrow or the next day. It's not supposed to rain for the rest of the week though."

"My guys are coming in around three." Fezz said through another mouthful. "F.Y.I."

"Are we ever going to get to see this masterpiece?" Haeli asked.

"It's close. Real close." Fezz said.

When the initial construction was done, Fezz announced he wanted to run with an idea he had for one of the rooms on the first floor. In the original plans, it was supposed to be a movie theater. But Fezz was so excited, everyone agreed to let him do whatever he wanted with the space.

Blake liked the idea of the surprise. It was the reason he had made it a point not to peek. And as far as he knew, no one else had either. The only thing they knew was that it wasn't a movie theater.

"Does that mean we have to clear out again?" Haeli asked.

# DETACHMENT

"If you don't mind," Fezz said. "Probably just need one or two more days. If my guys can get everything they need."

"I'll be in the basement all afternoon." Blake said. "I'll be out of your hair."

"Maybe Ima will want to go for a run," Haeli said. "Or maybe we'll go shopping. Where is Ima, anyway? Is she in her quarters?"

Fezz jammed the last eighth of the immense sandwich into his mouth. Then held his index finger out while he chewed it enough to manage forming words. "She took Ian to McQuade's. And she may have been stopping at the park. I don't know."

The mention of McQuade's Market sent a shiver down Blake's spine. It reminded him of Lucas. Or Robert Foster, to be more precise. Blake could still hear the quirky guy telling him about how he'd walk to McQuade's to pick up groceries for his aunt. He had taken such a liking to Lucas. At the time, he would have never guessed the guy would have turned out to be a monster. It was surreal how he gravitated back to this island, the small town of Jamestown, after all that had happened here.

But like all the other places in the world where bad things have happened—which, if Blake had done his math correctly, was everywhere—he'd have to learn to live with it. Live in it.

Christa, Gwyn, and Lucy were there. And now, his own chosen family was there. And that was all that mattered.

These were special days. When the construction was all done, when the tedium of normal life set in and the team was ready to answer the self-imposed call of duty, Blake knew the darker times would come. They always did. And these lazy days would have new meaning.

*Best enjoy them while we can.*

Blake picked up his sandwich and took a hardy bite.

"This is fantastic," he mumbled. "Thanks, Fezz."

Fezz grimaced. "Don't talk with your mouth full." He shook his head. "It's disgusting."

# CHAPTER 3

GENERAL JOHN "BUCK" Novak gripped the single sheet of paper with both hands. He had read it three times already.

His gaze jumped around the page, picking off random words and phrases, as if examining individual pieces of a jigsaw puzzle. "United States Department of Defense. Top Secret. Eyes Only. SECDEF. Effective Immediately."

The three main paragraphs of the order were clear and concise, but still made little sense. In all his years, Novak had not seen an official order quite like this one.

Novak stood and parted the blinds. He peered out across the hall. Through the smudged-glass window of his office, he saw Lieutenant General Kieran Brown listening with intensity to the business end of his desk phone's handset.

The message had been clear. Novak was to speak to no one about the operation, other than those responsible for carrying out the directive.

Even without reaching, this left some room for interpretation, he decided. Brown was integral to USSOCOM. And as his deputy commander, Brown deserved to be in the loop. Novak needed someone to be.

As soon as Brown hung up the phone, Novak cracked the door and called out, "Kieran. Come in here for a minute."

Fifteen thousand people worked at McDill Air Force Base every day.

Four percent of the population of Tampa. Buck Novak didn't trust any of them as much as he trusted Kieran Brown.

"What's going on?" Kieran said.

"Sit. I want you to look at something. This stays in this room. Agreed?"

Brown had the same top-level clearance as Novak did. Showing the order to Brown wasn't a legal issue, but an ethical one. It wasn't meant for Brown's eyes. But if Novak wanted a sanity check from anywhere, it would be from Brown.

"Of course." Kieran said.

Novak handed him the sheet of paper.

Brown read in silence.

Novak could have explained the situation to him, but it was something Brown would have to see to believe. An order from Ron Phillips to assassinate the Venezuelan president wasn't something any of them had expected to see come across their desk. Not today. Not ever.

Not that these types of actions didn't happen, but they were usually shadowy plots, orchestrated by the CIA and carried out by nationals. There was a possibility that the CIA's Special Activities Division would carry out something like this, if provided enough cover. But this was different. This involved the men and women of traditional special operations. Men and women unaccustomed to bathing in this level of filth.

"Wow." Brown said.

"'Wow'? That's it?"

"I don't know what to say, Buck. To be honest, I wish you hadn't shown me that."

"Sorry, it's just... I needed to bounce this off someone. And I trust you."

Brown handed Novak the sheet of paper. "What's there to bounce off? He's spelled it out. They want Delta. What else do you need to know? Pass it down to JSOC."

Brown was stating the obvious. Preparation and direct oversight of the mission would fall on the Joint Special Operations Command out of Fort Bragg, North Carolina. The ball would be squarely in JSOC commander

Lieutenant General Frank Eaton's court. That is, if Novak passed on the order.

"I know, Kieran. But don't you find this suspect?"

"What do you mean, suspect? It's a direct order."

"So it seems. But it can't be right? Right? I mean, did some wires get crossed somewhere? Circumventing the Pentagon, yet it comes through SOCOM anyway? Must be a mistake. Phillips might be a lot of things. Pompous. Bitter. But he's not stupid."

Brown shrugged. "Call him, then."

"Who? Phillips?"

"Yes, Phillips. Who else?"

"And say what?"

"I don't know. Ask him to verify."

Novak thought about it for a second. Based on the circumstances, it wouldn't be out of line for him to double check. He had the access, after all.

As USSOCOM commander, he reported to the Secretary of Defense. Because of this, he had built a rapport with the cantankerous ex-admiral. It wasn't friendly by any means. But they understood each other.

Novak picked up the phone and dialed. He held the handset to his chest. "I'm not crazy, right? This is off." He waved the floppy document in front of him.

Before Brown could answer the rhetorical question, a woman's voice came on the line.

"Department of Defense, how may I direct your call?"

"This is General Novak, SOCOM, verification alpha-zulu-five-eight-eight-lima, for the Secretary."

"Standby General Novak."

The line went dead for thirty seconds. Then the woman returned. "Hold the line for the Secretary."

Novak held the phone to his ear. He nodded at Brown, pointed at the handset, and gave a thumbs up. The line crackled to life.

"Buck, how are ya?"

"Fine, Mister Secretary. And you?"

"I just birdied the fourteenth at Baltimore, so better than fine, I'd say. To what do I owe the call?"

Novak knew Phillips well enough. He was acting as if everything was business as usual, which almost led Novak to believe the order was not only a mistake, but a complete fake. The fact that Phillips had taken the call on his cell phone, while on the golf course no less, meant he had instructed the switchboard to route the call ahead of time. No matter how nonchalant he might have seemed, he was expecting an inquiry.

"I received your communication, sir."

"Good. I expect you'll handle it expeditiously."

"Of course, sir. It's just—"

"Hold on, Buck."

Novak could hear the phone rustle and Phillips' distant voice talking to someone else. "Give me a minute, Bob," it sounded like he said. After a moment, Phillips returned to the forefront.

"What's the problem then, Buck?"

"There is no problem. I wanted to double check with you regarding the content of your communication."

"You understand that I am unable to provide any further clarification under current circumstances. Was my communication unclear?"

"No, very clear." Novak struggled to find a way to communicate his concern without transmitting classified information. The connection was encrypted, but it was protocol not to discuss such matters over the phone. He proceeded delicately. "The directive seemed unorthodox and, if I may be so bold, out of character. I'm simply calling to verify."

"Well, it sounds to me like you're questioning my orders. Of course, I know you would never think about doing such a thing. That would be, how did you say it? Out of character. Am I right?"

"Yes sir."

Novak knew he had overstepped the second the words came out of his mouth. The tone of Phillips' voice was confirmation that he was correct.

Phillips shouted. "Go ahead, Bob. I'll catch up." He lowered his voice again. "Buck, listen. Unorthodox as you might think it is, there are reasons. This is above even me, understand?"

"I do."

"Look, I've chosen to task you with this because I'm confident in your discretion, your judgment, and your capability of keeping tight control. You'll need to apply pressure to ensure this stays under wraps. Think of it as an opportunity. The kind that makes or breaks careers, if you get my drift. Don't screw it up."

"Roger that. Thank you, Mister Secretary. Oh, and that birdie—was that the fourteenth on East?"

"You better believe it," Phillips said. "Bob doesn't know it yet, but he's about to be two grand lighter. I'm having a hell of a round."

"Well, good luck, sir."

"Buck, I'm counting on you."

"Consider it done."

"I do." Phillips disconnected.

Novak took a moment to replay the peculiar conversation in his mind. Phillips had indicated that the order had come from above him. This part was no surprise. Something of this nature could only come at the direction of the President himself.

*"You'll need to apply pressure,"* Phillips had said. *"Makes or breaks careers."* Novak couldn't help but feel that Phillips had set him up as a sort of fall guy. Someone to blame when this thing went to shit. Which it likely would. Still, he was left with little choice.

"How'd that go?" Brown said.

Novak jerked. He had almost forgotten Brown was still sitting in front of him.

"Just like it sounded."

"So, are you going to pass it to JSOC?"

"I am."

"Do you want me to draw up the order?"

"No. I'll do it myself." Novak held the document toward Brown. "You can toss this in the burn box, if you don't mind."

Brown snatched the piece of paper, walked over to the industrial paper shredder, positioned against the wall just inside the door, flicked it on, and fed the document into its jaws. Then he opened the door, removed the basket, and carried it close to his chest. "On it."

As Brown left, Novak lingered in thought.

## DETACHMENT

As a young soldier in the field, he had operated in the gray area between right and wrong. He had brought violence with extreme prejudice. He had done what needed to be done. But behind it all was a backdrop of legality and morality. An internal compass that he and all men who first wore the uniform relied upon.

That was all in the past. With promotion came compromise. Of values. Of conviction.

His job was clear cut. Antiseptic. Sterile. The vestiges of personal dogma no longer played a part.

He would carry out his orders, like he always had.

What would Jackson and Robbie say if they knew?

Luckily, like everyone else in the world, they never would know.

# CHAPTER 4

IAN SAT on the floor with his legs outstretched under the coffee table. "E-five." He grinned.

Fezz rolled his eyes. "It's a hit. Of course."

"You have to say it," Ian pushed a red plastic pin into his playing board.

Fezz chucked. "Say what?"

"You know. You're supposed to say, 'You sunk my battleship.'"

"Oh," Fezz said. "I forgot."

"No, you didn't. You always say that."

It was true. Every time. And as far as Fezz was concerned, it never got old.

A few rounds of Battleship with Ian had become a daily ritual. Though he had yet to win a single game, Fezz was surprised at how much he enjoyed playing. Of course, it had nothing to do with the game and everything to do with the company.

Recently, Fezz had been spending a lot of time with Ian. And Ima, too. Taking walks, swimming. Whatever Ian wanted.

Two weeks prior, he, Ima, and Ian had taken a trip to town. Across from Cumberland Farms, a stop at the playscape had seen Fezz accompanying Ian on a mission to traverse the park's platforms, ladders, bridges, and truck tires without touching the ground. It was a critical mission because the ground, Ian had told him, was made of liquid magma.

Afterward, they'd taken a walk down Narragansett Avenue, toward the East Ferry.

It was there, on a table of used toys outside the Saint Matthews Episcopal Church thrift shop, that Ian had spotted Battleship.

Ian had been enthralled. In typical Ian fashion, he had questions.

"Haven't you seen the commercial?" Fezz had asked in return. "Ya know, 'You sunk my battleship!'"

Ian had just given him a blank look.

Ima had stepped in with an explanation he would understand. "It's a game of deduction, honey. Basically, a matrix where you try to determine the finite pattern the other player has set up. The trick is to use parity to cut the necessary guesses in half. Start toward the center of the board for a statistical advantage, and the rest is physiology. If you know your opponent, you'll know where to expect their ships. The more random they try to make them, the more predictable they become."

Ian's eyes widened. "Can we get it?"

"Done," Fezz had told him before going off into the shop to pay. When he'd returned, Ian was bouncing around like Charlie Sheen after a speedball, the ratty old box clutched in his hands.

"Thank you, thank you, Fezz. Can we play? I think I know where your ships will be."

Little did Fezz know that Ian hadn't been wrong. As it would turn out, he'd always know.

That was the wonder of Ian. And no one knew it better than Ima.

Fezz loved the way she connected with the boy. To an outsider, it would seem like she was talking to her math professor, rather than her own child. But Ian was different than most children. He didn't need coddling. He didn't want to be placated. What nourished him was information.

Still, Fezz sometimes forgot that Ian never had a real childhood. That he didn't fingerpaint in kindergarten or climb trees behind the elementary school. Hell, he had never heard of Battleship, or Monopoly, or Sesame Street.

In a way, Ian reminded Fezz of himself. Made him think about all the things he missed in his own life. A family. Stability. He wondered if it had all been worth it.

"If you're not going to say it, will you at least concede?" Ian asked.

"Concede? I still have my aircraft carrier left."

"I know. But either G-nine or F-eight will be a hit. So, I have six moves left at the most. You have ten, minimum."

"You got me." Fezz closed the clamshell board. "I concede. One of these days. I'm comin' for ya."

Ian giggled.

The rattle of the sliding door preceded the sounds of birds and ocean waves. Ima, wearing an open linen button-down and a bright green bikini, stepped inside and closed the door behind her.

"Guess what?" Fezz said.

"He sunk your Battleship?"

"You got it."

"He's getting better, Mom," Ian said.

"That's good. Did you take your shower like I asked? No, you didn't."

"I'm going now."

Ima walked into the kitchen, took her oversized sunglasses off and placed them on the counter.

"Fezz," Ian said as he tucked the boards back into the box. "When are we going to see your secret room?"

"It's not my secret room. It's a surprise. For everyone. And, soon."

"Okay." Ian put the box on the shelves built into the underside of the staircase. "Can we take a bike ride and get ice cream at Spinnakers today? You can use Khat's bike."

"I don't think I'd fit on Khat's bike. I'll take you for ice cream if you want, but not today. How about this weekend?"

"That's okay. We can play Battleship later then." Ian headed up the stairs.

"You know, you can say no if you don't want to play," Ima said.

"Come on. It's my favorite part of the day."

Ima cracked the fridge and fished out a can of Sierra Mist. "You should get outside. Get some air. It's gorgeous out there."

"I will." Fezz stood up and moved toward the kitchen. "You know, I was thinking about Ian. I hope this isn't overstepping, it's just a suggestion, but I was thinking maybe it's time you signed him up for school. He's been asking about it a lot. Don't you think he needs to meet some kids his own age?"

"Yeah. Our identities are pretty well established now. I just worry he'll be so bored sitting through classes. Unless he's enrolled in college, I'm not sure he'll learn anything. And even then, it'd be a stretch."

"Now that's where I disagree," Fezz said. "He'll learn how to be a kid. And he's got a lot of catching up to do. Anyway, maybe he'll teach *them* something."

Ima laughed. "Can you imagine what that teacher will have to put up with?"

"He does come out with some doozies. Like today, he told me that dogs can be allergic to humans. Of course, I looked it up. It's true."

"Do you know what he told me?" Ima asked. "That you and I should go on a date."

"He did?" Fezz felt his skin warming. He hadn't said anything to Ian about it, but the truth was, the idea had crossed his mind more than once. The kid was perceptive, that was for sure. "The crazy thing is, he's usually right."

"Yes, he is," Ima smiled.

Maybe he was imagining it, but he thought he caught a touch of nervous excitement in her voice. He wondered if she had also thought about it. Did she feel the same draw? After several awkward seconds, he decided there was only one way to find out. "In that case, we should probably consider it."

Ima lifted one shoulder and flashed a coy smile. "Are you asking me out on a date, Fezz?"

"Yes." Fezz straightened himself. "I guess I am."

## CHAPTER 5

PIPER PULLED to the edge of the roundabout and pressed the stop button. The gurgle of the engine dropped out, leaving only the persistent ringing in his ears.

Phillips already knew he had arrived. At ninety-four decibels, the growl of Piper's Porsche Carrera S convertible made sure of it. Besides, he was right on time for their weekly meet.

Piper stepped out and looked up at the squarish mansion. With its arching front door, white stone pillars, and ornate cresting along the edges of its flat roof, it looked like a miniature White House. Knowing Phillips, this similarity was the whole reason he selected it.

Taking the path around to the right, he circumvented the main entrance and headed toward the back yard. There, he knew he would find Phillips on the patio, with a glass of tequila on the rocks and a copy of the Washington Post in his hands.

*Sure enough.*

"Piper," Phillips lowered the paper and removed his reading glasses. "Tequila?"

"No, thanks."

Every week Phillips offered. Every week, Piper declined.

It had been several years since Piper had so much as taken a sip of alcohol. Not since the day he quit cold turkey. He hadn't planned on it. It just happened. He remembered thinking to himself that he had enough vices. Girls, gambling, fast cars, the occasional bump. He decided he could do without the booze.

"I got your message," Piper said. "You got something for us?"

"No. Not exactly. Not yet. Please, sit."

Piper pulled up a chair across the table from Phillips. "What's happening?"

"We've got a bit of an issue," Phillips said. "Moore's got his panties in a bunch about these protests in Caracas. David Butler, that half-witted prick, he's got Moore's ear. Convinced him to move on Maduro."

"Move on him? You mean, take him out?"

"Yes, Piper. I mean take him out." Phillips shook his head. "It's a goddamn debacle."

Piper understood. It put them both in a predicament. Though he didn't know what Phillips needed from him and his team, he couldn't imagine that Phillips was on board with the President's plan. "We're not doing that, right?"

"You're not. But he's insisting it be done."

"That will seriously screw us."

"Indeed." Phillips folded the paper, placed it on the table, and took a swig of tequila. "Are you familiar with Buck Novak?"

"SOCOM?" Piper asked.

"Yes. This is going through him."

"So you're actually pushing this through? What are we gonna do about it? Venezuela's gonna be pissed."

"I know," Phillips said. "I've already been in contact with them. I've given them the heads up and told them I'll keep them apprised. Maduro's unhappy, but I think I've salvaged the deal. He understands my hands are tied."

"Can you talk Moore out of it?"

"It's a delicate situation. As lucrative as Caracas has been, Maduro's only a piece of the pie. I know you realize what's at stake. The most important thing is staying in Moore's good graces. I lose access and we lose everything, right?"

Phillips was right. Maduro was one of many sources. There were always governments willing to pay bribes to United States insiders. Especially those in positions as influential as Phillips'.

Piper benefited from these arrangements, more than anyone else on the team. Phillips was generous that way. Sure, Piper had paid his dues. But he owed Phillips, too. It went both ways.

Out of subconscious compulsion, Piper reached up and ran his finger in the grove of scar tissue that crossed his face from his temple, across his nose, and to his jaw.

As a loyal soldier, Piper had gone above and beyond for Phillips. He had almost lost his life, and later, his freedom. But Phillips had never abandoned him. He saved him from a lifetime of incarceration. He took him in after his court martial and dishonorable discharge.

Then again, it was because of Phillips that he and his team had been in that position in the first place.

Now it was all dirty water under the proverbial bridge. No matter the circumstance that led to it, they had established trust. The kind of confidence that could only be forged in the muck and mire. It was what drove Piper to kill for him. It was what compelled Phillips to share everything he had built. And above all, it was what solidified their mutual resentment of their government.

"So, we're standing down on this one," Piper said.

"For now. But I wanted you to be aware. The situation is fluid. Right now, my main concern is Novak. He already pushed back a bit. In my assessment, people like Novak are our biggest threat. The high-and-mighty types. The conscience dwellers. They're erratic. Prone to loose lips. And if this leaks out, we lose control. If we lose control, we risk exposure."

"You want us to handle Novak?"

"No. Not now, anyway. Just need to keep an eye on him, and on Eaton over at JSOC. But I'm not as concerned about Eaton. He knows the drill. As far as the teams, they won't know shit until they're on the plane."

"It's a death sentence, you know. Maduro will kill them." The idea of setting up their own didn't sit well with Piper. But they all had their crosses to bear. And if there was one thing he'd learned, enemies and allies weren't mutually exclusive. Everyone was susceptible to becoming collateral damage.

"I'll work that out with Caracas," Phillips said. "In the meantime, I need you to take a run to Lebanon. We're having a bit of a 'collection' problem in Syria."

"Again?"

"Again."

"Okay. Roger that. I'll rally the troops. Rip's gonna shit when he finds out we're going back. You know how he feels about Syria."

Phillips nodded. "Tell Rip there's a little extra in it for him this time around. But you're going to have to make it quick. This thing's ramping up within days."

"Good." Piper got up from his seat. "I'll call you when it's done. Tell Moore I said, 'Screw you.'"

Phillips laughed. "Sure thing."

Piper leapt over the flowers and onto the path, to avoid the extra ten steps. Phillips unfolded his paper and disappeared behind it.

## CHAPTER 6

IRVING OAKLEY STRAIGHTENED his tie and waited for the butler to open the double doors to the west sitting room.

This was Oakley's third invitation to the President's private residence —if one counted being summoned as being invited.

When the doors opened, Oakley entered with as much confidence as he could muster.

Inside, Moore was sitting on the couch in front of the large lunette window. He didn't get up.

"Sit down, Irving."

Oakley complied. He eased himself down as though he were a hot air balloon that had run out of propane.

Moore wasted no time on pleasantries. "What was that? In the situation room."

"You know what that was, Bill. You've lost your mind." Oakley's tone was confrontational, but it wasn't how he'd intended it to come out. He tried to walk it back before the coiled asp lashed out. "What I mean is—"

"Who the hell do you think you are?" Moore stood up and pointed at his index finger at Oakley's face. "How dare you challenge me in there? In front of the cabinet!"

Oakley felt vulnerable. Not because Moore was the leader of the free world, but because Oakley was sunk deep into the overstuffed chair while

# DETACHMENT

Moore hovered over him. He pushed himself to his feet to meet the moment with dignity. "I'm the vice president. Who you chose, I might add. I think that affords me a little leeway to throw in my two cents every so often. Besides, everyone else in the room was thinking it, except for your little crony Butler. They just didn't have the guts to say it."

Moore bent over, then ran his hand through his hair. He paced in a small circle. "I did choose you, Irving, because I thought I could count on you to back me up. We're supposed to be a united front, you and me. But time and time again, you're a disappointment."

A pit formed in Oakley's stomach. He tried not to let it show, but he was affected by Moore's callous rant.

When Moore had offered him the job, Oakley and his wife Beth went back and forth, late into the night. Should he take it? Should he not? At the time, he'd been a senior senator. Head of the intelligence committee. A shoo-in for majority leader. The public had respected him, and he'd accomplished things that mattered to his constituents.

The allure of being a step away from the highest office in the land had clouded his judgment. He had let it intoxicate him, just as it intoxicated Beth.

Oakley and Beth both knew that Moore was a bastard. That he cared more about power and status than the people. He was a banker, after all. They also knew that he would win the election.

In the end, Oakley accepted. And it was a decision he replayed in his mind each and every day.

"That's not fair, Bill. We're not talking about budget cuts here. We're talking about assassinating a world leader. Who are you, Mussolini?"

"I'm acting in the best interest of the United States!" Moore yelled. Spittle flew from his mouth. "That's the job. And that's why you lay your head down at the observatory and not in this house!"

In an uncharacteristic moment of exasperation, Oakley raised his voice, letting out a growl. "You're an asshole, you know that?"

Moore paused for a moment. Oakley was sure he was about to lunge at him. Instead, Moore sat himself on the edge of the chair opposite him and blew out a long, loud puff of air.

"Effective immediately," Moore started, his voice low and ominous, "you will no longer be read in on the situation in Venezuela. You will refrain from talking about it to the cabinet. You will refrain from talking about it to anyone. Including me. Your briefings will be redacted and access to the oval and situation room will be restricted."

"Bill! Are you serious?"

"You tell me, Irving. Am I?"

The question did not need or deserve a response. He was serious. Crazy. But serious.

"On Wednesday," Moore said, as if the previous several minutes had not existed, "you'll go to the International Energy Summit in Oslo in my stead. There, you'll try not to embarrass me or this administration."

"You know this will end badly, Bill. Maduro's shifty. If he survives, he'll have you over a barrel. You could let it play out. You could focus on diplomacy."

Moore stood up, walked to the door, and opened it. "Thank you, Irving, for your counsel. Please, enjoy your evening."

Oakley made his way into the second-floor foyer. A bewildered traveler on treacherous terrain.

"And Irving."

"Yes, Mister President?"

"The next time you mention Venezuela, I'll ban you from the West Wing and set you up with an office in Annapolis. Are we clear?"

"Crystal. Thank you, Mister President."

# CHAPTER 7

"THIS IS the layout of the compound, as close as we can determine." Master Sergeant Musa directed the handheld laser pointer at the projection screen. "This, gentlemen, is the target's main living quarters. Guys from the 20th engineer brigade are slapping together an approximation of this area as we speak, in a hanger at Pope. If we're lucky, we'll have enough time for about five or six run-throughs in the shoot house. If that. You each have a copy of this schematic. I want you to study it tonight."

Jackson Novak flipped through his binder and found the copy of the architectural drawing.

In the past hour, a large amount of information had transferred to the dozen men in the room—the tactics they would employ, the insertion and extraction plan, the equipment they would need, the type of environment they should expect—everything except where they were going and who they were supposed to kill.

Wherever and whatever they were up against, Jackson couldn't have been more pleased with the choice of teammates for this mission. The best of the best, in his opinion.

The assignment was based on a hurried selection process in which team members were pulled from a pool of volunteers. Jackson had thrown his name into the hat as soon as he heard the words, "high level target." Still, even as a current team leader, Jackson had to undergo an interview and service review process. Command ultimately selected him as a member of the team, but not as team leader. That honor went to Master Sergeant Akin Musa.

Although Jackson and Musa shared the same rank, Musa had more time in the Unit and a lot more experience in the field. The fact of the matter was that the big Nigerian was a born leader and consummate warrior. And he was smart. As much as Jackson would have liked to lead the mission, he had to admit that Musa was the right choice.

"Any questions?" Musa asked.

Master Chief Petty Officer Preston raised his hand. "How long is the trek, and what's the total time on the ground?"

One of a few Navy SEALs in Delta Force and the only non-Army member of this mission, Preston was an exceptional operator. Jackson had been skeptical at first since Preston had come to OTC after washing out of DEVGRU. But it had become apparent that it was SEAL Team Six who got the short end of the stick.

"Two hour trek. Twenty minutes hot, tops. If you can un-ass yourselves in less than that, we're out of country in under four and a half." Musa looked around. "Anyone else?"

Jackson had a hundred questions, none of which he could answer. Even Musa was operating in the dark, only regurgitating the little he'd been told. Chances were, most of the finer details wouldn't be relayed until they were airborne.

"No? Good. Get your shit put together and go rest up. We rally at O four hundred."

Jackson unwedged himself from the desk-chair-combination and stretched his back. He followed Preston out. Ashton Furst trailed behind them.

In the hallway, Jackson waited for Preston to fish his phone out of a plastic bin.

"Whatever this is, it's gotta be important," Jackson said over Preston's shoulder. "Otherwise they would have just had DEVGRU handle it."

Preston snickered. "If they did that, they'd probably end up sending us to rescue them anyway."

# DETACHMENT

"Who do you think it is?" Furst joined Jackson and Preston in the hallway. He shifted to the right to allow the other men through the door.

"I bet it's al-Zawahiri," Preston said.

"Why? You hear something?" Jackson picked his phone off the pile. He turned it on and slipped it into his pocket.

"No. But who else?"

"We're going jungle, ya dopes." Furst shook his head. "al-Zawahiri? You serious?"

Furst was right. They were gearing up with woodland camo. This wasn't one of the usual suspects. Not Iraq or Afghanistan. In fact, the entire Middle East was out. If Jackson had to guess, they were headed for Southeast Asia. He threw out a couple of suggestions of his own, but they were equally uninformed. "Philippines, maybe. Or North Korea."

"Aw." Furst flashed a maniacal, toothy grin. "I hope it's Kim Jong-un. Tell me we're gonna pop that prick. I'm gonna be the one to do it, too."

"You think so," Preston said. "Why don't you put your money where your mouth is? A hundred bucks each. Whoever pops him takes the pot."

"Done," Furst said. "How 'bout you, Jackey? You in?"

"I don't want your money. Not with all those baby-mamas you gotta pay for." Jackson slapped Furst in the abdomen with the back of his hand. "Besides, it's gonna be hard for you to get a shot while you're guardin' the perimeter."

"Whatever," Furst said. "See if I help you when you're gettin' your ass handed to you by a bunch of ninjas."

Preston laughed. "You're an idiot."

Jackson's phone buzzed in his pocket. He stepped away to let Preston and Furst bicker while he checked the screen. A notification showed a text message from Pop.

It had been a week since he'd heard from his father, which was a lifetime for them. Normally, Jackson would check in every other day or so. Just to say hi. But he'd been preoccupied. Especially in the last twenty-four hours.

Jackson touched the notification to bring up the message. It read, "Hey Jackson. Just wanted to let you know your brother is taking a couple days to come down to Florida. Thought maybe you could too. Need to talk. Let me know. Love ya."

As nice as it sounded to spend a few days with Robbie and his father, the timing couldn't have been worse. Fortunately, if anyone would understand the unpredictable nature of the job, it was those two.

For as long as Jackson could remember, he had wanted to follow in his father's footsteps. He signed up for the Army on his eighteenth birthday, just as his brother would two years later. Each of them with full intentions of someday standing where he now stood.

They had done well, but their connection to the great Buck Novak had allowed them the opportunities. For that, both he and Robbie were forever grateful.

*Sorry Pop. Not this time.*

Jackson looked up from his phone. Preston and Furst, exhausting their repertoire of insults, were heading off in separate ways.

Wandering back into the empty briefing room, Jackson leaned against the wall and typed out his response. "Hey Pop. Sounds great, but I can't make it. Something came up at work. Something big. Looks like I'll be tied up. I'll take a raincheck tho. TTYL. Love ya."

In what seemed like the same instant he touched the send button, his phone rang.

He answered.

"Hey Pop, I just texted you."

"I know," Buck said. "I saw it. We need to talk. You're taking the assignment?"

"Yeah. I assume you know what this is all about."

"Listen, son, why don't you sit this one out. Come down to Tampa. Spend a few days with your brother and me. It's been a while since we've all been together. We'll do a little fishing. Catch up."

"Sit it out? Why? I volunteered. I can't bag out now. Would you have sat it out? I don't think so."

"I'm asking, Jackson. When do I ever ask anything of you, huh? Do this for me. Just hop on a flight. I'll make sure the leave is taken care of."

"I'm sorry, Pop. It's not happening. I won't leave the team high and dry.

## DETACHMENT

This is what I signed up for. I'll come see you when I get back if you want. All right?

There was silence at the other end of the line.

"I've gotta go, Pop."

"Jackson–"

"Love ya," Jackson blurted. And disconnected the call.

# CHAPTER 8

BLAKE PINNED THE THROTTLE. The three four-hundred-fifty cubic-inch outboard engines rocketed the thirty-eight-foot Mako over the crest of the swell.

Haeli stood at his side, grasping one of the chrome hard top supports. Her eyes were closed, her mouth was drawn up in an effortless smile, and her dark hair whipped in every direction.

From where Blake was standing, she was a vision. Medusa, herself. Only more beautiful. And more deadly.

The sun hovered half-way off the horizon, casting a shimmer as far as the eye could see. He took a deep breath of salty air.

There was something about being on the water that invigorated a person. Blake might not have had Haeli's grace, but he felt just like she looked.

When they purchased the boat, they were all in agreement it was a necessity. For Blake, it was also a guilty pleasure.

*Gem-ini*, he'd named it. Though the other guys ragged on it, he was happy with the choice. It was a nod to Haeli. To what made all of it possible—the house, the toys, the future. She had laughed when he'd unveiled the decal. As far as he was concerned, it was a win.

"Is that them?" Khat yelled over the roar of the engines.

His sunglasses were heavily tinted, but the glare off the water made it difficult to make out the small shape dotting the water, a half mile ahead of them. Blake shielded his eyes with his hand. "Gotta be."

Blake glanced at the chart plotter. They were almost on top of the agreed-upon waypoint— 41.08494537218554, -71.09116409584296. A little over twenty-six miles off Beavertail, and twice the distance of what was considered international waters.

They had taken down their American ensign once they reached the twelve nautical mile mark. The closest country outside of the United States was Canada, and they were still four hundred miles from Nova Scotia. Still, Khat had insisted they take down the flag. He argued they could only be prosecuted under the ensign they flew.

Blake had started to explain that the boat had been registered in the United States, so they were already on the hook if they got caught. It made Khat happy though, so he let it go.

The same was not true for the people they were meeting. A contact out of Baltimore, Mutt, arranged this meeting with sailors on a Norwegian container ship, heading to New Jersey. Technically, the sailors fell under the jurisdiction of Norway as long as they remained in international waters. And they were a long way from home. Unless the long arm of the law was thousands of miles long, these men didn't have much to worry about.

As was expected when dealing with Mutt, a lot of holes remained unfilled. Blake still wasn't sure how the sailors would be able to pull it off, but Mutt was confident they were capable. And more importantly, trustworthy.

The shipment of military equipment did not originate in Norway. Several factories throughout Europe trucked the equipment there. Somewhere between Norway and here, the inside-men were to gather the team's shopping list, then rendezvous with another of Mutt's contacts with a speedboat. That was according to Mutt, anyway.

As Blake understood it, the men intended to make the drop and return to their ship before the "wrong people" realized they were gone.

It was a gamble, but as the bobbing dot on the horizon grew into the outline of a candy-apple red cigarette boat, it looked as though all had gone to plan. Otherwise, they wouldn't be there at all.

"You've got the cash?" Blake asked.

Haeli tilted the cockpit bench cushion upward and withdrew a bulky manilla envelope from the compartment underneath. She showed it to Blake and then tucked it into her armpit.

Blake pulled back on the throttle.

"Keep your eyes peeled when we get over there," Khat said. "I don't like this. We're sitting ducks out here."

"Relax," Blake said. "We'll be in and out in two minutes. Mutt hasn't screwed us yet, has he? He moved the diamonds. I don't even think he skimmed any off the top."

The truth was, there was no way to know if he did.

"Haeli, grab the line," Blake said. "I'll pull us up alongside. You toss the line over. Khat, put the fenders out."

Blake took a wide arc, negotiating the waves and current. As they approached, they saw three men on the long, slender craft. Two of them had bleach-blonde hair and pasty white skin. The man at the helm had a darker complexion and wore a baseball cap.

"We've been waiting," one of the blonde men said. His accent was thick and carried the intonation of Scandinavia.

"Seventeen hundred hours," Khat snarked. "It's sixteen fifty-eight."

"Do you have the money?" the man asked.

Haeli pulled the envelope from under her arm and waved it at the group. "Toss it over."

"Not until we see the merchandise," Blake said.

"It's right there." The taller of the two blonde men pointed at a wooden crate, sitting on the seats at the stern of the cigarette boat.

"That's it?" Haeli asked. "That's everything?"

"Yes. Everything. You want to look, be our guest," the tall man said.

Haeli shot Blake a look as if to say, "This isn't good."

"What the hell, I told you," Khat said.

Haeli and Khat weren't overreacting. Haeli was holding fifty-thousand dollars in cash. For that, they expected a laundry list of equipment. Rifles, new night vision apparatus, explosives, body armor, and more. There was no way it would all fit in one small crate.

"I'll go take a look," Blake said. "Haeli, you take the helm."

"You stay at the wheel, Khat and I will go," Haeli said.

"Everything you asked for," the man said. "Fifty-thousand, American."

Haeli stepped up onto the gunwale and climbed over the railing. Khat moved in behind her.

The edges of the two boats undulated with the swells. Haeli waited a moment for them to settle before hopping over the two-foot gap and landing on the deck of the speedboat.

Khat climbed over the metal rail and steadied himself against it. Just as he began to step forward, a wave sent the cigarette boat upward two or three feet. He grabbed hold of the railing, just in time to prevent himself from going in the drink.

"Damn it," Khat said. But Blake couldn't hear it over the scream of the water jet drive.

The bow of the cigarette boat lifted high in the area as the pilot jerked the wheel and jammed the throttle.

Haeli reached out over the side as if hoping Blake would pull her back to safety, but she was already twenty feet away.

"Hold on," Blake yelled. He shifted into gear and pushed the power to its max.

"Hurry, they're getting away!" Khat hollered back.

"I know!"

A gush of sea spray covered them as Blake smashed head-on into a wave. He gripped the wheel tight and willed the powder-blue Mako to pick up speed.

"We're never going to catch them," Khat said.

Blake pushed on the throttle, but it was already as far as it could go.

"No," Blake said. "We're gaining on them."

Of course, he was lying to himself. With every foot they traveled, the fifty-foot speedboat gained two.

Khat was right. They had Haeli. And there was no way they would catch up.

Blake would have given them the money. The guns. Whatever they wanted. He wanted to kick himself for letting her board first. How could he have not seen it coming?

With the Mako at full speed, planing over the swell, the cigarette boat continued to increase its distance. Before long, it would be out of sight.

Still, Blake refused to give up. He checked the gas gauge. Three quarters of a tank. It would run until he spent the last drop of gas. He would never give up, even if it killed him.

"Look!" Khat slapped Blake on the shoulder and pointed out ahead.

Blake couldn't believe it. They were gaining on it. And fast.

It was almost as if the cigarette boat had slowed to a stop.

No, it had stopped.

Within seconds, the Mako was closing in on fifty feet. Twenty.

Just before smashing into the other vessel, Blake spun the wheel, whipping the stern around until it bumped up against the hull of the other boat.

There, standing alone on the deck of the pirate's ship, was Haeli. Alone.

"Took you long enough," she shouted.

"What happened?"

"The guys went for a swim," she said. "Weird time to take a dip, in the middle of a kidnapping and all."

Blake let out a peculiar noise. Something between a laugh and a sign of relief. "You're gonna be the death of me, woman."

Haeli grinned. "Throw the line, Khat."

Khat grabbed the rope near the cleat and pulled it from the water. He tossed it to Haeli, who tied it to a cleat on the other side.

Blake wondered why he even worried. It was because he knew her as a sweet, caring, and fun-loving companion. He sometimes forgot who she really was. A weapon.

"Hang here," Blake said.

Khat nodded.

By the time Blake boarded, Haeli had already pried the top of the crate free and was standing over it. A bewildered look on her face.

"What?"

"Just come here and look at this," Haeli said.

Blake pushed in next to her and peered into the box.

There, nestled in a pile of straw, were a half dozen weird little porcelain statues. Gnomes, they looked like. The kind you'd find in a garden.

"Bastards."

"Guess we're gonna be short on weaponry," Haeli said.

"Nah. We've got plenty of guns," Blake said. "It's the other stuff we needed. Especially the explosives. C-4 isn't so easy to come by these days."

"You think Mutt set us up?"

"I don't know. Maybe. Or the Norwegians played him. Now he's down one man, though. And one cigarette boat."

"We'd better get back."

"Yeah."

Haeli hopped up on the side and leapt onto the Mako.

Blake started to follow, then paused. He reached into the crate and pulled out one of the ugly little statues.

"What are you doing?" Khat asked.

"For the garden," Blake said. "I kinda like it."

# CHAPTER 9

"I HEAR YOU'RE LEAVING US." Ernie hovered his spoon above a yogurt parfait in a clear plastic cup.

"Leaving you?" Archer Wade pushed back from his cubicle and swiveled his chair to face the sixty-two-year-old veteran reporter. "I'm just gettin started."

"Not the Globe," Ernie said, "the bullpen. I heard Robertson's old office has your name written all over it."

Penelope peeked over her divider. "What? You're leaving us?"

"No. Don't listen to Ernie. This is my desk. I like it here." Wade smiled. "In the slums with you guys."

"I've been here for twenty-three years. I've never been offered an office."

Wade grunted. "Again, I haven't been offered an office." He scooted his chair back to his desk. "Don't you have work to do?"

Wade's phone rang. With recent and increasing reluctance, he answered. "Boston Globe. Wade speaking. Sure, yes. No, I don't have my calendar in front of me, but shoot me an email and I'll give you a shout back. No, I haven't made any commitments yet. Yes, yes, I'm familiar. Okay, thanks."

He hung up.

"Who this time?" Penelope asked.

# DETACHMENT

"The Today Show," Wade said.

"In New York?" Ernie said, a glob of yogurt covering his teeth.

"No, in Boise. Yes, New York, Ernie. Where else?"

Out of the corner of his eye, Wade noticed a man in a dark gray suit who had been walking to the elevators but deviated from his path to cut through the bullpen. He was heading straight for Wade.

"Archer, excellent work." The man patted Wade on the back.

"Thanks," Wade said.

"That's talent right there," the man announced to an audience of unaffected faces. "Well, keep it up. See ya around."

When the men left, Wade waited a beat, and then stood up. "Who the hell was that?"

"I don't know." Ernie shrugged.

"Never seen him before," Penelope added.

"Jesus," Wade said. "Maybe I should ask for that office. Just to get some peace and quiet."

Since his story broke, Wade had become something of a celebrity. Emails and phone calls were flooding in. Now, apparently, men in fancy suits were stopping by to visit. It wasn't what he was going for, but he had to admit, the validation was nice.

Looking back, the choice to push for the assignment was a no-brainer, but there were times when he thought he might end up with egg on his face. He had fought hard to convince Clint Taylor, the Globe's new editor-in-chief, that it was worth the time and expense. And boy did it turn out to be.

Two months prior, Wade had gotten a tip that a Boston-based Petroleum exploration company, Boxwood Petrocom, had discovered a large oil reserve off the coast of Mauritania, West Africa. An anonymous British Petroleum executive had provided documents showing that BP had drilled in the very same area a year prior and had come up dry.

When Wade investigated Boxwood's claims, he found that the company had yet to release any of the technical details of their findings. Their press release was vague and over-sensationalized.

It was only a hunch to start with. But he knew in his heart there was a story. A big one.

Probably based on Wade's sheer determination, Taylor had given in to his groveling. He'd authorized a trip to Mauritania and allowed Wade to forgo his usual weekly assignments.

Worried about being scooped, Wade had put in hundreds of hours and ended up traveling to Europe and Canada, as well. The more he uncovered, the more involved it got.

In the first few days, the motivation for falsifying the discovery had seemed shrouded in mystery. Wade had to assume it was rooted in financial gain. It usually was. And within days, it was clear his assumptions were correct. Boxwood Petrocom's market share had shot up from fifty million to over nine-hundred million in the matter of a week.

After being stonewalled by Boxwood's attorneys, he'd realized that he needed help getting access to information. He'd employed the help of a Boston attorney and former Federal Prosecutor, Joseph Berg.

As it turned out, the two had ended up helping each other. Based on the information they'd gathered, timed with the release of the featured article, Berg had ended up filing a class action lawsuit on behalf of the investors.

There'd been no oil where Boxwood claimed. Not a year ago, not today, not ever. How they'd thought they would get away with the scam, Wade couldn't begin to guess. Now, with the Associated Press picking up the story, half the world would know every grimy detail.

The phone rang.

*Not again.*

"Wade speaking. Sure. Of course. Right away."

"Who now?" Only Penelope's forehead and eyes were visible over the top of her cubicle. It meant she had her heels on. "Dateline?"

"Dateline? Does that even exist anymore? No, that was Taylor, he wants to see me."

"To give you your office," Ernie chimed in.

Normally, when Taylor called a reporter into his office, an ass-chewing was sure to follow. But in this instance, Wade was confident it wouldn't be that kind of meeting.

"Be right back," Wade said.

"We'll be here," Ernie grumbled.

# DETACHMENT

Wade headed to the elevator, took it to the top floor, and found his way to Taylor's door. The door was open, but he knocked anyway.

"You wanted to see me?" Wade poked his head through the door's opening.

"Come in," Taylor said. "Look at this."

Wade stepped in. Taylor was standing in front of a large TV screen tuned to CNBC, holding a remote control. His sleeves were rolled up and his tie was loosened. A prerequisite look for the editor of a newspaper, he thought.

"The stock is plummeting. Vultures are shorting. By the end of the closing bell, Boxwood Petrocom will be no more."

"Can't say they didn't have it coming. Not good news for the investors, though."

"No." Taylor stared for another silent moment, then switched the TV off. He walked around and sat behind his cluttered desk. "Take a seat."

Wade complied.

"I just wanted to congratulate you in person. This was excellent work, Archer. I mean it. Superb."

"Glad you think so. It was stressful. A lot on the line, ya know. I appreciate you taking a flier on me."

"I have to admit, I had second thoughts. But I figured, 'What the hell, give the kid a shot.'"

It had been a long while since anyone called him a kid. At thirty-eight years old, he figured that ship had sailed. But he pegged Taylor for early sixties, so compared to him, Wade was a young buck.

Taylor had the reputation of being tough but fair. And they had hit it off when Taylor first took the job. John Henry had courted Taylor and offered an obscene amount of money to come over to the Globe and leave his editor position at the Washington Post. The pay raise was a factor, but as the diehard Red Sox fan had confided in Henry during their first conversation, it was access to Henry's private box at Fenway Park that sealed the deal.

Wade crossed one leg over the other, resting an ankle on the opposing knee. "Well, now that it's all wrapped up, I can get started on my backlog.

A lot of inquiring minds out there need to know what Kim Kardashian's been up to."

"No, no more fluff for you. You need something hard-hitting. I'll tell you what, why don't you take a few days, think about what you might want to do next. If something juicy comes in, I'll bring it to you first. Deal?"

"Sure. That would be great."

"Great."

"Okay, then." Wade stood up. "This celebrity status thing is working out after all." He offered his hand.

Taylor stood and accepted with a hardy handshake.

Wade headed for the door.

"Wade."

"Yes?"

"Why don't you move into Richardson's old office, eh? You've earned it."

Wade chuckled. "Thanks, Boss. But I'm good where I'm at."

## CHAPTER 10

JACKSON PANTED. The terrain wasn't the worst he'd endured, but the pace was demanding. If they were to stay on schedule, there would be no letting up.

In the civilian world, there was a general misconception about the elite fighting forces. Many assumed that top level operators were superhuman. They clearly never tired. Never sweated. Never failed.

Nothing could have been further from the truth. They were always exhausted. Perpetually sweaty. And whatever could go wrong usually did.

Jackson could attest to the reality. Carrying fifty pounds of gear, soaking wet from a river crossing, and barreling through the darkness while viewing the world through what might as well have been a green-tinted toilet paper tube, his legs muscles burned, and he was battered and bruised from smashing into every tree branch and rock he could find.

Sure, the men around him possessed extraordinary skill in a multitude of disciplines. But the only physical difference between them and the man or woman clocking an hour or two a day at the local gym was a complete disregard for their bodies. The more difficult it got, the harder they went. At whatever cost.

"Clearing," Musa's voice blared in Jackson's ear.

Jackson reached inside his blouse and adjusted the volume on the receiver, then repositioned it to prevent the fabric from jostling the knob again.

Ahead, the team converged at the edge of the tree line. Jackson fell into the stack.

"Looks clear." Panone squatted a few feet into the open and panned his night vision goggles back and forth. "Good to go."

Musa took one step past Panone, scanned the distance, and set the team sprinting again with a hand signal.

Jackson darted, wrapping his forearm under his rifle to stop it from bouncing.

Just east of the Columbian Border, the landscape was rural, but not jungle. Before seeing the aerial photos, most had expected to be plodding through the rainforest. Instead, they'd been trekking through a savanna spotted with dense, wooded patches, intermingled with swathes of open land. While they had planned their route to stay within the forest's cover as much as possible, there was no way to get where they were going without crossing several sections of open plains.

They risked someone spotting them, but there was no other option. Using few sources of artificial light, they were blessed with the blanketing cover of near complete darkness.

Jackson kept his eye on Preston, directly in front of him. He picked up his pace to match his teammate's, and made a conscious effort to slow his breathing, syncing each exhale with exactly four long strides. Around a quarter mile ahead, the inky splotch of the next stretch of trees began to fill the glowing green frame.

They were getting close. Somewhere around the tenth or eleventh mile of the twelve-mile trek.

Jackson felt compelled to check the GPS unit attached to his wrist, but decided he'd wait until he reached the tree line. His current location wasn't important, and the last thing he wanted was to be out in the open any longer than he had to be.

While the small screen was configured for viewing through night-vision, the binocular device strapped to his face all but eliminated his depth perception. Traversing the uneven terrain was a task and a half. Add in a small bouncing screen to the mix and he was liable to end up

# DETACHMENT

with a mouthful of Venezuelan dirt. Or face-to-face with an angry bushmaster.

Three hundred and fourteen strides later, Jackson reached the next waypoint. He dropped to one knee and worked on catching his breath.

"We got everyone?" Musa bobbed his index finger with each man he counted.

"Fifteen minutes out." Preston bubbled with excitement. "Get ready boys."

Jackson checked his wrist. One more waypoint. One more field. Then it was on. The main event.

Musa stood. "Ready?"

The men answered in a hushed *Hooah*. For several seconds, no one moved. The sound of twelve men sucking wind overpowered the backdrop of prattling crickets and quibbling frogs.

It was a well-deserved respite, however short.

Fewer than two hours earlier, they had stepped off a plane onto the tarmac of the Los Colonizadores Airport, near the town of Saravena, Columbia.

They had chosen Los Colonizadores because it was the closest out-of-country airstrip to their target. Only a few miles from the Venezuelan border, it was ideal for rapid insertion. More importantly, the area had a strong military presence—that is to say, control.

With a little mutual backscratching, the resulting arrangement had allowed the team to circumvent customary channels and provided them with resources, security, and a degree of anonymity.

Unlike the sparsely populated region beyond the border, Saravena was a town of around forty-seven thousand. There would be no skulking around in the bushes, and it wasn't like they could march down the street in formation. They'd needed a ride. And the Columbia military had been kind enough to oblige. For a fee.

Columbian officials had dropped them off at the end of a dirt road, a hundred yards from the sandy banks of the Rio Arauca. Their escorts had left three vehicles off the path to use on their return.

Naturally, the river crossing—or crossings—would have been the first hurdle. It had ensured they were all nice and soaked for the rest of the hike, thus maximizing the amount of chafing that would occur.

Luckily, it had been drier than normal. While usually overflowing its banks, the Arauca hadn't been a solid, wide waterway. The low water level had reduced it to a series of converging offshoots, flowing around a lattice of small islands. It had been an advantage—trading a long, dangerous swim for a cluster of short hops.

Still, it had been just as wet in the end.

At around four miles in, there was another river. It was narrow, and crossing was trivial.

All in all, Jackson was surprised how smooth the insertion had gone thus far. But just as soon as the thought popped up, he pushed it from his mind. They weren't there yet, and this type of presumption often tempted the gods.

The team trudged its way to the edge of the outcropping. Like a half dozen times before, they set out across the half mile stretch of grassland.

Running. Breathing. Burning.

Before Jackson knew it, they were under a leafy canopy once again. Only this time, there wouldn't be another. Not until they were on their way out.

"Everyone good?" Musa asked.

"Good," Furst said. The question was meant to be rhetorical—the kind that should only be answered in the negative.

"The main house is two hundred yards that way." Musa spelled it out, even though each man could see the target on their wrist and had run through the plan several times. "Rocket, Furst. Left flank. Brosch, Fang, Right. The rest of you, with me."

The four men split off to get eyes on the east and west sides of the compound. Jackson joined the core group of eight, who made their way to the wood line and took up a ready position. Jackson proned himself next to Preston. Musa was on the other side of him.

"Exactly like the models," Preston said.

He was right. Three-dimensional digital models had been created, allowing the team to use virtual reality headsets to explore the exterior of the property. The virtual version was accurate, right down to the peeling paint and the stack of rusted fifty-gallon drums just outside the wall. It instilled confidence. A feeling of familiarity.

There were several buildings on the property. The two-story main house, three small outbuildings close by, and a large barn-like structure with a corrugated steel roof a few hundred yards north. From their vantage point, they could see the south side of the main house and one of the smaller structures. The barn was too far away and any view of it was blocked by the main brick structure.

"I don't like this already," Musa said. "Where is everyone?"

Jackson got the same eerie feeling. The place was quiet. Devoid of any life. No lights. No guards. Granted, it was the middle of the night, but aerial images from the night before showed a dozen troops along the perimeter.

Musa didn't say what he was thinking. He didn't have to. They were all thinking the same thing.

*Madura's gone.*

"Alpha, Bravo." Musa's voice came over Jackson's earpiece. "You guys have eyes? Any movement?"

Rocket keyed in. "We're set up. Nothing showing on the west side."

"Same here," Broach added.

A second later, the comms crackled, and Broach came back on. "Hold up, we've got something. A patrol. Four guys coming around the west side. You should pick them up in a second."

Jackson watched and waited. Sure enough, four uniformed men appeared at the east corner and moved along the south wall of the building.

"He's here," Jackson said.

"Standby," Musa said into the mic. "Alpha, Bravo, hold your positions. Provide cover fire if needed. When the patrol rounds the west side, we're going."

"Roger, Alpha."

"Roger, Bravo."

Jackson got off his belly and into a crouched position.

"Hold," Musa said. "On me."

The four men stopped for a moment, as if surveying the scene to the south. There was no indication they had spotted anything in the trees. They continued moving, until they disappeared around the building.

"Now."

The group pushed out in the open and hurried toward the four foot stone wall, separating the residence from the rest of the world. They held their weapons at eye level, itchy fingers resting on the edges of the trigger guards.

Musa reached the wall first, then Rosini, Preston, and Jackson. Musa vaulted the wall and dropped into the compound. Rosini and Preston followed.

As Jackson pushed himself onto the wall and swung one leg over, his night vision went stark. By instinct, he reached up and ripped the binoculars from his face.

Disoriented by several large flood lights mounted to the main house, it took Jackson an extra split second to realize what was happening.

From either side of the building, two or three dozen troops crowded in toward them. They yelled and whooped a medieval war cry.

Atop the wall, Jackson had a perfect view of the disaster unfolding. He turned to the men behind him. "Go! Retreat!" he yelled.

Musa, Rosini, and Preston tried to scramble back to the wall. It was too late. The hoard of presidential guard were only a few feet away.

In those few seconds, Jackson had a choice. He could join his team leader. Try to fight off the enemy. But there were too many.

If he joined the rest of the team and fled to the woods, they stood a chance of escape. Possibly, a chance to regroup and coordinate a rescue.

That was, if the captured men weren't executed immediately.

With a heavy heart, Jackson made his choice.

Dropping onto the grass, he bolted with the others toward the tree line.

The teammate in front of him, Espinosa, stopped dead in his tracks. Jackson slammed into his back.

"Why'd you—"

Jackson didn't need to finish his question. From the east and west, dozens more soldiers filed out of the woods. To the east, Brosch and Fang were prodded along in front of the group, no longer carrying their rifles.

To the west, only Rocket was visible. One of the Venezuelans helped another, who appeared to bleed from the groin.

"What do we do?" Espinosa asked.

"We're screwed," one of the other three said, although Jackson didn't know who.

"We're surrounded," Jackson said. "Completely outmanned and outgunned. There's only one thing we can do."

The soldiers approached quickly. Jackson knew they needed to take decisive action. He stepped forward, laid his rifle on the ground, knelt down, and put his hands in the air.

Surrender was the last thing he ever thought he would do. He didn't care if he died fighting. And he knew that every one of his teammates felt the same. It was why he needed to set an example. To make it okay to lay down their arms. For their sake. For their families. For their children. If they could live another day, there would be hope where there wasn't any before.

"Get off me," Rocket said, as one soldier shoved him to the ground next to Jackson.

The soldiers were all yelling at the same time, and although Jackson knew enough Spanish to get by, he couldn't discern the rapid, overlapping orders.

On all fours, Rocket lifted his head. The look on his face, pure pain. "He's dead."

"What?"

"Furst. He's dead." Rocket turned toward a group of soldiers holding the team at gunpoint. "But not before he blew the balls off one of these assholes."

The closest soldier reared back his rifle and drove the butt into Rocket's skull. He collapsed in a heap.

"Okay, okay. Please," Jackson waved his hands in the air. "We're not going to give you any trouble. No te vamos a dar problemas. Espinosa, tell them."

"They know. They're saying it's us that are in trouble."

"¡Vamos!" One of the soldiers waggled his gun toward the compound.

Jackson and the others climbed to their feet. The soldiers herded them around to the east and through an open gate.

There, Musa, Preston, and Rossini stood against the brick wall. Stripped of all their equipment. Bloodied but very much alive.

The Venezuelans searched Jackson, collected his equipment, and told him to line up against the wall with the others. He fell in next to Musa.

"Furst is dead."

Musa shook his head. "I'm telling you right now, they knew we were coming. They knew when and how."

"Are you saying what I think you're saying?"

"There's no other explanation. We were set up."

# CHAPTER 11

PHILLIPS SHIFTED IN HIS SEAT. Most people would have considered it an honor to sit in the oval office. To have an audience with the President of the United States. He wasn't most people.

Twenty minutes ago, Moore's chief of staff, Donovan Macdara, had deposited Phillips in the empty office. He had passed on Moore's explicit instructions that Phillips was to wait until the President's arrival. According to Macdara, Marine One was scheduled to land "momentarily."

Phillips stood and circled the room for the umpteenth time. During the first few laps, he considered taking a seat behind the Resolute desk. Just for a minute. In the end, he couldn't bring himself to do it.

It was peaceful in here, he had to admit.

That changed in a hurry.

"Give me ten minutes." Moore barged in, Macdara at his side. "And tell Kristina I want that bill on my desk by the end of the day. If she can't work it out, I'll do it by executive order. Then neither side will be happy. Okay?"

"Fine." Macdara jotted notes on a small pad. "Anything else?"

"Bring me Beth Oakley," Moore said. "Ten minutes."

Macdara nodded and left the room, closing the door behind him and sealing out the cacophony of the west wing.

Moore sat behind his desk and let out a sigh. "What the hell happened, Ron?"

"Our men were ambushed, sir."

"Yes, I know. I'm asking how. Why? We were supposed to have some of our best men on this."

Phillips slid the antique chair from beside the desk, placed it across from Moore, and sat. "U2 footage showed the team reaching the compound without incident. They attempted an assault, but Maduro had amassed more troops than we realized. Our men were overpowered almost immediately."

"How did we not know there were so many soldiers? We had surveillance around the clock."

"No one knows," Phillips said. "Brought them in slowly? Kept them hidden in the compound? As far as we knew, there were only a dozen or so at any given time."

Of course, Phillips did know. Or assumed, at least. Once Phillips provided Maduro's people with the particulars of the mission, it was up to them to prepare how they saw fit.

"What's the status with the men? Can we confirm that Maduro actually has them?"

"Yes. We believe most are still alive. We've been able to identify eleven of the twelve from the footage. A kid named Furst is unaccounted for. It's possible that he's evaded capture and may have hunkered down somewhere in the area. The Venezuelans brought them to a barn near the compound. We believe they're still there now."

"'We believe.' You keep saying that. 'We believe, We believe.' Is there anything you *know*?"

"Sorry. Yes. We *know* they are still there now."

"God damn it, Ron. This is a catastrophic failure. Now, I've got Caracas making demands."

Phillips wasn't surprised. It figured that Maduro wouldn't be satisfied with simply evading death. He'd try to leverage the situation for all it was worth. Phillips couldn't say he blamed him. In some ways, they were cut from the same cloth. As long as the communist pigs kept paying, it was none of Phillips' concern what they did. Moore could go to hell for all he cared. Now, it was all about keeping up appearances. "What are they saying?" Phillips asked.

"Maduro's threatening to expose the assassination plot and execute the men if the United States refuses to denounce the coup, publicly support his presidency, and provide financial aid. That son of a bitch!" Moore slammed his fist on the desk, then stood and swiped his forearm across it. Papers flew across the room and settled on the floor.

Phillips waited for Moore to regain his composure. "Feel better?"

"No." Moore turned his back and looked out the window toward the rose garden. "How many other people know about this?"

"Only a few. Novak, of course, and a couple guys at JSOC. It's well-contained."

"Okay. Make sure it says that way. We need to buy ourselves time."

"There's one other thing," Phillips said. "It's about Novak."

"What about him?"

"It turns out that his son Jackson is one of the hostages."

"What? Why would you allow Novak's son on the mission? What is wrong with you? If Novak gets a hair across his ass over this—"

"I didn't know until after the fact. I never would have—"

"It's your job to know. Jesus Christ, Ron."

"You're right. It was sloppy. There's no excuse."

"I'm calling a cabinet meeting. Situation room in two hours. Be there."

"Yes, sir."

"Now go. And tell Macdara to get in here."

"Of course." Phillips took his leave with haste and, all things considered, relatively unscathed.

# CHAPTER 12

"L-TWENTY." Griff touched the probes of the tracing transmitter to the exposed copper.

Blake waved the detector at a bundle of wires, home-run to a six-foot-tall panel in a separate room at the far side of the vault. When the intermittent beeping turned to a solid tone, he plucked the closest wire from the bundle and attached his own probes to confirm it was the same as Griff held at the other end.

"L-twenty." Blake used a blue Sharpie to write on the adhesive label, then peeled it off the sheet and wrapped it around the newly identified cable.

Like a well-oiled machine, both men went to work installing the terminals. In this case, an RJ-45 port on Griff's end and an RJ-45 connector on Blake's.

Over the past several weeks, Blake and Griff had spent time in the last unfinished portion of the underground bunker—or "the lab," as the team liked to call it—transforming it from a seven-hundred square foot concrete box into three separate rooms: the panel room, the equipment room, and the workroom.

No bigger than a standard closet, the panel room didn't house any actual computer equipment. Its purpose was routing and organizing

# DETACHMENT

wired connections for data or power. Signal conditioners, battery back-ups, dumb switches, and the like.

The equipment room was where the bulk of the computing power would live. Server racks. GPU arrays. Ima liked to call it the "brains of the operation."

Then there was the workroom. Long built-in tables lined every inch of available wall space and held giant screens, tower cases, and keyboards. This was the center of operations. The human interface. Enough for Blake, Griff, and Ima to each work with multiple terminals at once.

Like the rest of the underground bunker, the first step had been skinning the concrete walls with metal studs. Then, they ran the thousands of combined feet of wiring and laid out the wall boxes. Lastly, they installed the floors, drywall, and drop ceiling panels.

Now, it was just a matter of putting it all together and setting up the equipment.

"Far cry from the cave, eh?" Griff popped the finished port into the slot on the box cover.

Blake shrugged. "Maybe a little."

"The cave," was Griff's name for Blake's former computer room in the old Alexandria, Virginia townhouse. While Blake held an affinity for his old bunker, there was no denying this setup was "next level."

As part of a larger underground structure, the lab represented only a small piece of the puzzle. With two bunk rooms, an armory, a supply room, a conference room, a kitchen, and three full bathrooms, the bunker was a home beneath a home. Bomb rated, fully stocked, and sealed at its three access points by thick metal doors, the entire team could survive within its confines for at least a year.

The most important part of the design was the air handling systems. Filtered ventilation and climate control were a must. Especially with the amount of computer equipment they would run.

Air exchange systems were cleverly integrated into the utility room of the pool house, just above the lab. The air conditioning condenser was mixed in with several others along the north side of the main house.

Blake's old setup had been sufficient for the time. A smaller version of this, for all intents and purposes. It just had one major drawback. It had only one point of egress by a staircase off the kitchen.

When designing for the new build, Blake had prioritized including multiple points of access.

At the back of the pantry in the main house, the entire wall, shelves and all, could swing out to reveal a staircase. At the bottom, a steel door connected with the subterranean conference room. It was the most used entrance. However, the other two were even more useful.

Its beefy bulkhead doors hidden under the base of the wooden dock, a long tunnel connected the bunker to the shoreline. It would be useful for the covert loading of equipment or to escape by boat if needed. When phase two of construction started—which included the inground pool and underlying structures—the shoreline tunnel seemed like an overreach. But after a few design iterations, it came to fruition on schedule.

Finally, there was the garage. A hatch concealed by a roll-away tool chest at the back, opened to a shorter tunnel at the bottom of the steel ladder bolted to the side of the concrete cavity. Like its counterpart, the tunnel allowed for easy resupply and quick escape by vehicle should the need arise.

Two of the garage bays shared a double door, allowing them the space to back in a box truck. With the help of a sling hoist and a couple of hand-trucks, they had loaded most provisions and equipment through this entrance.

"L-twenty-two." Griff held the probes and waited for Blake to locate the next cable. "I don't think we're going to get through all of these today."

"That's okay," Blake said. "It's not like we have a deadline."

"I know. It's just..."

Blake waited for the rest, but it didn't come. "What's on your mind?"

"Nothing. I just want to make sure you haven't forgotten the whole point of all this."

"You think I've forgotten?"

"I don't know." Griff said. "The past few weeks, you've spent most of your time sitting on the porch of the guest house, staring at the water, or whatever. I think everyone's wondering where we're going with all this. I

# DETACHMENT

mean, don't get me wrong, this place is great. I guess everyone's just worried we're on a permanent vacation."

Blake made a conscious effort not to defend himself. Griff was right. At least partially. Blake had every intention of fulfilling the promises he'd made. That they all had made. He could feel the pull of complacency. After all he had been through, he wanted to tell himself he'd earned a retirement.

But that wasn't him. Any more than it was the rest of them.

"Trust me, Griff. We're just getting started. We'll finish this up, tie up a couple other loose ends and when Kook gets back from Las Vegas, we'll hit the ground running. Okay?"

"Sure." Griff held up the cable, probes still attached. "You got the other end of this one or what?"

"Yep. Good to go."

From the work room, Blake could hear Haeli's tinny voice through the intercom speaker embedded in the wall. "Blake? Honey? You out in the garage?"

*Honey?*

Blake couldn't remember Haeli ever calling him 'honey.'

"What's up with her?" Griff asked. "She knows we're down here. Why would you be in the garage?"

"Something's wrong." Blake dropped what he was doing, went to the intercom, and pressed the talk button. "Everything okay?"

"Yes. We have visitors. The neighbors were nice enough to stop by."

*Oh no.*

"Thanks sweetie," Blake said. "I'll be right in."

It was a matter of time. Blake had seen them peeking out their window whenever he drove in or out of the shared portion of the driveway. It was a wonder they hadn't shown up sooner.

"Neighbors?" Griff's attention remained on wrangling the tiny strands of copper into their respective slot on the plastic port fitting. "I forgot we had neighbors."

"Be right back." Blake darted off through the bunker and into the kitchen. He punched in the code, releasing the locks on the heavy door.

Within a few seconds, he reached the end of the tunnel and climbed the metal rungs.

When he reached the top, he unlatched the hatch, then backed down a few rungs to allow the trap door to swing downward. He climbed again and used one hand to push the rolling tool chest out of the way while he gripped the top rung with the other hand.

After getting to the garage and repositioning the tool chest, he grabbed a rag from a milk carton the workers had left behind. A bottle of gun oil sat on the workbench. For added effect, he squirted a small amount on the rag and bunched it into his palm.

He activated the overhead door and stepped out to the circular driveway. Outside was a panel truck belonging to the three-man crew helping Fezz with his project.

Blake made his way up the path and through the front door.

"Hi there," a man dressed in khaki shorts and a purple polo shirt said. "You must be Blake. I'm Cornelius. Cornelius Baldwin." He offered his hand.

Blake made a show of wiping his hands with the rag, then accepted the handshake. "Sorry, I was just working on the car."

"No worries, friend," Cornelius said. "Oh, and this is my wife, Margaux. That's with an 'AUX', not an 'O'."

Margaux stepped forward to shake Blake's hand. "Hi Neighbor."

After she let go, Blake could see her glance at her hand and then hold the stiffened appendage out to the side of her hip as if she were afraid of brushing her clothing with it.

"Sorry about the grease." Blake headed toward the kitchen island. "Let me just wash up."

"It's so refreshing that you work on your own car," Margaux said. "Is that, like, a hobby?"

Blake was going to respond, but decided anything that came out wouldn't have been well received.

"Blake, darling, Cornelius and Margaux were kind enough to bring us a cake." Haeli's back to the pretentious pair, she made a face like she had smelled a dead skunk. "Isn't that nice?"

# DETACHMENT

"So nice." Blake shook off his wet hands, then grabbed the towel draped over the handle of the dishwasher.

"Nice place you got here," Cornelius said. "Quite an operation you had going for a while. What a mess, am I right? Came out nice, though."

Blake walked over to Haeli and put his arm around her. "Thanks. These things are a process."

"Indeed." Cornelius said.

"I won't lie," Margaux started, "we were a little worried when we found out someone was building on this lot. But when we saw you were leaving the trees in between and that it wasn't, well, you know."

"No, I don't." Blake wasn't being facetious. He had no idea what she was getting at.

"What Margaux means is, we were worried about home values. I'm sure you can understand. Could have been, how do I say this, the lower class, God forbid.

Blake squeezed Haeli. She squeezed him back. Neither of them had to speak to know what the other was thinking. *Man, I'd like to punch these two in the face.*

"Anyhow." Cornelius looked around the great room as if he had lost something somewhere near the ceiling, "Olivia here tells me you're in tech."

"Olivia." Blake said. Haeli's lips parted into a slight smile. "Right. Well, Olivia is right. I mean, I'm retired now. My company invented an image processing algorithm. Google bought the company, lock, stock, and barrel. So here we are."

"Must have been a pretty penny," Cornelius said.

"I did okay. How about you? What business are you in?"

"Oil."

"Really?"

"Well, my great grandfather was."

"I'm told Cornelius here was named after Cornelius Vanderbilt," Haeli said. "Isn't that interesting?"

"The railroad magnate." Blake said. "Are you related?"

"No," Margaux let out an awkward giggle. "He's not."

From behind Blake and Haeli, Fezz and three other men barreled in from the hallway off the kitchen. "—and I never saw her again. Swear to God."

The men laughed.

Fezz, noticing Cornelius and Margaux's presence, froze in his tracks. "Who are you?"

"Butch, this is Cornelius and Margaux, our neighbors. This is Butch, our, um. Groundskeeper."

By the look on Fezz's face, Blake wasn't sure if he was about to protest or to laugh. He did neither. "I—We were just wrapping up in the theater, boss. We'll get out of your hair." Fezz motioned to the three workers. Without a word, the four men hauled their five-gallon buckets and canvas bags through the front door.

"Theater?" Margaux said. "How modern. Can we see?"

"No!" Fezz blurted. "I mean, it's not safe. There's nails. Lots of nails. And wet paint."

"Butch is meticulous," Haeli said. "A true craftsman."

Cornelius looked puzzled. "I thought he was the groundskeeper."

"He is," Blake said. "But he does a lot of odd jobs around here. Jack of all trades. Right, Butch?"

"Right," Fezz said. "Anyway, I've gotta get to the guesthouse and fix that thing you asked for."

"You know, Margaux's been wanting to have the oak refinished in the salon. Maybe we could hire Butch."

"I don't know," Fezz said. "I've got a lot of work to do around here still."

"Nonsense." Blake attempted to keep his amusement at bay. "We don't mind loaning him out."

"Wonderful." Margaux took Cornelius by the hand and started moving him toward the door. "We're having a small gathering this weekend. A meeting of the Jamestown Historical Society. I'm the treasurer—not that it matters. But in case you were interested. Anyway, you can start on Monday."

"He'll be there." Blake turned to Fezz and released a huge, mischievous grin. "With bells on."

## CHAPTER 13

"MISTER PRESIDENT." Butler leapt from his seat.

"Sit." Moore hurried around the table and took his spot at the head. "Has Ron filled you in?"

"Yes." Conway acknowledged.

"Good. Then you all understand the predicament we're in. Ron, have you reached out to SOCOM?"

"Not yet," Phillips said.

"What are you waiting for? People, listen. It's time to circle the wagons. I need everyone focused. Dave, what are you hearing?"

"We're picking up a lot of chatter," Butler said. "CIA. NSA. Word's getting around that Maduro claims to have hostages. It's all over Venezuela. He's using it as anti-American propaganda."

"David's right," Laurel said. "Resistance leaders have gotten word. Hernandez has publicly denounced any support from the United States. This is exactly what I—"

"No," Moore interrupted. "Don't even think about playing the 'I told you so' game. This is all our asses. Like it or not."

"It is," Conway said. "But right now, the most important thing is getting our boys home. I think we can all agree on that. What are we doing to organize a rescue? Ron?"

Phillips looked at Conway and then at Butler. Their expressions were almost identical, as if the work of a single sculptor. If there was one supposition the pensive faces relayed, it was that they were not going to like the answer. He turned to Moore, then to Conway, and back to Moore. "Bill?"

"There won't be a rescue mission, Laurel." Moore said.

"Hold on a minute," Butler said. "We're giving in to his demands?"

"We're not doing that either."

Conway scoffed. "Maduro won't release them out of the kindness of his heart. We're going to have to give him what he wants. Or we'll to have to go back in."

"You're not listening," Moore said. "We're not doing either. We can't risk another mission. And I refuse to negotiate with this terrorist."

"The intelligence community will not be behind this," Butler said. "They're already clamoring for a rescue mission. The Special Activities Division has already put itself on standby. They know our guys are in there. They're not going to let it go."

"Wrong," Moore said. "They don't know. They only think. We can issue a public statement acknowledging the rumor and debunking it."

"And what happens when Maduro releases video of his captives?" Butler asked.

"I have to agree," Phillips said. "There shouldn't be any acknowledgement, even to dispel the rumors. Internally, we can plant word that a rescue mission has been conducted and that our guys have been recovered, safe and sound. Anything that comes out of Venezuela at that point will be considered a desperate ploy and withheld from the public as a national security issue."

"We're not just going to leave them there to die," Conway said. "We can't do that."

"We don't have a choice," Moore said. "We took our shot, and we failed."

Phillips chuckled under his breath. That word. "We." Three times in one sentence, no less. The last time they sat together, in the very same chairs, Moore hadn't uttered the word once. Then, it was about "his" plan. "His" will. Now, all of a sudden, he was a "we."

"Let me at least see what Langley can come up with," Butler said. "Let me bring it to you. We might be able to do this quietly and still get our guys out."

"I thought this wasn't one for the CIA, Dave," Phillips said. "Wasn't that what you said?"

"If you hadn't screwed it up—"

"Enough," Moore barked. "I don't want to hear any more talk about rescue or anything else. We're going to handle this by keeping our mouths shut and doing nothing. Dave, you do what you have to do to knock down the chatter as false information. Categorically deny all of it. If Maduro takes it to the next level, I'm going to need some insulation. Plausible deniability. Do you understand?"

"Are you saying you want us to take the hit for this?" Butler's skin blanched and his forehead glistened in the overhead lights.

"No," Phillips said. "He wants me to."

Moore bowed his head. "I'm sorry, Ron. It would have to be you. You took it upon yourself to issue the order, based on intelligence you received. Neither I, nor any other member of the Cabinet were aware. I won't lie to you, it would mean your resignation, and I'm sure the Attorney General would insist on filing charges. Of course, I would pardon you as soon as I'm sworn in for my second term and you would be taken care of financially." Moore slapped the table and shifted his voice to an upbeat tone. "But let's not get ahead of ourselves. We're talking worst-case scenario here."

Conway and Butler sat silent. No doubt dumbfounded by the soliloquy they had just witnessed.

Phillips couldn't say he was as surprised. Of course, there was no way he would take the fall for the likes of Moore, but Moore didn't need to know that. Besides, it would never come to be. Phillips would make sure of it. "Of course, Mister President. I understand."

"Good. I mean, thank you." Moore stood up. None of the other three budged, including Butler. "We'll reconvene tomorrow."

Moore rushed out. The others sat in silence.

Even in Moore's absence, a sense of foreboding lingered in the air.

After a few moments, Conway spoke. Her tone was solemn and introspective, as if she were praying. "This isn't what I signed up for."

Phillips took a deep breath and rose to his feet. "Well, then. Tomorrow." He walked toward the door.

Butler twisted and spoke over his shoulder. "Ron–"

Phillips stopped and raised his hand, palm toward Butler. "I know."

Butler sank back into his chair.

As Phillips cleared the doorway, he could hear Conway grumble, "And where the hell is Oakley?"

# CHAPTER 14

"KIERAN," Buck Novak called across the hall.

"What?"

"Come in here for a second."

Kieran Brown took off his reading glasses and placed them next to his keyboard.

Novak returned to his seat behind his desk.

A few seconds later, Brown ambled across the hall and pulled his usual chair from under Novak's desk.

"Close the door," Novak said.

"Really?"

"Yes. I need to get your take on something."

Brown hesitated. "This better not be about the thing I said I didn't want to know about."

"It's not. Will you close the door, please?"

With the enthusiasm of erosion, Brown pushed it closed. "There. What's going on?"

"It's about Venezuela."

"Jesus, Buck. I told you, I don't want to know anything about it. Why do you insist on dragging me into this?"

"I'm not trying to drag you into anything, Kieran. This conversation never happened. You know I would never throw you under the bus."

"There's no bus. I don't know anything about it."

Novak raised his voice. "I don't know anything about it, either. That's the problem."

"Then what are you carryin' on about? Just forget about it."

"You don't understand, Kieran. Jackson is on the team."

Brown sat up straight. "No." His jaw hung open.

"I tried to talk him out of it. He wouldn't have it."

"You've got to stop him, Buck. Have him pulled. You can't let him get mixed up in this thing."

"It's too late. He already left."

Novak tried to hold himself together. He had received a message from his son two days prior. "Heading out," it read. "Looks like I'll be back in time to make that visit after all. Talk to you tomorrow. Love ya."

*Talk to you tomorrow.*

Since then, Novak had sent at least two dozen text messages and tried to call as many times. He knew Jackson wouldn't have his phone with him on deployment.

"He was supposed to be back already," Novak said.

"Did you call Eaton?"

"Several times. He hasn't called me back."

"Then I'll call him."

"I thought you didn't want to be involved."

"I don't. But Jackson..."

Novak's inclination was to brush it off as a ridiculous suggestion. What good would it do to have Brown call? Then again, if something had gone wrong—if it had to do with Jackson—it was possible Eaton was avoiding him.

Leaning forward, Novak lifted his finger and waggled it at Brown. He didn't say anything, but the message was specific. *You—You, my friend, are a genius.*

"Let's call him from your office," Novak said.

"Now?" Brown asked.

"Yes, now."

Brown stood up. At his usual pace, he opened the door and headed across the hall. Novak followed close behind.

"What are you going to say?" Novak asked.

"I don't know. What do you want me to say?" Brown replied.

"Just see if he picks up."

Brown sat at his desk. After clicking the mouse a few times, the contact for General Frank Eaton appeared on the screen. Brown dialed and held the handset to his ear.

After around three seconds, he spoke. "Frank. It's Kieran Brown."

Novak snatched the phone from Brown's hand. The cord clotheslined him across the neck.

"Frank, Buck Novak here."

"General Novak. I was just about to call you back." Eaton said.

"Cut the crap, Frank. What's going on with Jackson? Where is he? Did something go wrong?"

"I don't know what you mean."

"Bullshit. You know exactly what I mean. I know Jackson is on the team. What happened?"

There was only silence from the other end of the line.

"Frank. Tell me right now. What happened to Jackson?"

"I don't know anything about Jackson. I don't know what you're getting at. I'm sorry, I wish I could be of more help."

"You don't know what I'm talking about? Venezuela, Frank. I'm talking about Venezuela. Did you forget? I issued *you* the goddamn order!"

Over the course of three sentences, Novak's voice morphed from seething snarl, to growl, to full-out yell. Brown jumped out of his chair and slammed his door closed to contain the ruckus.

"You want me to spell it out for you, Frank?" Novak's eyes glistened and his skin turned an unhealthy shade of red. "You sent my kid to Venezuela to assassinate a president! And I haven't heard from him since! Does that ring a bell for you?"

Silence on the other end of the line. Novak wanted to slam down the phone, but he kept his composure enough to wait for a response. Something. Anything.

"Buck," Eaton finally said. "Listen to me closely."

Novak was listening.

"I've been told—" Eaton enunciated each word as if he were

concerned Novak would miss one "—there was no such order. There was no such mission. Do you understand what I'm saying?"

*No such mission.*

Novak understood. He understood completely. The mission had gone south. The White House was cutting its losses. The bastards would sweep the whole thing under the rug. "Can you just tell me, Frank? Is he alive?"

"I've gotta go, Buck."

The line disconnected.

Novak lowered the phone. The blood drained from his face.

"Buck, I..." Brown placed his hand on Novak's shoulder.

Novak appreciated the gesture, but he couldn't help but feel a twinge of resentment. Brown didn't have children. He couldn't possibly have known what it felt like.

"Leave me," Novak said.

'This is my—"

"Now." Novak sat and squeezed the sides of his skull with his palms. He heard the door open but didn't look up to see if Brown had left. It didn't matter.

As his eyes welled, and his stomach churned, Novak thought out loud. "Please be alive, Jackey. Please be alive."

# CHAPTER 15

BUCK NOVAK SLOGGED across the cobblestone, lost in thought.

Thunder Alley, they called it—the open stone-paved area beside the main entrance to Amalie arena.

Still daylight, the video montage of Steven Stamkos' highlights projected on the parking garage structure was barely visible. Later, the game would be broadcast there. Those who couldn't get seats or didn't want to pay the exorbitant price, could gather in Thunder Alley with a few thousand friends to watch the Tampa Bay Lightning make another run at the Stanley Cup.

Crowds were already filling in, and it would only get worse.

When Novak bought the tickets from a coworker a week prior, he was excited that he and Robbie would get to see another playoff hockey game together. It would be like old times.

Now, Novak couldn't care less. The only thing on his mind was Jackson and how he'd break the news to Robbie.

Any minute now, his youngest boy would be texting him, asking where he was in the crowd. There would be no happy reunion. Only solemn conversation.

Novak wished he had answers. Anything he could share. A reason for hope.

He didn't have those.

Not that he hadn't tried. The only thing he came away with were more questions.

Since he spoke with Frank Eaton, he wanted nothing more than to call Phillips himself. To give him a piece of his mind. Demand something be done.

As much as his phone had been burning a hole in his pocket, he had decided it wouldn't be a smart career move to chew out the Secretary of Defense. Although he could no longer remember why.

What was the worst that could happen? A demotion. Forced retirement. What did it matter? They could take the job for all he cared. This was his family.

Without conscious intention, Novak slipped his phone from his pocket.

*I could call.*

Novak scanned the crowd in case Robbie was wandering around looking for him. He didn't expect so. He had already asked him to text as soon as he arrived downtown, and there hadn't been any messages yet.

If he called Phillips now, he would at least have something to tell Robbie. Even if it was only that he went to bat for Jackson.

*Screw it.*

Novak held the microphone close to his mouth to allow the voice assistant to pick up his words over the background noise. "Call D.O.D."

"Calling D.O.D.," the phone answered back in the familiar female voice.

The call connected.

"Department of Defense, how may I direct your call?"

"This is General Novak, SOCOM, verification alpha-zulu-five-eight-eight-lima, for the Secretary."

"Standby General Novak."

After around forty-five seconds, the operator returned with the usual directive. "Hold the line for the Secretary."

The line clicked several times.

Phillips came on. "Thanks for calling back, Buck."

"Calling you back?"

"Did you get my messages?"

# DETACHMENT

"No," Novak said. "I'm not in the office." A sense of relief washed over him. Maybe Eaton had gotten his wires crossed. There was no cover-up. Phillips had reached out to *him*. "Do you have news?"

"News? No." Phillips said. "What is that noise? Are you on a cell phone?"

"Yes."

"For Christ's sake, Buck. How am I going to—"

"Why were you calling?"

Phillips spoke slowly, as if vetting each word as it was formed. "I wanted to touch base with you to reiterate your obligations. My boss —*our* boss—appreciates your continued loyalty to your country and trusts that you understand the consequences for any actions that would threaten national security."

"You're questioning my loyalty? Are you serious right now? My son is on that team. Do you know that? My son is down there right now, and I want to know what we're going to do about it!"

Novak felt dizzy. The world around him faded in the background. Amid hundreds of festive fans, he might as well have been standing on a deserted island.

"Watch your tone, General."

Novak dropped the phone to his chest and took a breath. Maybe he could appeal to Phillips' conscience. There was some remnant of humanity in there somewhere, Novak was sure of it.

"Cut the order. Please. I'll have our guys on a flight tonight. Do it for me, Ron. I'm begging you. You talk to me about loyalty to the country. What about the country's loyalty to its men? Men who have given all of themselves to fight for it. Like you and I both did."

"There will be no order, Buck. I'm sorry. Look, I understand. I do. When it comes to family, it can be difficult."

Novak's hands trembled. "If you're not going to send a team back in there, I'll put it together myself."

"See, that's the kind of thing I hate to hear, Buck. I know you're emotional. How about this? This one time, I'll forget you said that, okay? In return, you won't speak about this ever again. And I mean ever, Buck, is that clear?"

Novak seethed but provided no response.

"Answer me. Are we clear? For the sake of your—let's say, your longevity. And I'm not talking about the job, Buck. You know what I mean?"

Novak's top lip quivered. He cupped the bottom of the phone with both hands and spoke softly. "You're a bastard. All of you are."

As Novak dropped the phone from his ear and pressed the 'End Call' button, a hand gripped his shoulder. It took him a second to even register the touch.

"Pop? Hey, I texted but——"

Novak turned and looked at this son. Tears welled in his eyes.

"You okay, Pop?"

"No. I'm not okay."

"What's wrong?"

Novak thought about telling Robbie everything. Spilling it all out there at their feet. Right then and there. But if he did, Robbie would be involved. And there would be no reversing it.

"Rough day, that's all. Come here, kid." Pulling his son close, Novak embraced him.

"We don't have to stay for the game if you're not up for it, Pop."

"No, I'm good." Novak cleared his throat and turned to face the monolithic arena. "Let's go, Bolts."

# CHAPTER 16

TWENTY-TWO SAILBOATS. That's how many Blake counted in the last half-hour.

In the chair he claimed on the small guesthouse porch he built for this very purpose, Blake took in the sights and sounds of the West Passage.

Boating season was ramping up and traffic on the narrow section of Narragansett Bay increased by the day. It didn't bother Blake. Just the opposite. He could sit there for hours, watching them.

Jamestown and neighboring Newport were sailing towns through-and-through. While the Mako powerboat was convenient, he wondered if he shouldn't take the plunge and add one more toy to the inventory. The long private pier had plenty of room on the opposite side of the Mako for at least a forty-foot sailboat. And it would be a shame to waste the space.

In his mind's eye, he could picture sailing off for a weekend to Block Island or Martha's Vineyard. Blake at the helm. Haeli next to him, arm in arm. Nothing but open water ahead of them.

Throughout his years, Blake had always allowed himself to dream. Now and then, he could linger in a made-up moment. Experience what could be. Sometimes, the idea was within the realm of possibility. Other times, it was far out of reach.

Now, there was no such thing. Everything that money could buy was obtainable. For that reason, he often reminded himself—The things that matter in life can't be bought.

Blake glanced at his watch. In a few minutes, he should fire up the grill.

As he stood, walked to the end of the porch, and stepped down to the path back to the pool, he kept his eyes on the scene beyond the shoreline as if afraid he'd miss something important.

Around the back side of the guest house, the newly planted flowers were starting to bloom. There was grass already, too. A pleasant contrast to the muddy pit that had existed for many months before.

Ahead, Blake could see the crew taking advantage of the first truly nice day of the season. It was unusually hot for the time of year. And no one was letting it go to waste.

He paused to take in the tableau. It was the best part of this place. The chance to see the people he cared about enjoying themselves. Without a care in the world. At least for the afternoon.

Poolside, Haeli was lying on her back. Her lounger tilted back until almost horizontal. She wore a black bikini, and her skin already had a smooth, sun-kissed glow.

*She is flawless*, he thought. And he was sure very few people would disagree.

Next to Haeli, Ima reclined on a matching lounger. She sat upright with a book on her lap but paid it no attention. She and Haeli were engrossed in a rather unanimated conversation.

In the shade of a juvenile tree, Ian sat at the glass table, scribbling in a notebook. Blake could hardly guess what he was working on. Probably something with merit. Ian wasn't one to occupy himself with trivialities.

In the pool, Khat floated on a wedge-shaped raft printed to look like a piece of pizza. He gripped a plastic Tervis tumbler in his left hand, half-submerged in the water. Although his sunglasses made it impossible to tell, it was a decent bet he was fast asleep.

Blake swung open the gate and closed it behind him. "Who's hungry? Should I throw on some burgers and dogs?"

Haeli continued facing the sky. "In a bit. Come and sit."

"In a bit," Blake repeated.

DETACHMENT

He was about to ask where Fezz and Griff were, then remembered that today was the day Griff was picking up his new Tesla. He had enlisted Fezz to drop him off at the dealership. How could he forget? Griff had been like a giddy child when he found out it came in.

It was part of a pact made with each other. To use some of the money to do things they'd always wanted to. Within reason, of course. Blake figured he could make a case for the sailboat. Who could say when he came up with the idea, right?

Ian was wearing his bathing suit but was as dry as a bone. "Ian, why don't you go in the pool?" Blake asked.

"I don't want to. There's no one to play with. Only Khat, and he's busy day-drinking."

Blake laughed out loud. "How do you know about day-drinking?"

"My mom says it's how you know you're on vacation."

Ima reached down and picked up her glass off the stone deck. It was filled with a pink concoction. She raised it in Blake's direction.

"Fair enough," Blake said.

Ian turned his attention back to his notebook.

"Well, I'm gonna start the grill. If anyone wants anything, let me know." Blake kicked his sandals off and pushed them under one of the four empty loungers with his bare foot.

"Hello?" A gentle voice came from near the corner of the house.

Peeking around the stone facade was Christa Kohler, with Lucy right behind her.

"Christa," Blake said. "Come on in. Glad you decided to stop by."

Lucy passed Christa and gave Blake a hug.

Blake squeezed and gave her back a rub. "Good to see you, Lucy. How's everything?"

"Good," she said.

Christa dropped her canvas tote bag next to Haeli's chair. "I rang the doorbell, but—"

"Yeah, we're out enjoying the weather. Grab a seat. Or jump in the pool. I'm about to cook some burgers if you want anything."

Haeli lifted her sunglasses to her forehead. "Welcome to paradise."

"So it is." Christa said.

"Hi, Lucy!" Ian abandoned his notebook to fly in and grab Lucy's hand. "Wanna go swimming with me?"

"Of course I do," Lucy said.

Lucy was Ian's favorite. Probably because she never tired of going along with whatever Ian had on his agenda. She set about taking off her outer clothing, and then tossed her shirt and shorts on the ground near Christa's bag.

"Let's go." Lucy turned and jumped into the water. Ian ran, and with a howl, cannonballed a few feet from her.

Khat stirred. He lifted his head for a moment, then rested back down on the inflatable pillow.

"I'll go in and grab some towels," Blake said.

"No worries," Christa said. "I really appreciate the invite."

"Of course. You don't need an invite, you know. Just stop in. Any time."

"Can I get you a drink?" Ima swung her legs over the side of the lounger and stood up. "I'm going in to make another, anyway."

"Sure."

"Cosmo?"

"Cosmo sounds good."

Ima picked up the towel she'd knocked onto the ground and draped it over her chair. Christa watched as Lucy and Ian splashed each other, laughing like hyenas.

"I love how Lucy is with him," Christa said. "She's so good with younger kids."

"Don't let him fool you," Ima chimed in. "He's older than me." She headed off to the kitchen.

"So, did you sell the house?" Blake always made it a point to show interest in Christa's work. She was proud of it. And for good reason. She had made a name for herself as one of the top real estate agents on the island.

"I did. They close in two weeks."

"Congrats," Blake said. "Who's better than you?"

"It has nothing to do with me. That place is beautiful. Four-million-dollar house on the water. What's not to like?"

DETACHMENT

Blake looked around. *What's not to like, indeed.* "We're on for Sunday, right?"

A few months prior, Christa and Gwyn invited Blake over for dinner. Since then, it had become something of a Sunday tradition.

"Absolutely. But there's a stipulation. Gwyn's rules, not mine. Haeli has to agree to come this time."

"Are you kidding?" Haeli said. "I'm absolutely in. I hear it's the hottest table in town."

Blake gave a sheepish grin. "I may have raved a bit about Gwyn's cooking. I mean, you have to admit, the woman's a master."

"She is. You should all come to the restaurant some night," Christa suggested. "Gwyn would love it."

"I was just thinking the same thing yesterday," Blake said.

He was being sincere. He thought it was strange they hadn't all gone to Gwyn's restaurant, O'hana, as a group. Gwyn was plenty busy and wasn't hurting for customers, but it was the least they could do to show their support. Plus, the food was out of this world.

"It's settled then," Christa said. "You'll be our guests. Next week maybe?"

Ima threw open the slider, ducked back into the house for a second, then emerged with the three glasses of Cosmopolitan pressed to her chest. She closed the slider with her foot.

"I come bearing gifts," she said.

Behind her, the sliding door whooshed open again. In the doorway stood Kook.

"This is what you've been doing while I was gone?"

"Kook!" Haeli sat up.

"Hey buddy, you're back!" Blake left the women and met Kook halfway between the door and the pool. They shared a G-lock handshake and a pat on the back. "How was Vegas?"

"Same," Kook said. "Much better without having to deal with the ex-wife. Got a few things taken care of. I think they'll be good without me for a while."

As the owner of a sightseeing company and a small fleet of aircraft, Kook had to check in now and again to make sure everything ran smoothly. On this trip, he was bringing his new business manager up to speed.

Kook walked over to the edge of the pool. "Look at these animals. How's the water?"

"Tepid," Ian said. "You should come in."

"You think so?" Kook's eyes widened in mock surprise. "Now?"

"Yeah," Ian giggled.

Kook took his wallet and phone out of his pocket and dropped them on the chair between Haeli's legs. He stripped off his t-shirt, kicked off his Birkenstocks, and jumped in.

Knowing what was coming, Ian fled toward the deep end.

Kook chased with hands out as if bearing his claws, growling like a werewolf.

"No." Ian laughed. "You can't catch me."

Lucy jumped on Kook's back. "I'll save you."

Kook knocked into Khat's raft, tipping him into the water.

Without missing a beat, Khat lifted his drink in the air and, with one hand, paddled himself to where he could stand. He plodded his way to the stairs.

"I've got him, Ian, run!" Lucy shouted.

Ima smiled. "Ya know, if Lucy ever wants to do a little babysitting."

Dripping wet, Khat walked over, grabbed Ima's towel from her chair, and started drying himself off. "Babysitting? There's like thirty people living here. I think we've got it covered."

Christa put her hands on Khat's shoulders and moved him a foot to the left so she could see Ima. "Whenever you need it. She'd be happy to."

## CHAPTER 17

DOWN THE HALL, the morning meeting was in full swing.

Buck Novak had excused himself without explanation, only to close himself into his office.

Over the past few years, there were times when he'd almost forgotten anything existed outside these four walls. Countless hours spent. Wasted.

Time had flown by. No matter how much he wished it hadn't. He regretted not spending more time with his family. They might still be one if he had.

But his was important work. Necessary work. And it required sacrifice.

Few people in the United States were aware of the dangers posed to their way of life every single day. Intelligence, law enforcement, the military—the thin line between equilibrium and disaster. No group of people were more instrumental than the special forces.

As commander, he bore a heavy burden. Lives were on the line, every single day. The weight he carried wasn't only for the soldier or sailor, but for every freedom-loving person in the world. Now, he felt gravity conspiring against him.

On a few minutes of sleep a night, his mind was dulling. Self-doubt—the opportunistic scavenger it could be—was ever present. Lying in his bed at night, memories bombarded him like a horror movie marathon.

He wondered if he was losing it. Did he no longer have the stomach for war?

It wasn't that he was averse to violence. Death and destruction were as much a part of his life as his morning coffee. As a result of his decisions, good people had died. The lives of those left behind, shattered. And yet he had never lost a moment of sleep. How? What was so different about this?

*Jackson is my son, that's what.* The obvious answer. The wrong answer.

Yes, Jackson's life was in extreme danger. That was a fact. It tore at his gut in more excruciating ways than the shrapnel still lodged there from a lifetime ago. But Novak had prepared for this day. Almost expected it.

In all his years, he had never sent a man into hell unless he believed in the cause. Unless he knew in his heart, that man believed enough to lay down his life.

Above all of it, there was the creed. The tenet permeating every reach of the military mindset.

*Never leave a man behind.*

It was an unwritten contract between the United States of America and those who served her. In Novak's mind, this contract was unwavering and eternal.

He was wrong.

Cloistered within the same graying walls where minutes had turned into years, time stood still.

Without him, the meeting down the hall still took place. Battles were being won and lost. Secret wars were being waged. Time ticked on. And he was helpless.

*That's it.* The thought hit him like a mortar shell.

It wasn't only about Jackson, or honor, or morality, or code. Helplessness had kept him up at night. Impotence where there was once strength.

*I will not give up on you, Jackey.*

Novak picked up the phone. Another call. Another step toward the end of the proverbial plank.

"Switchboard," the operator said. "How may I direct your call?"

"Personal call for the Vice President. Tell him it's Buck Novak. Please."

"Thank you. Please hold."

Years ago, Robbie and Oakley's oldest, Trevor, had attended the same boarding school in Avon, Connecticut. The boys had become close friends, bringing Novak and Oakley together for social occasions. Birthday parties, Fourth of July barbeques, New Year's Celebrations. Although it had been years, Novak considered Irving Oakley a friend. Which is why Novak had avoided putting him in this position. Until now.

"Buck?" Oakley connected without warning.

"Irving. How are you? Long time."

"No kidding. How is everyone? The boys? I heard about the divorce. Was sorry to hear that. Anyway, what's the good word?"

"I need your help, Irving. You know I wouldn't normally call, but—"

"Of course, Buck. What's on your mind?"

*What's on my mind? What do you think?*

"Venezuela, Irving. Venezuela is on my mind."

"Venezuela? What, the protests going on down there? Why?"

"Come on, Irving, please don't play games. We're on a secure line. I'm read in, all right? I know. I cut the damn order myself."

"Okay. Sorry. I didn't know if—ya know. So why do you need my help? If it's information you want, I'm afraid I don't have it."

Novak sighed. Where his frustration once manifested itself as anger, it now took a more pathetic form. "We go back, you and me. And I've never come to you for anything. But this—"

"You're misunderstanding," Oakley said. "I'm saying I'm out of the loop on this one. I know—it's a long story. Honestly, at this point, I'm fine with it. No offense, Buck, but I'm on the other side of the fence with this. It's not right, in my opinion."

"What side do you think I'm on?" Novak raised his voice. "He's my son, for Christ's sake."

"Hold on. I'm not following. Did something happen to Robbie? I thought we were talking about something else. Is he in trouble?"

"Not Robbie. Jackson! Are you screwing with me right now, or do you really not know what I'm talking about?" Novak rubbed his head. Could it be that the Vice President of the United States was unaware of something of this magnitude? It was unfathomable.

"Are you saying Jackson is mixed up in Venezuela?"

"Listen to me, Irving. I can't believe I'm saying this, but I need to bring you up to speed. Ron Phillips, I assume by the direction of the President, sent a unit into Venezuela to assassinate Maduro. The unit was captured. And now, instead of organizing a rescue, everyone's scrambling to cover it up. When these boys shouldn't have been there in the first place! So, no, I don't need information. I need us to go back in there and bring our boys home."

When Novak finished his rant, there was silence from the other end of the line.

"Irving?" Novak held his forehead in his hand, trembling in anticipation.

"That scumbag," Oakley whispered.

Novak waited for more.

"Jackson is part of the unit." Oakley finally guessed. "They're holding him captive."

"Yes." Novak let out the breath he didn't realize he was holding in. Finally, they were getting somewhere.

"I'm so sorry, Buck. I didn't know. I knew about the plan, but then..."

"You have to fix this, Irving. You have to talk to the President. Talk some sense into him."

"It's not that easy." Oakley said. "I mean, I tried. You have to believe that."

"Try again."

"I will. You know I will. But listen, I'm not going to give you false hope. It wouldn't be fair to you. Or to Jackson or Robbie or Cheri. It kills me to say it, but he won't back down. It's not in his nature."

"Please just do what you can. Cheri doesn't even know. She'll never know. If Jackson doesn't make it back, what am I supposed to tell her?"

Oakley didn't have an answer. Instead, he offered a solemn statement. "Jesus, Buck. I'm so, so sorry."

Novak knew what he meant. Although he was, Oakley wasn't saying he was sorry about Jackson. He was apologizing for already having failed. Oakley was saying that it was over.

"Yeah," Novak said. "So am I."

## CHAPTER 18

BUCK NOVAK SAT at the kitchen table. The clock on the wall pointed to eight o'clock. Any other day, he'd have already been at work for a half-hour. Then again, on a normal morning, he would have gone to bed the night before.

Beside the ticking clock and chirping birds somewhere beyond the kitchen window, the sound of a door squeaking and the slapping of bare feet against the hardwood were the first sounds Novak had heard in hours.

Robbie shuffled in from the hallway wearing a pair of gym shorts. The hair on the right side of his head was perfectly manicured. On the left, it stood on end. "Mornin'."

"Mornin'," Novak grumbled.

As tired and as tormented as he was, Novak was happy for the company. It was why he'd bought the two-bedroom condo. In case one of his sons wanted to stay over. Up until a day ago, the second bedroom had never been used.

"Running late?" Robbie cracked the fridge and rooted around inside, as if looking for something that wasn't there.

"I don't think I'm going in today."

Robbie swung the fridge door closed and turned to his father, abandoning his search. Novak could feel his son's stare. He sat as still as his body would allow, offering himself as a visual specimen. An oddity in a glass jar.

"What?" Novak asked with a mild affect.

"You sure you're feeling okay? Wanna talk about it?"

*Do I?*

It was all he wanted to do. He wanted to shout it out to the world.

"No. It's fine." Novak said.

"Okay," Robbie shrugged. "I'm here if you do." He grabbed two Oreo cookies from an open package on the counter and shoved them in his mouth. Then he started back towards his room.

"Robbie," Novak said.

"Yeah?"

"Come and sit down for a minute."

With a narrow focus and tilted eyebrows, Robbie made his way to the table and sat down. As he chewed and swallowed, his cheeks retracted like a python, digesting its prey.

"I want to tell you something. But I don't. Something I'm not allowed to tell you. In fact, just knowing this could jeopardize your job. Maybe even put you in danger. It's beyond classified, if you get what I'm saying."

"Then don't."

"But I believe it's something you should know. That you have the right to know. And I need to get it off my chest."

"Fine. Then tell me."

"I just want to make sure you're okay with me putting you in that position, that's all."

"Are you going to tell me, already? It's not like anyone would ever know, anyway."

"Okay." Novak rested his elbows on the table. "Do you know where your brother is?"

"No. I mean, I know he's deployed. He couldn't say where. Why? Does this have to do with him?"

"It does. Very much so."

"Is he all right? Stop talking in circles, Pop. Just tell me, is Jackson all right?"

"No. He's not all right, son. He's been taken hostage in Venezuela."

Robbie's jaw dropped open. "Are you serious? Venezuela? What the hell is he doing in Venezuela?"

"Let me start at the beginning."

For the better part of a half-hour, Novak explained every detail. Rehashed every conversation. By the time he was done, Robbie's demeanor had turned from shock to fury. His muscles tensed and his eyes smoldered.

"I can't believe the President would just abandon them! There has to be something we can do. I'll grab some guys and go get them. I'll kill every last one of those bastards if I have to."

"There is no doubt in my mind that every single one of your teammates would line up to help, I know I would have. Think about it, though. How would you get the equipment you'd need? How would you even get in? Let's say you could. Without support, it'd be a death sentence."

"Pop, you run special operations. Get me the resources."

"It doesn't work like that, Robbie, and you know it. I could cut an order, and then what? As soon as I made a single call, it would be shut down. No one is going to disobey a direct order from Phillips or the President himself. I'd steal you a plane myself if I thought it would help. Without authority, you'd set off an international incident. You'd be deemed rogue. Insubordinate. You'd be court-martialed and probably spend twenty years in prison. I might lose one son, Robbie. I'm not going to risk losing another."

"Maybe if everyone knew what was happening here, they'd be forced to do something about it."

"That's why they'll do anything to keep it quiet."

Robbie stood and kicked the wooden chair he was sitting on. It toppled over but didn't break. "Then we go to the press. Tell them everything we know. If we can't do it ourselves, we force their hand."

"Don't you think I thought of that already? Use your head. There is no proof that this mission ever existed. No record of who is there. It would be discredited immediately, and we would be back in the same boat."

"What do you mean there's no record?" Robbie yelled. "You said you cut orders. You said you received orders. Those are the proof we need right there!"

Novak found himself raising his voice to match his son's. "These things aren't just lying around the office, Robbie. Come on! We destroy paper copies and encrypt digital communications in secure facilities. I'm watched like a hawk. It's not like I can call up JSOC and say, 'Hey, you know that thing I sent you that we're never supposed to talk about ever again? Yeah, can you go ahead and send that back to me?'"

"If I were a General, yeah, I guess that's exactly what I would do."

"Don't be an ass, Robbie. You know that's ridiculous. It's not like I wouldn't go to the press. I would in a heartbeat. I know exactly who I'd go to. But even Clint wouldn't do anything with a fairy tale just because I said to take my word for it."

"These orders—you said they'd be archived at JSOC?" Robbie asked.

"The one I sent, yes, for sure. Along with any other materials related to the mission."

"Which means maps, schematics, equipment lists, everything, right?"

"Yes, likely," Novak said.

"I think I can get them."

"Who?"

"No. The files. I think I can get copies of the files."

"How would you do that?"

"Don't worry about that. But I think I have a way in."

For a moment, Novak figured his son was just blowing off some steam. Dreaming up a poorly thought-out, yet somehow foolproof plan to slay the dragon. Because, as Novak had come to realize, it was better than admitting the dragon was unbeatable. Still, something in his son's expression told Novak that he was as serious as he was sober.

"I can't let you do that, Robbie."

"You can't stop me, either. Unless you're going to report me and have me arrested."

"That's not funny."

"Let me do this, Pop. It's our best chance. Our only chance. You have a contact you trust. We'll be protected. No one will know how the files were leaked. We can force them to take action through public shaming. But we need to move before it's too late."

Novak swallowed hard. "It might already be too late."

"So, is that a yes?"

"Fine, but I don't want you taking any unnecessary risks. If it's dodgy, we call it off. We'll try something else."

"Great." Robbie hustled toward the hallway. "I've gotta get a flight back to North Carolina."

## CHAPTER 19

"KHAT!" Blake hollered from the bottom of the stairs. "Ima! Come down here for a minute. Team meeting."

"Coming," Ima called back.

"Khat?"

"One sec."

In the great room, Haeli, Fezz, Griff, and Kook had already settled into the sectional. Blake went into the dining room and dragged out two of the kingwood chairs. He positioned them in front of the fireplace and sat on the left.

Through the windows, the landscape lights mingled with their own reflections.

"Glad to see you made it back, Kook," Fezz said. "I thought maybe a poker table ate you."

Kook chuckled. "That's *why* I'm back. That reminds me, you got five bucks I can borrow?"

"How's the sightseeing business?" Griff asked.

"Fine. How's the new car?"

"Fast as hell. You've gotta check it out."

"I don't know," Fezz said. "If I'm gonna spend eighty grand for a car, I want it to come with an engine."

"At least when I roll in now, I don't rattle the windows like Mick."

"That's fair," Blake said.

Six months earlier, Blake had traded in his Challenger for a newer model. The SRT Hellcat Redeye Widebody's six-point-two-liter Hemi V8 put out seven hundred ninety-seven horsepower and the decibels to match.

Ima flittered down the stairs. "Where should I sit?"

"Wherever you want. Is Khat coming down?"

"I don't know." She slotted into the open spot between Fezz and Kook, and patted Fezz on the knee.

Blake noticed Ian sitting on the top step. "Hey bud, you want to join us?"

"Can I?"

"Team meeting," Blake said. "You're part of the team, aren't you?"

"Don't encourage him," Ima said. "He already believes that."

"Yes, I am!" Ian ran downstairs and climbed over the back of the couch. He squeezed between Fezz and Ima, then slid onto the floor by his mother's feet. "What's the meeting about?"

Haeli laughed. "We thought you were going to tell us."

"There he is," Griff said as Khat appeared from the upstairs hallway. "Right on time."

Khat held his arms up while he descended, one dramatic step at a time. It was an entrance worthy of a debutant at The Queen Charlotte's ball. "Behold!"

Haeli craned her neck to watch the show behind her. "Oh my god. You shaved."

"Holy cripes," Fezz said. "You don't look like The Cherchen Man anymore."

"You look weird," Ian giggled.

"Ian, that's not nice." Ima put her hands on his shoulders. "We're just not used to seeing his face. I think you look handsome."

"Thank you. I try." Khat took the chair next to Blake. "So, what are we doing here? Playing charades?"

Blake rested his elbows on his knees. "I know everyone's been getting a little antsy. I figured, now that this place is in order, that we should discuss our next steps."

"Ah." Kook smiled. "You want to know what we want to be when we grow up."

Ian raised his hand. "I want to be an astronaut."

"That's what every kid wants to be," Griff said.

"Yeah," Fezz added. "But how many kids do you know who are actually qualified?"

Kook reached for his drink. The condensation left a wet circle on the coffee table. "Fezz's got a point."

Haeli stood and leaned over the table to reach the small drawer at Kook's knees. She pulled it open, took one of the cork coasters, and slapped it on the table.

Kook moved the coaster over to cover the wet spot and rested his glass on it. He bumped Ian's thigh with his foot. "Watch out for the coaster police."

"Come on," Blake said. "Let's focus for just a minute. Does anyone have any ideas they'd like to throw out there?"

"I'll go." Haeli said. "I think we need to advertise—"

"Advertise?" Khat scoffed. "What are we, Kentucky Fried Chicken?"

Blake held out his hand. "Let her finish."

"I mean, we have to create a buzz. I don't know if that means a social media campaign, or what, but we need to start getting the word out."

"Haeli's right," Fezz said. "But I don't think we can get people's attention unless they see something to back it up. Something high profile."

Kook flapped his lips. "Sort of a chicken and the egg situation."

"What if—" Khat paused.

Blake was sure he could see smoke leaking from his ears. "What if what?"

"What if we monitored the news? Watched for something good. An ongoing crisis, like a hostage situation or a bomb threat. As long as it was close enough, we could swoop in, handle the situation, and get out. The press would eat it up."

"That's a dumb idea," Ian said.

"There are no dumb ideas, honey," Ima said. "Except maybe that one."

"Might be a little too much exposure, I agree," Blake said. "When the press and the authorities are already involved, we probably shouldn't be."

"Obviously," Fezz said. "The way I understood it, one of our primary goals is to keep our faces *off* the news."

Khat grunted. "We'd wear masks."

"Oh, masks?" Fezz laughed. "Do we get capes too?"

"Hold on," Ima said. "Maybe Haeli was onto something. We could advertise on the dark web. Lay it all out there like we're a law firm. Here are our services. Here are our rates. Nice, professional website. The whole bit."

"Easy enough," Griff said, "but the people we're looking to help won't be on the dark web. I say we keep it simple. We set up a secure telephone number, proxied and encrypted on this end so it can't be traced. We blanket social media using untraceable accounts with simple messages like, 'Nowhere else to turn? Call one-two-three etcetera.' We can let people leave messages, and if anything sticks out, do a little vetting and maybe look at helping."

"Perfect," Blake said. "Does anyone have any issue with that?"

"Not me," Fezz said. "Sounds like a plan."

"I'm good with it," Kook added.

"What's our name?" Ian asked.

The room fell silent for a moment. Blake assumed everyone else was thinking what he was thinking. *Did we ever have one?*

Ian looked puzzled. "What would people call us if we didn't have a name?"

There was wisdom in that logic. At some point, there would be a name. Everything and everyone was assigned one, whether they liked it or not. The question was, did they want it chosen for them?

"I think Ian's right," Blake said. "We need to control everything about this. Not only who we help and for what reasons, but the image, the narrative, all of it."

"Why not?" Fezz said. "This whole thing is ninety-nine percent bonkers, anyway. Why not take it all the way?"

"It would have to be dark and mysterious, like a codeword." Haeli put on her best movie-trailer voice. "'Project Prism.' or 'Task Force Searchlight.'"

"I have one," Khat said. "The Bad News Bears."

Kook shot back. "The Presumed Deadheads."

The group broke into laughter and the names flowed in rapid succession from all directions.

"Black Bonnet."

"The Revengers."

"Deus Ex Machina."

"Freedom Pirates."

"Vigilant-T."

"Project Purple Heart."

Blake sat back and laughed along. It didn't matter how goofy the conversation had become. The group carried a sense of revitalized energy. The resurgence of camaraderie. It was exactly what Blake was hoping for.

As the night went on, they would drink and plan. Laugh and scheme. And it would keep them all going.

Blake had called the meeting to remind the others that things weren't stagnant, only in flux. He ended up reminding himself.

## CHAPTER 20

"BACK BAY," the conductor announced.

Robbie looped his arm through the strap on his knapsack and lifted it off the floor. His back was stiff, but no worse than expected from almost eight hours in an uncomfortable seat. No one ever said the Amtrak economy class was the lap of luxury.

Soon after leaving Fayetteville, Robbie had noticed a black sedan in the distance behind him. For four and a half hours, he had let his mind run wild, even stopping at a rest stop for fifteen minutes to ease his overactive imagination. He had taken the opportunity to use the bathroom and grab a snack from a vending machine. Sure enough, once he was back on I-95, there it was again. The black sedan, in his rearview mirror.

Could it have been a coincidence? Maybe. He couldn't say for sure it was the same car. Given the circumstances, it wasn't worth the risk.

By the time he'd reached Washington D.C., he had decided to take evasive action. If for nothing else, then for his own sanity.

Having lived in D.C. while his father worked at the Pentagon, he knew the streets well enough to try to shake the tail, if it existed at all.

For twenty minutes, he'd snaked through the city until he was satisfied no one was following. It was during that time he'd come up with an idea.

Pulled over next to a fire hydrant, he'd searched up the Amtrak schedule. It was already after three in the afternoon and behind schedule. The one-fifty-five train out of Union Station fit the bill close enough. It would mean he'd arrive in Boston at nine-forty-five at night—slightly later than he intended. It wasn't so bad that it derailed the plan beyond repair. Or so he'd hoped.

After messaging his contact, he'd made his way to Union Station and ditched his car in the parking garage. As luck would have it, he had enough cash to buy the ticket. He'd seen enough spy movies to know it was never a good idea to use a credit card if someone was following you.

In the back of his mind, Robbie knew he was being paranoid. He didn't care. No one ever regretted taking too much precaution.

By the time he'd boarded the train, he had already received a reply from the contact. A reporter with the Boston Globe named Archer Wade.

Wade had been hand-selected by Robbie's father's friend. To hear his father retell it, he was the second coming. An investigative-reporting messiah. And exactly who they needed to blow this story wide open.

That was yet to be seen.

According to Wade's response, the plan would remain the same. Only the times would shift.

Once in Boston, he would get off in Back Bay and make his way north to the Fairmont hotel in Copley Square. In the lobby, there would be a black Labrador. Its name was Catie, if Wade was to be believed. Robbie was to pet the dog and if anyone spoke to him, he was to say, "I had a lab just like her. Her name was Catie, too."

That was it. The whole clandestine meeting was supposed to be kicked off by petting a dog. Why a Labrador? And why was it in the lobby of a hotel? Robbie didn't know. *It is what it is*, he thought.

Robbie looked around as the train pulled into the station and slowed to a stop. No one moved or seemed interested in him.

He unzipped the small pocket on the front of his bag, pulled out the thumb drive, and transferred it to his front pants pocket. Made of plastic and a few bits of metal, it was a pedestrian object. But considering what was on it, Robbie might as well have carried a nuclear warhead. The people he was afraid of, the people in power, would treat it as such.

In a way, he felt dirty having it on his person. Like a criminal. Although, that was a fair appraisal. The information *was* stolen.

The fact that he had stolen it wasn't what put the knot in his stomach. It was *how* he stole it. He had used his girlfriend's brother to get access. He had put Darrell in a precarious position. And if anyone ever found out, Darrell would be held accountable.

As dense as Darrell appeared, he could have already been wise to Robbie's ruse. He had tried calling Darrell several times since and was sent to voicemail. It was unlike Darrell. Always eager to connect, he'd usually answer on the first ring, or text back within seconds, like he was sitting by the phone waiting for someone to reach out. Not this time. Nicole had tried to reach him too, also to no avail.

Was he just busy?

Another thought crossed Robbie's mind. Darrell could already be in custody. He could have given Robbie up, for all he knew.

What if Darrell's boss audited the file transfer records? He seemed irritated with Robbie's presence. It would at least explain the black sedan.

It was too much. Confused and racked with guilt, he could barely keep his head on straight. But there was one thing he did know. If he didn't give himself a reality check, he'd be wearing a tinfoil hat by morning.

When the train doors opened, Robbie wasted no time finding his way to the exit. He looked behind him every other step. Through the crowd, it was hard to tell if anyone was tracking his movements.

As he approached the exterior doors, he gave one last glance over his shoulder.

Thirty to forty feet behind, he saw two men dressed in jeans and black t-shirts. Ex-military maybe. They seemed to notice him looking in their direction.

Robbie caught them bowing their heads and drifting away from each other. It was awkward. Out of place. Robbie's gut told him this wasn't a coincidence.

The Google Maps directions showed he was to exit onto Dartmouth St and walk two blocks north to the hotel.

Did the pair know where he was going? Were they monitoring his phone?

Valid questions. But no. If they knew where he was going, they would just intercept him when he got there, not follow him all the way from North Carolina. If they'd been up on his phone, he would have never seen them coming.

Robbie rubbed his forearm against the butt of the nine-millimeter tucked into a holster inside his waistline. He could just imagine what his brother would say. "What? Are you worried about these two blockheads?"

The truth was, he wasn't. Not at all. But the last thing he wanted to do was put this reporter in any danger, or worse, jeopardize the mission.

Until he could be sure, he would have to steer clear of the Fairmont. Then, if it came down to a fight, he was up for it.

Cutting around a large group of commuters to the left, Robbie hunched over and blended in as best he could. As he emerged into a gap between one group and another, he could see the two men hustling toward the doors, their heads swiveling back and forth.

Robbie bolted toward the east side of the station, zigzagging to avoid the last few stragglers from the train.

If he could put some distance between them, it was still possible to get to Wade.

He headed for a row of doors under a giant glass arch—the mirror image of the ones on the west, leading out to Dartmouth St.

Without stopping, he shouldered one open, pushing through into the warm night.

A row of buses sat idled along one side of a driveway. He darted to the left, following the sidewalk behind the buses and out of view. Flanked by the brick exterior wall of a parking structure, he kept moving toward the street.

As he reached the end, about to disappear around the parking garage, he gave in to the urge to look behind. Just in time to spot the two men coming around the front of the furthest bus. The problem was, they spotted him, too.

There were only two directions he could travel. Left or right. Across the street, the sidewalk and guardrail marked a thirty-foot drop to a highway, which seemed to materialize from deep within the earth.

Before he made a conscious choice, his legs were already pumping. Left. North. Toward the Fairmont.

He crossed the street in a diagonal trajectory, shedding his backpack and abandoning it in the middle of the roadway. He checked behind him. The two men hadn't yet come into view. He still had a chance of losing them.

On the right was a small street. The sign said Stanhope. From the open space afforded by the highway below, he had a clear view down Stanhope, all the way to the next corner. He needed more distance. A better option.

One more glance behind. The men had cleared the garage and now ran in a full sprint. Robbie pushed harder.

Half a block later, he noticed an opening between two stone buildings. A narrow, unmarked street.

Without looking behind him again, he took the corner.

It was his moment. Out of view for at least a few seconds, he needed to find a cutout, or a vestibule. Somewhere he could duck behind and wait. If he could catch one of them off guard, he could level the playing field. One on one, the battle was as good as won.

The results of his visual assessment were as unfortunate as they should have been foreseen. The situation proved less than ideal.

To the left was a building wrapped in construction netting. The row of aging brick buildings on the right looked to be buttoned up tight. While there were at least two steel doors, they didn't have exterior handles.

Two equally poor options remained. A fire escape, the grated steps and platforms of which offered zero cover. Or a set of three green dumpsters, tucked beside a protruding, rusted air duct.

*The dumpsters.*

Robbie slipped behind the far side of the last garbage bin and dropped to one knee. Edging slowly, he peered around the bin toward the main street.

What he saw was peculiar.

About twenty feet in, both men stopped and stood in the middle of the road.

Keeping his eye on the men, Robbie reached into his pocket, pulled out the thumb drive, and squeezed it in his palm. He looked around for a place to hide it. Somewhere he could be sure it would be safe until he returned to retrieve it.

Attached to the building, he saw a downspout, an inch from the edge of a dumpster. The flimsy sheet aluminum was battered to the point where the open end was almost crimped shut.

Robbie shoved the thumb drive as far inside as his fingers would reach, then lifted his shirt, removed the Glock from its holster, and crept over for another peek.

He wasn't sure what he expected to find. Either the men would be bearing down on him, or maybe they'd left altogether. What he found was neither. The men held their position.

*What the hell?*

If this was a waiting game, he could play it for days. Why though? What were they waiting for?

The answer came from behind. Separated into several distinct and horrifying parts.

Before he registered the sound of the booming report, he heard the ping of the bullet ricocheting off the metal after it passed below his right shoulder blade. Next came the searing pain, the blood, the gasping wheeze of his perforated lung. All in one instance. And eons apart.

Robbie spun around and pressed his back against the cold steel. The nine-millimeter bounced off the pavement. His right arm hung useless at his side.

He could see two more shadowy figures, fifty feet down the poorly lit alley. They advanced on him.

*That's what they were waiting for. Back up.*

With his left hand, he reached over his right thigh, picked up the pistol, pointed, and pulled the trigger twice.

The two additional men scrambled for cover. They found it behind a parked sedan.

Robbie waited for a glimmer of movement. When he saw it, he fired again.

Glass shattered.

*Eleven more shots.*

It wouldn't be enough. He was exposed. Incapacitated. Struggling to breathe. And two men covered each direction.

The silhouette of the car broadened as one of the men poked halfway out. Robbie lifted his pistol.

He was fading fast.

*Steady.*

From over his shoulder, two hands reached in and twisted the gun out of Robbie's grasp.

Robbie groaned and let his left arm drop to his lap. Legs outstretched in a pool of his own blood, Robbie used his remaining strength to turn towards the man hovering over him. His vision had started to blur, but he could make out the man's features.

One feature stood out. A long nasty scar stretching from one side of his face to the other.

*I know you. I think.*

The man crouched down, eye to eye, and shoved the muzzle of Robbie's own pistol against his forehead. "Where is it?"

Robbie didn't hear the words, but an echo of them. An ethereal droning from somewhere far away.

His eyes were open, he thought, but he saw nothing but blackness. He thought of his father. His brother. He fought to hang on. For them.

In a second's time, a bullet would leave the barrel of the Glock and find its way deep into Robbie's brain. But Robbie would never know.

He was already gone.

# CHAPTER 21

ARCHER WADE STOOD with his hands in his pockets. Yellow crime scene tape flapped against his abdomen.

Twenty or thirty feet ahead, a body lay on the payment, shrouded by a white bedsheet, and bathed in the warm glow of dawn. The latest contribution to the city's crime statistics.

As cities went, Boston was tame. With around fifty murders per year, violent incidents still garnered fleeting attention from the press and the public. This one seemed to have enticed more networks and publications than usual.

Back Bay was a safe area compared to some of the seedier sections. People tended to feel comfortable walking its streets at night. Word of this case was sure to spark fear among the residents. And fear was what the news was selling.

For Wade, the fear was much closer to home.

He suspected the murder was more than a coincidence. His source had failed to show up, despite their communication during his trip into town. Then, a man turns up dead, a block away from the Fairmont.

When Wade called his editor to inform him the contact didn't show, he referred to the contact as "a ghost." Now, he had a sinking feeling the expression was more literal than he intended.

*I have to get closer.*

## DETACHMENT

The entire roadway from Clarendon to Berkeley Street had been cordoned off. Designated as a staging area for the press, the taped-in corral on Stuart Street was well inside the outer perimeter. It was still far enough removed that he couldn't overhear the discussions taking place in the heart of the scene.

Television crews had it worse. They were forced to keep their cameras beyond the outer perimeter. Most of them gathered on Clarendon Street, but some tried their luck at the east end.

The press pool exuded a certain energy. Reporters held pads and voice recorders at the ready and chattered about their own theories and wild speculations.

Wade felt it too. But his mind was occupied by heavier matters. Yes, he worried about what he had gotten himself into, but it wasn't his primary concern. He had been skeptical about his source's story. But if his contact and the man under the sheet were one and the same, the story was deeper and more sinister than he would have ever imagined.

Stories like this, no matter how sordid, always started with a single step. A lone piece of information. In this case, the first step was to find out if the dead man was who Wade thought he was.

"Officer?" Wade waved at a uniformed policeman speaking with a second man off to the side. Wearing a hoodie and blue-jeans, Wade could have mistaken the second man for a suspect if it weren't for the gun on his hip and the badge around his neck. The officer looked Wade's way, then returned to his conversation.

At least two dozen cops swarmed the scene. Among them, several crime scene technicians in white coveralls and booties collected samples and other evidence. None of them appeared up for a chat.

"Officer?" Wade tried again. "Can I talk to you for a second?"

This time it was the plain-clothes detective who broke off his conversation. He and his gruff expression moved toward Wade. "Sir, this is an ongoing investigation. If ya want a comment, call the Office of Media Relations."

"I'm not looking to ask you any questions," Wade said. "I may have some information about this crime. If you have two minutes, we could talk away from the others. I could just—" He took the police tape between his thumb and forefinger, lifted it a few inches, and waited for a response.

The detective looked over his shoulder, then sighed. "Fine. Two minutes."

Wade slipped under the tape. The other reporters protested.

The man walked him just far enough to escape prying ears.

"Whatta ya know?"

"I was supposed to meet someone around the corner last night and he didn't show up. I think this may be him.

"And why do ya think that?"

"I don't know," Wade said. "Just a hunch. He was nervous. Thought he was being followed. What if he *was* being followed?"

The detective pulled a ratty looking mini notebook from his back pocket and flipped through the pages until he found a blank one. "What's this guy's name?"

"I don't know that either," Wade said. "We hadn't met yet." Half of the statement was true. They hadn't met.

"Do you know your name?"

"Archer Wade."

The detective scribbled in the notebook. "Archer Wade. Right. So, let me get it straight. A guy, whose name you don't know and have never met, blew you off in a city of three-quarters of a million people, and you figure our dead guy has to be him because you have a hunch. Nice try, get behind the line with your other googly-eyed friends."

"There's more to it. I just can't—" Wade didn't know how much he wanted to say. He needed more information before he started talking out of school. If at all. "Just not here, that's all."

"Fine. I'll tell you what. Here." He handed Wade a department issued business card.

Wade had seen many like it. He looked at the printed name. "Detective O'Connor."

"That's me. Now do me a favor and go over to D-Four on Harrison. I'll call over and have someone take a statement from you. Tell the desk I sent ya."

"Okay, thanks." Wade slowly turned away. It hadn't gone as expected.

Not only did he glean no information, but he involved himself in something he was sure he didn't want to be a part of.

"Hey Bobby, come 'ere." Someone said from behind.

O'Connor started over toward the where the body lay. By instinct, Wade followed behind. There was no doubt in his mind that the detective would chew him out, but Wade was good at playing stupid. "Oh, I thought you still needed me," he'd say. Or something to that effect.

A crime scene tech hovered over the body. The sheet was pulled back, revealing the man's torso and legs. He looked muscular. Fit.

"Military ID. Right front pocket." The tech held up the card in his gloved hand, never acknowledging that Wade had crept in, not far behind O'Connor. The guy probably assumed he had O'Connor's blessing. "Robert Novak, it says."

Wade's stomach sank. He felt as though he would vomit. Robert Novak. The man he was supposed to meet.

Before O'Connor was any wiser, Wade scurried back toward the press pool without looking behind him. Relieved that no angry tirade followed him, he ducked under the tape and resumed his front row position.

Wade had little information about who Robert Novak was or what he would reveal. But he knew it was supposed to be big. Something involving government conspiracy. And now, murder.

"I don't suppose you'll tell us what you found out?" The young, blonde reporter standing next to him batted her eyelids. It was shameless, and probably often effective. Just not on him. Not today.

"I got nothing," he said.

"Sure you didn't."

The truth was, he did get something. A name. A confirmation. An invitation into what just might be the biggest story of his career.

The blonde startled as though she were poked with a sharp stick. "Wait. I think they found something." She turned to the man to her left. A twenty-something with an eyebrow ring and an oxford. "You see?" She pointed. "What is it?"

She was right. At the brick wall, a few feet behind the body, several people crouched and crowded. One of the techs pulled something from the base of a downspout. The group looked on with approving professionalism as if the tech were a surgeon who had just successfully removed a hard-to-reach brain tumor. A second tech held open a small paper bag. The surgeon deposited something into it.

Wade had a feeling he knew exactly what it was. And if he was right, it meant Robert Novak's killer had failed.

Still clutching the business card in his left hand, he brought it toward his waist and smoothed the creased paper with his right. A minute ago, he had no intention of following O'Connor's directions. Now, the situation had taken an abrupt turn.

He would give that statement. And he would find out what was in that bag.

# CHAPTER 22

NEXT IN LINE, Wade abandoned the online Boston Globe news feed and dropped his phone into his pocket.

He tapped his foot and looked at his watch three times before the guy in front of him with the floppy green mohawk and matching lipstick even picked up the wall-mounted phone. If patience were the only virtue in life, Wade would have had to chalk himself up as depraved.

When Wade arrived at Boston Police Headquarters, there had been four people in front of him. A woman who wanted to file a restraining order, a very large man in an electric wheelchair who wanted to report his rent money stolen, and the person currently being served, who wasn't sure what he wanted.

Headquarters was nothing like the district office where Wade had given his written statement earlier that morning. That one was smaller and less busy. He had commented to the desk officer on how empty it was. The officer said, "Give it time. The usual customers don't roll out of bed 'til noon."

City cops were a colorful bunch. Wade had learned this the moment he'd stepped onto the beat in Beantown. In Colorado, the cops seemed happy. Rested. As if anyone should be so lucky to wear the badge. If he had to describe his professional interactions with the police back then, he'd use the word cooperative. A healthy give-and-take relationship.

Not so much in Boston. Many of the guys seemed bewildered. He couldn't say he blamed them. After the comedy of errors performed for his viewing pleasure over the past few minutes, the idea of jumping off a bridge looked more appealing.

Riley, the officer he'd spoken with at D-Four, was friendly and accommodating. No more than twenty-five years old, the Southy native had come across as sharp and efficient. The issue was the lack of information transfer. Not that Officer Riley had been stingy, he just hadn't known anything about the case.

It wasn't to say that Wade had come up empty handed.

As Wade reviewed his statement to put his signature on it, another man in plain clothes had come into the interview room. Wade had gotten the impression the man was a supervisor. He'd asked if Wade knew anything about a thumb drive.

*Thumb drive.*

The two words Wade had been waiting to hear. It confirmed that the object the crime scene unit found was the digital storage device Robert Novak had intended to give to him at the Fairmont.

Confirmation aside, there was still the matter of the question. In the moment, it had been hard for him to spit out an outright lie. Instead, he'd tried talking in a lazy circle. No one had bought it.

Yes, he knew about the thumb drive. No, he didn't know what was on it.

What he hadn't said was that the drive was encrypted and only he and Robert Novak—or he alone now—had the password. He'd decided to save that tidbit for the meeting he'd hoped to have in the very near future.

"Next," the desk officer said through a speaker of the phone as soon as Lady Gaga hung up the receiver.

Seated behind thick glass, the officer no doubt enjoyed the blissful silence of his cocoon. He motioned to Wade to pick up the phone.

"How can I help you?" he asked.

"I'd like to speak to someone in your digital forensics department," Wade said.

"What's it regarding?"

# DETACHMENT

"I have information regarding the murder last night."

"Hold on." The phone clicked. Wade could see the officer dialing.

A year prior, Wade had worked on an embezzlement piece involving a slew of digital evidence. During that time, he'd become well-versed in the Boston Police Department's digital forensic techniques, procedures, and capabilities. He had a good understanding of the division's structure and how they handled evidence. This experience had given him confidence that he'd come to the right place.

*Beep.* A new voice came on the line. Ten times higher and a thousand times sweeter than the officer in the oversized fish tank.

"Jones," she said.

"Hi, is this the digital forensics department?"

"That's right. Who am I speaking with?"

"My name is Archer Wade. I was hoping to speak to you regarding the murder last night. If that's possible?"

"I'm listening."

"On the phone? I mean, are you in the building?" Wade looked around as if he would find her waving back at him from a duplicate wall-mounted phone at the other side of the lobby.

"What's this about?"

"It's about a thumb drive found at the scene. It's encrypted, right?"

"How did you—" Jones paused. "I'll be right down." The phone disconnected.

Wade replaced the receiver.

"Next," the speaker blared.

From behind Wade, a man with dried blood all over his face stepped up to the window.

Wade took a seat in one of the airport terminal-style chairs. When he thought about it, the entire place looked like an airport. Huge windows spanned the length of the lobby, looking out to the would-be tarmac. If only there were a Dunkin' Donuts.

Within two minutes, a door opened and a petite young woman stepped out. "Archer Wade?"

"That's me," Wade said. He went to her and offered his hand. "Thank you for seeing me. Nice to meet you."

"Detective Jones." She shook his hand. "Right this way."

Jones led him to a small room, not far from the lobby. Inside, he saw a table and two chairs. Much like the room he'd spent his morning in.

"Take a seat." Jones waited until Wade sat down to do the same.

"I'm assuming you've already tried to look at the thumb drive," Wade said.

"I can't comment on an open investigation, Mister Wade."

"Please. Call me Archer. And I understand. But please hear me out, okay?"

"Sure."

"Great. Where to begin? Okay. I'm a reporter with the Boston Globe and—"

"A reporter?" Jones interrupted.

"It's not what you think. I'm not here for a story. Not exactly. Last night, I was supposed to meet a man. I've been assigned a story, and this man was my source. A whistleblower of sorts. He was supposed to provide me with a thumb drive with some very important information on it. Only—" Wade paused. "Well, you know what happened to him."

"Go on," Jones said.

"That's it. I mean, I wasn't there when it happened. And I never actually met him. But when we set up the meeting, he told me he would give me a thumb drive. He said it would be encrypted and password protected."

"And you know the password?"

"I'm the one who made it up. He asked me what I wanted it to be. Based on what I know about this type of thing, I'm guessing you've already tried to get into it. Right? Except you can't. Can you?"

"I can't comment—"

"I know," Wade said. "But I think we can help each other."

"You can help me by giving me the password."

"I would gladly do that," Wade said, "but I'll need something in return."

"What's that?"

"A copy."

# DETACHMENT

"You can't be serious," Jones said. "Out of the question. Whatever is on that drive is evidence in a homicide."

"I know it is. That's why I need to see it. It was intended for me. The only way I'll get to the bottom of this is to get a look at it. See? We're both after the same thing."

"Look. Archer. Even if I wanted to, I couldn't help you. It'd cost me my career. You seem like a smart guy. You didn't really think we'd turn over evidence to you, right?"

"I figured you could make a copy and no one would be the wiser. You probably already did. It's protocol, isn't it? Digital Evidence Retention, Section three point two. Immediate forensic imaging before the source is logged in and transferred to the Property Division, right? Then you work on the copy so as to not risk damaging the original."

"So you've read the regs. Good for you. That doesn't change anything. Copies or not, it's off the table." Jones put her elbows on the table and clasped her hands together. "Here's what I can offer you. You give me the password so I can do my analysis. After the case is adjudicated, I'll let you know and you can submit a Freedom of Information request with the records department."

"That will take years," Wade complained.

"And the story will still be there."

"It's not about the story. I mean, it is, but if this conspiracy runs deep, more people could be in danger. Who knows, it could affect every citizen of this country." Wade winced at his own hyperbole. "I know it sounds crazy, but I wouldn't be surprised if more important people than me come looking for that drive. People with power and influence, you know what I mean?"

"I appreciate the concern, but it's just not happening. What about civic duty? Don't you want to help solve this? See justice for the victim?"

Wade sighed. "More than you know."

"Then give me the password. Do the right thing."

Wade bowed his head for a few seconds. Then stood up. "I'm sorry, Detective Jones. I'm afraid I don't know what that is."

## CHAPTER 23

"STOP. WATCH FOR TRAFFIC." Fezz straddled his bicycle, his feet planted on the ground. From the stop sign at the bottom of Hamilton Avenue, they could see enough of Walcott Avenue for a safe crossing.

Ian looked both ways, then pushed off.

As Fezz pushed down on one pedal, he struggled to keep the front wheel straight until he could hoist his other leg up to help give him some momentum. With each pump, a knee grazed the handlebars. The verdict was in. He was too big to ride a bicycle.

As Ian hit the decline towards downtown, he stood on his pedals and coasted.

"Slow down," Fezz hollered from fifty feet behind.

When Fezz agreed to take a bike ride with Ian to get ice cream at Spinnakers, he thought he'd load the bikes in his truck and take them somewhere close. Somewhere flat.

Ian had different plans.

"That's no fun," Ian had complained. "I want to ride all the way. You need the exercise, anyway."

Impolite as the statement might have been, Ian was right. Fezz did need the exercise. Over the past few months, he had been getting lazier and, as a result, heavier. He hadn't fallen over the cliff. Yet. But a few more pints of India Pale Ale could well tip him over the edge.

## DETACHMENT

Anyway, the issue wasn't one of lethargy, but one of comfort. From Fezz's perspective, Khat's bike might as well have been made for a child. The first part of the ride wasn't bad. In fact, flying down the hill on Beavertail Road toward Mackerel Cove beach had been a blast. Fresh air. A little speed. It was all good. Until they'd passed the beach and headed up Hamilton Avenue. The twenty-five hundred feet long, thirty percent incline had been effective at knocking the wind right out of his sails, and his lungs.

Now, on the last stretch down Conanicus Avenue, he decided it was worth it. Ian was having fun. And that was all that mattered.

For some reason Fezz couldn't quite explain, he would do just about anything for that kid. Maybe he saw himself in Ian. Maybe he felt bad for him. But there was a connection he'd never felt before.

The desire to protect wasn't new to Fezz. He had been protecting his whole life. This was different. The closer he got to Ian, the more responsible he felt for the boy.

Ahead, Ian pulled over to the curb and looked down at the water. Fezz caught up and stopped behind him.

"Can we do that?"

Fezz looked in the approximate direction Ian was looking—the piers, jutting from behind and to the south of the main marina building. "What? The boats? We can go out on ours anytime you want."

"No," Ian said. "The kayaks."

On a small floating dock attached to the taller pier by a wooden ladder were several red and yellow kayaks, tied off in a row. Two people in oversized life jackets climbed into a tandem. The sign, affixed to the piling, announced that the small paddle boats were for rent by the hour.

"Sure, we can do that," Fezz said. "Why don't we buy a couple of them for the house? You and I can build a rack down by the beach. It'll be fun."

"Are you sure? I've never been on a kayak. What if I don't like it?"

"What's not to like?" Fezz figured this sound logic. "Anyway, how much can a couple of tiny plastic boats cost?"

Ian shrugged. "I don't know."

"Ya know, I get it. It'll take some getting used to, but you don't have to worry about money anymore. We can do anything we want to." Ima had told Fezz about her time in the United Arab Emirates. How Ian had owned only one pair of shoes. Now, he could have several closets full if he wanted. "You'll be able to go to college. Move away. Start a life of your own someday."

"I don't want to go to college. I don't want a life of my own. I'm part of the team. When I get older, I'll be bigger and stronger, and I can do what you do."

"Don't say that," Fezz snapped. "You have so many opportunities ahead of you."

Ian looked at Fezz with a blank expression. Probably unable to decipher what was behind Fezz's outburst.

The truth was, this was no place for a kid. Sure, it seemed quiet and safe, compared to what Ian had been through. But the false utopia wouldn't last. It would be replaced by some degree of stress, heartache, violence. Neither Ian nor Ima were cut out for it. Nor did they deserve it.

"Let's get that ice cream," Fezz said.

In his obedient manner, Ian jerked his bike so it pointed down the road and hopped onto the seat.

A minute later, Ian and his wobbly pet circus bear were both turning into the parking lot.

"What are you going to get?" Ian asked.

"Don't know. What should I get?"

"Rocky Road, I think."

Fezz chuckled. "Is that what you're getting?"

"No, I'm getting black raspberry."

"Black raspberry? Don't you want chocolate, or caramel, or peanut butter?"

"Those flavors are so pedestrian." Ian's assessment carried the seriousness of a federal prosecutor delivering his opening arguments. "Black raspberry is for those with a more discerning palette."

*Pedestrian? Discerning palette?*

Fezz often wondered if the words that came out of Ian's mouth were weird by design. An inside joke, constructed for his own personal amusement, as if he got a kick out of watching people react to him like he had a third eye. For that reason, Fezz often tried to avoid taking the bait. "Hey, you do you, Anthony Bourdain."

Toward the edge of the wharf, there was a bike rack. Fezz and Ian rolled over to it, dismounted, and shoved the front wheels of their bikes between its slats.

As Fezz started walking toward Spinnakers, Ian took hold of Fezz's hand—or a portion of it.

Through an exterior window, a worker handed ice cream cones to a group of people gathered on the adjacent sidewalk. Hand in hand, Fezz and Ian fell in behind the group to wait their turn.

Toward the back of the group was a woman wearing a striped, sleeveless shirt. The man closest to the window turned to pass her a plastic spoon and a paper cup with two large scoops of purple ice cream.

"Black raspberry?" Fezz asked.

"It's the best, isn't it?" The woman smiled and dug in.

Fezz squeezed Ian's hand and held back an inappropriate laugh.

"Where are you from?" The woman asked.

"Here," Fezz said.

Based on the way the group was dressed and the fact that two of them carried dry bags over their shoulders, Fezz figured they were boaters. Probably one of the larger yachts along the main pier.

"How nice," the woman said. "Is this your son?"

Without a second thought, Fezz answered. "Yes. This is my son, Ian."

Noticing that the man at the window had finished paying and the group had started moving on, the woman jabbed the spoon into the mound of ice cream and picked up her purse from where it rested against her right ankle. "What a handsome young man," she said. "You both have a lovely day."

As the group moved on, Fezz looked down at Ian. With a tilted head and furrowed brow, Ian stared right back up at him.

Fezz worried that he'd freaked Ian out with his response to the woman's inquiry.

Ian was not his son. But Fezz would be damn proud if he was.

Still, he realized Ian might think it presumptuous.

Fezz crouched down until he and Ian were at eye level. "Hey. I didn't mean anything by that. I mean, I hope you don't think I—"

Ian threw his arms around Fezz's neck and hugged him tight.

# CHAPTER 24

ONE HUNDRED PERCENT.

Three of the four monitors displayed data from several different cases, all temporarily abandoned for the fourth, showing only a stagnant blue progress bar.

Andrea Jones stared at the screen in annoyance. To her mind, a hundred percent should mean 'complete.' Yet, it always seemed to take an extra few minutes before the machine caught up to its claims.

Since she'd met with Archer Wade, only one case had been occupying her mind. The murder of Robert Novak.

On its face, the case shouldn't have been of any particular interest, at least from a digital forensics standpoint. However, Wade's allusion to a deeper, broad-reaching conspiracy had piqued her interest.

Wade was right about protocol. The forensics team never examined on the original evidence. Hard drives, flash media—these items were prone to corruption and failure. Especially with the amount of processing needed to find and parse useful information. Instead, the team used a write-blocker to create a bit-for-bit, read-only copy of the original to preserve its integrity. They could then analyze the copy with scientific confidence that it was identical to its source.

When crime scene techs collected any device, they would take it to the Digital Forensics Unit office, where it would be stored in a walk-in vault they called "Intake." From there, the team would photograph, disassemble, image, repackage, and transfer the device to the Department's Property Division for permanent storage. With only one sergeant and five detectives working the unit, they had a backlog spanning several months.

High priority cases like homicide were often bumped to the front of the line. The Robert Novak case was no different. While Wade had assumed the team had made copies and attempted methods to circumvent any encryption scheme, they hadn't. In fact, the task case hadn't even been assigned.

Upon returning to the office, Jones had taken it upon herself to locate the thumb drive in the intake vault and image it. If she could get a look at the data and confirm that Wade was correct about its encryption, she would include it in her write-up of their conversation. Plus, she couldn't help but take a peek.

It wasn't all an exercise in curiosity, though. She intended to petition the sergeant to assign the analysis to her. She hoped she could leverage what little rapport she'd established to convince Wade to change his mind about cooperating.

*Finally.*

On the screen, the blue was replaced with a list of files representing the segments of the completed image.

Using a rubber glove which she hadn't bothered to put all the way on, she pulled the thumb drive and dropped it back into the paper bag. At some point, she would have to complete the process by photographing, sealing, and signing the item for transfer. But for now, it could wait.

Jones walked to the vault and set the paper bag back on the shelf. She returned to her desk to take a crack at opening the newly acquired image.

"Right this way." Sergeant Peligro keyed his way in. Behind him were two men wearing green formal military uniforms, like her own dress blues. Unlike hers, both suits were adorned with an assortment of colorful ribbons. Maybe she was supposed to, but Jones didn't recognize either of them. "Jones. Where's Ward?"

The office was small. Consisting of one main area, the vault, a faraday

## DETACHMENT

room, and Peligro's small side office, there was no mistaking when someone else was present. Of the six L-shaped cubicles that made up the main area, Jones' was the only one occupied at that moment.

"I don't know," Jones said. "Everyone's out. Burgess is up in the north end helping A-One get video from a break-in. Rodriquez is—"

"Never mind. Did Ward bring in property from the homicide last night?"

"Yes," Jones said. "It's in the vault."

Peligro went to the vault while the two other men stood just inside the door. Jones noticed one of them carried several larger paper bags, a Boston Police evidence sticker attached to each.

"Everything all right?" Jones asked. The question wasn't directed at one person, but to any who could answer. She received none.

Peligro returned with the same small paper bag Jones had replaced only seconds before. He gave it to the empty-handed man. "That's all there is."

The soldier opened the bag, looked inside, then handed it to his partner, who added it to his payload. "Are there any copies?"

"No," Peligro said. "It just came in." Peligro turned to Jones. "Right?"

Jones froze. It wasn't like she would be in trouble for having already imaged the device. It was part of her job, and she was taking initiative. All she had to say was, "Yes." But for some unknown reason, she couldn't bring herself to say it. "No, not yet. Were we supposed to?"

Peligro turned back to his escorts. "There you have it. Is there anything else, gentlemen?"

"As a matter of national security," the empty-handed man started, "I must remind you that you are not to discuss anything about this case with anyone. The Suffolk County District Attorney's office has closed the case and has ordered any evidence be destroyed. It is of utmost importance that no information about this young man's suicide gets out to the public. Is that clear?"

*Suicide? Bull.*

Jones knew by looking at the initial responding officer's report that an off-duty corrections officer had called 911 after hearing the shots and seeing two men running from the area of Stanhope Street. Before the police arrived, the prison guard had taken it upon himself to investigate the source of the gunshots. He found Robert Novak deceased, an estimated two minutes after his initial call, and one minute before the arrival of the first Boston Police officer. No firearm was found on or near the scene, nor on the correction officer's person. If this was a suicide, it was by magic.

"Of course," Peligro said. "Forgotten."

The two soldiers stared at Jones. After a second, she realized they were waiting for her verbal acknowledgement. "Oh. What suicide? Never heard of it."

With faces made of stone, the two soldiers glanced at each other, then turned to head out the door.

Peligro watched the door pull shut by its pneumatic closer. His shoulders dropped at the same rate.

"What was that about?" Jones asked.

"I don't know. Never seen anything like it."

"So we're supposed to just forget about an entire homicide investigation?"

"Suicide," Peligro said. "It came from the Superintendent. Called me directly."

"Don't you find this whole thing strange?"

Peligro blew a puff of air through his teeth. "Everything about this place is strange. I just do what I'm told. You'll learn. Don't ask questions and everyone's happy." Without any further explanation, he walked to his office and closed the door.

Jones was left with her thoughts and the copy she now knew as contraband.

There was no question she needed to get the files off her machine, and fast. It would be easy enough. One keystroke could secure-delete the image files, sending them forever into the weird past.

Yes, that was exactly what she would do.

*Control-A, Select all. And delet*—her pointer finger hovered over the delete button, repelled by an unseen force like two magnets with matching polarity.

## DETACHMENT

She couldn't keep them. She couldn't give them to the reporter, Archer Wade. But there was something she could do. Something that would absolve her of guilt. Or at least, pass the buck.

## CHAPTER 25

"SURE, SEND HER UP." Andrew Harrison hung up the phone, gathered the papers strewn about his desk, and tucked them into a file folder.

Andrea Jones from the Boston Police Department. An unexpected visitor, but a welcome one.

The last time Harrison had spoken with Jones, she was on loan to one of the FBI's Cyber Crimes task forces. Made up of federal, state, and local law enforcement agencies, these task forces were meant to foster cooperation between jurisdictions. The municipal and state officers, temporarily sworn in with federal arrest powers, would take the lead on cases that originated in their own jurisdictions.

When Harrison had first met Jones, she had been working a high-profile bank fraud. Since many of the target's assets had been in Massachusetts and Rhode Island, Harrison had found himself overseeing much of the investigation. He'd been impressed with Jones' work, and even helped her out by asking Blake Brier to help track down the international bank accounts.

Blake passed on the information he'd found to Jones as an anonymous tip. Eventually, after arresting the suspect, both Jones and Harrison had reaped the benefits of a job well-done. This was a favor Harrison had yet to repay to Blake.

Harrison opened the door and waited for Jones to step off the elevator. He called across the bullpen to her. "Andrea. Hi. Come on in."

Jones snaked through the desks, waving at a few people she recognized, then joined Harrison in his office. He shut the door behind her.

"What are you doing in Providence? How long are you in town?" he asked.

"I'm not in town. I mean, I am, but I just drove in. I was hoping to catch you." Jones motioned to one of the two green nineteen-seventies style chairs in front of Harrison's desk. "Do you mind?"

"No, of course. Sit." Harrison dropped in behind his desk. "You didn't come all the way down here to see me, did you?"

"I did."

Harrison liked the young woman. He'd even say they were friends. But they had never gotten together outside of work, and he would never have dreamed she would make a special trip to visit. Something was off. He could feel it in his bones. "Is everything okay? Do you need help?"

"Something strange happened, and I just can't stop thinking about it. I needed to talk to someone, and I know I can trust you."

"Sure you can." Harrison took on a soothing, drawn out tone, hoping to allay her visible anxiety. "What's wrong?"

"If I tell you, you have to promise you won't tell anyone. I could get in big trouble. Not just with the department. I mean, this could be serious."

Harrison wasn't sure he wanted to make that promise. What if she told him she had kidnapped someone and had them in the trunk of her car? He wasn't trying to sign himself up to be an accomplice. But he felt he knew Andrea Jones. He trusted her good nature and moral compass. Plus, what was he going to say, "Sorry, go somewhere else?"

Still, he had to be sure.

"You haven't committed a crime, have you?"

Jones' eyes welled, and she instantly broke down. "Yes. I have," she sobbed.

*Damn it. I shouldn't have asked.*

Now, he was all the way in. There was no way to leave it there.

"Is it bad?" he asked.

"I don't know. I mean, I didn't hurt anyone or anything."

At least there was that, Harrison figured. If no one was hurt, maybe it was fixable. "Okay. Take a breath. What happened?"

Jones wiped her eyes and cleared her throat. As fast as she fell apart, she pulled herself back together.

"We had this case, the night before last. A homicide. A guy was gunned down in the middle of the street. Our guys located a thumb drive near the body. From a nasty old drainpipe. Only it was clean, like it was just hidden there. The next morning, a reporter came into the station, and I spoke with him. I didn't know anything about the case at the time, but the reporter—Archer was his name—he told me he had the password to the thumb drive because the victim was a whistleblower who was going to give him information about some kind of big conspiracy." She paused and looked him in the eyes. "You with me?"

"I'm with you."

"Archer refused to reveal the password unless I gave him a copy of the drive."

"You didn't."

"No, I didn't. I wouldn't. But after that, I was interested. I mean, was this guy for real? That's why I imaged the drive, so I could take a look."

"It doesn't sound like there was anything wrong with that."

"Not normally. But right after that, the military came in and confiscated everything to do with the case. Every piece of evidence. Every report. They made the whole thing disappear. They said it was for the sake of national security."

Harrison was no stranger to keeping secrets in the name of national security. As part of the job, he retained a top-secret security clearance. Cases involving terrorism or espionage were deemed classified, and the information and materials were handled as such. Jones herself had to be cleared when she first joined the FBI task force. Still, he had never heard of the military coming into a municipality to confiscate evidence. Sure, it was possible Jones was mistaken, but given what he knew about her, it wasn't likely.

"They asked me straight to my face if I had any copies." She paused. "And I said no."

"You did? Why?"

"I don't know. I guess I felt like it wasn't right. Like they were trying to hide something."

"Yeah, Andrea, that's what classified means."

"No, listen to me. This isn't about classified information. This is something else. They were trying to cover their asses. Whatever is on that drive, I think a man got himself killed over it. And I'm pretty sure our own military is involved in the murder."

Harrison took a deep breath. "You didn't destroy it, did you?"

Jones bowed her head, then pulled a purple USB stick from her packet and tossed it onto Harrison's desk. It clattered against the dark wood veneer. "I couldn't give it to the reporter. If he used it for his story, that'd put my ass on the line. So I thought I could give it to you."

"Me? Why me? What am I supposed to do with it?"

"Remember the Laroche case? When I got that tip about the bank account numbers? I know that was you."

"What was me?"

"I overheard you on the phone with someone, asking them to look into it. Plus, the way you acted when I told you about how I got the information. I could just tell you already knew."

Harrison leaned back in his chair and chuckled. "Oh Andrea. You don't miss a thing, do you?" As it turned out, she was better at keeping a secret than he thought. "You want me to reach out to my guy? Even if you find out what's on it, you can't do anything about it. The best you can do is go home and forget it ever happened."

"I don't care if you give it to your guy or smash it to bits. I just needed to give it to somebody. To get it off my back. I figured, since you were willing to go outside the law in the past, I could trust you. Or maybe you'd want to investigate it. Either way, it's yours now. Do whatever you want."

Harrison said nothing, just stroked his goatee. For a quiet moment, both of their attentions were fixed on the small plastic device sitting on the desktop between them—two grandmasters over a chess board.

Jones was the first to move. "I better get going."

"Yeah. Hey, it was good to see you."

"You too. Thanks for listening."

"Sure." Harrison walked to the door and opened it for her. "I think I will pass it on to my guy."

"Okay," she said. "But do me a favor. Don't ever tell me what you find."

## CHAPTER 26

BLAKE PULLED ONTO THE GRAVEL. The tires of his Dodge Challenger crunched as they sunk into the pea stone.

Lucy sat on the front porch of the small Cape Cod-style house with a book in her hands. She looked up and waved.

Blake and Haeli waved back.

As he stepped out of the car, a bottle of Merlot in hand, Blake noted the progress of the renovations next door. Since the tragedy involving the former owner, a retired couple from Massachusetts had bought the place and completely gutted it. Most recently, the exterior had been finished. New Siding. New windows. New landscaping. It was a completely different house.

"You should have seen the inside of that place before they fixed it up," Blake said.

"I'll pass," Haeli said. "Your description was plenty."

Of course, Blake had relayed every gory detail of the experience. Not right away and not all at once, but by now, there wasn't much about his first trip to Jamestown that she didn't know.

When he and Haeli had first arrived together, after getting back from Europe, Blake took her around the island to give her the lay of the land. They had driven by Christa and Gwyn's house, but didn't stop. He didn't know if she had been by since, but he did know that this would be her first official visit.

Blake pushed the car door closed with a *thunk*.

"Hi Blake." Lucy smiled.

"Hey Lucy. Enjoying some quiet time?"

"Studying. I have finals this week."

Blake climbed the single step and placed the bottle atop the half-wall lining the porch on three sides. "Ah. Look at you, all studious and whatnot. Don't get up." He bent over to give her a hug.

Blake was proud of her. It never ceased to amaze him how well adjusted she had become in spite of everything that had happened to her in her life. She had gone through a bit of a rebellious streak, that much he knew, but by the time he met her, he saw no sign of it. It was funny how life-threatening experiences helped put things in perspective. And no one knew that better than Blake.

"Here, let me give you a proper hug." Haeli flitted in, parked herself on the rocking settee next to Lucy, and wrapped her arms around her. "What subject is it?"

"Biology. Pretty boring stuff."

"Come on," Haeli said. "I'm sure some of it's interesting. Have you gotten into molecular genetics?"

"Like DNA and stuff?"

"Yeah, like DNA and stuff. Biotech. It's incredible what they can do nowadays." Haeli shot Blake a cheesy smile. The inside joke flew over Lucy's head.

"I guess."

Blake picked up the bottle of wine. "Your mom inside?"

"Yep," Lucy said. "Both of 'em. Look out though, they're running around like chickens with their heads cut off in there. Everything has to be perfect, ya know. Especially since Haeli's here."

"Oh no," Haeli grimaced. "I hope they didn't go to too much trouble on my account."

"Let's go see." Blake rapped on the glass panel of the storm door. It rattled like he had punched it. He opened it before getting a response. "Hello?"

## DETACHMENT

"Blake. Haeli. Welcome!" Christa rushed over from the dining room. A slight sheen covered her forehead.

Blake gave her a kiss on the cheek and moved into the dining room to set the Merlot on the table while she and Haeli said their hellos. In the adjoining kitchen, Gwyn was hard at work as usual. A flaming cast iron skillet in her hand and a bandana on her head. Compared to Christa, Gwyn was in a full out sweat.

"Hi Gwyn," Blake said.

Gwyn used her free hand to blow Blake a kiss. "Almost done. Grab a drink, hang out on the porch if you want. Christa will go out with you. I'm just finishing up."

"Smells delicious," Haeli said. "Thanks for having us."

"Our pleasure," Christa said. "And we have a surprise guest tonight as well."

"Fun," Haeli giggled.

"You want a Cosmo? I already have some made."

Haeli giggled again. "I thought you'd never ask."

Blake thought it was funny how fast Haeli could slip into girl mode. Once averse to manicures, spa treatments, and gossip, as soon as Haeli got together with Christa, she became a sorority girl.

It was one reason Blake was happy Ima had decided to stay. Ima and Haeli would spend hours chit-chatting, shopping, and watching old movies. He could tell it was important to Haeli. Another woman to offset the tide of testosterone. Not that everyone on the team wasn't respectful, but they weren't the most genteel. Plus, it wasn't likely any of them would be up for sipping Chardonnay and talking about their feelings.

At the back counter of the kitchen, where Christa filled two Martini glasses from a frosty metal shaker, Blake reached around Haeli and grabbed the bottle of Balvenie. He poured himself a dram, and the three carted their libations to the front porch.

"I feel like I should be helping Gwyn," Haeli said.

Christa laughed. "It's safer out here."

"I used to say the same thing," Blake said. "But I learned. Gwyn does not want anyone in her way. Trust me."

Lucy scooted so the three adults could sit next to each other. Her nose remained planted in her book.

"So who's this special guest?" Haeli asked.

"You'll see."

"Is it Chief?" Blake asked

"No, it's not Chief. But I wouldn't be surprised if he wandered by at some point."

Christa's neighbor, John Perrington, was a long-retired former Chief of Police for the town. Somewhere along the way, the title stuck and became a nickname. He was a fantastic guy with a million and one funny stories. As a testament to his good nature, Chief was still friendly with Blake, even after he'd accused the old man of being a serial killer.

"How's he doing?" Blake asked.

"Good," Christa said. "Just had surgery on his knee. But he's getting around. Hey, speaking of Chiefs, guess who else stopped by a few days ago."

"Charlie Fuller?" Blake guessed.

"You're getting warmer. Try again."

"No way." Blake said. "Tom Hopkins."

"Yep. Tom was driving by and saw me outside. He ended up staying for over an hour."

"What's he up to?"

"Woodworking, from what I gathered. Still sober. And he's got a new lady friend."

"Hey now," Blake chuckled. "Good for him. I have to reach out, maybe get together for a coffee or something. Now that all the dust has settled."

"He said the same thing." Christa put her glass on the table, reached behind her, and fluffed up the pillow. "God, I need to get new cushions and throw pillows out here. You only get a couple seasons out of them with the mugginess. Just one of the hundred things I need to do around here."

"Your home is lovely," Haeli said. "So nicely decorated. It's very inviting."

Blake agreed. But it wasn't the decor or the location that made it so. It

# DETACHMENT

was the people, content just to be together. Warm and generous, they'd make any house the perfect home.

"Thank you," Christa said. "Little by little, we're gettin' there."

Out front, a black Ford Taurus slowed and made the turn into the driveway. The mystery guest had revealed himself. "The great and powerful Andrew Harrison," Blake announced.

Christa smiled. "I usually catch up with him on the phone once every week or two. I always extend an invitation and he always takes a raincheck. Yesterday I mentioned you two were coming and asked if he wanted to join, and he finally accepted. Surprise."

Harrison popped out of the car with a grin on his face. "Is this where the party's at?"

"It is now," Blake said.

"Sorry I'm a little late. Got tied up at the office. And I had to stop at the packy." Harrison opened the rear door and retrieved a twelve pack of Sam Adams Boston Lager. He made his way onto the porch, swinging the cardboard box by its cutout handle. "Which fridge do you want this in?"

Christa got up, took the box, and kissed Harrison on the cheek. "I've got it, you sit." She ripped the top of the box, pulled out a bottle, and handed it to him before retreating inside.

"Thanks, Christa." He turned to the group. "Blake, how are ya? Lucy, good to see you, hon. And this must be Haeli. We finally meet in the flesh."

"I forgot, you two have never actually met. It's crazy, right? After all this time. Well, Harrison, meet Haeli. Haeli, Harrison."

"Cheers." Harrison leaned with his butt against the half-wall and brought his beer bottle to his lips before realizing it was still closed. "Uh. Anyone have a popper-topper?"

Lucy looked up from her book, kicked off her flip-flop, and tossed it at Harrison.

After a couple of bobbles, he managed to pin it between his stomach and forearm. "What's this?"

"It's got a bottle opener on the bottom," Lucy said.

"I hope this is for soda pop, young lady." He levered the cap.

"Of course." She giggled.

Sans bandana, Gwyn swung open the storm door. "Hi Andrew. Dinner is ready, everyone."

Blake got up and wrapped his arm around Harrison's neck. "Real good to see you, buddy. Hope you brought your appetite."

The group moved inside for an evening of fun and laughter, food and wine, and family.

---

"I'M STUFFED." Harrison dropped onto the settee next to Blake.

The women were in the kitchen, finishing cleaning up. They had banished Harrison and Blake to the front porch. Blake could hear them laughing inside.

After sunset, it got dark fast. With two hours until the moonrise, the only source of light was an oil lamp on the coffee table. Blake loved the ambience. It brought back memories.

*The perfect end to the perfect night.*

"She's great," Harrison said.

"Haeli? Yeah, she's a keeper." Blake poured another two ounces of scotch in his glass, then did the same to an empty one he had brought out for Harrison. He was okay with taking the bottle out with him. After all, he had stashed it there for these very occasions. "Here." He handed the glass to Harrison.

"Thanks." Harrison raised his glass. "To starting over."

Blake laughed. "I'll drink to that." He took a sip.

"Speaking of starting over, have you given any thought to what you'll do next?"

"We just had a discussion about it. The whole group. We're at the point where we're ready to stick our toes in the water, I think. But no specifics yet."

"Well, I have something you might be interested in."

"What's up?"

Harrison took the purple USB drive from his pocket and tossed it. Blake snatched it out of the air.

"What's on it?"

"Good question," Harrison said. "It's encrypted. Just the way you like it."

"Okay. Where'd ya get it? You gotta give me something."

"A friend of mine in Boston went through some trouble to get that to me. It came off a dead guy. Murdered on a city street. A guy named Robert Novak. I looked into him. He was one of yours. Spec Ops. My contact seems to think the killing was an inside job."

"Government?"

"You tell me, once you get a look at it."

"Forensics must be all over it already."

"Not so much. After the military paid a visit to the PD, they didn't leave so much as a scrap of paper. I tried making a couple calls. They're so freaked out over in Boston, no one would talk to me. And these are guys I know well. The only one with the balls to stand up was the person who snuck that copy out before they confiscated the original."

"Maybe our dead guy was a spy. Passing information to foreign operatives. Do we know what he was doing in Boston? Does he live there?"

"He lives in North Carolina. He's with the First Special Forces Operational Detachment. Or was, anyway. I don't think he was passing information to another government. It seemed like he was trying to pass it to the press. Why in Boston, who knows? I'm just the messenger."

"All right. I'm intrigued."

"Don't get too excited. It may turn out to be nothing."

"If there was a cleanup on aisle seven, it's not nothing. Anyway, it'll give us a chance to put the new system through its paces. I hope it's at least AES-128 encryption. Otherwise, it wouldn't be much of a challenge."

Blake was being cheeky, of course. AES-128 would ensure that all the computers in the world couldn't decipher the key within any useful timeframe. But if the data was being passed to someone, it was likely there was a memorable password. And non-random passwords were a whole different ball of wax.

"Well, you can go geek out over it all you want," Harrison said. "Just let me know if you need anything from me. I owe you one."

"If this turns out to be what I think it is, I'll owe you. Big time."

## CHAPTER 27

BLAKE TURNED off Beavertail Road into the shared driveway. The big F-250 shuddered. He was no mechanic, but it didn't sound good. Hopefully, it was benign. He would never hear the end of it if Fezz's truck crapped out during the two hours Blake had borrowed it.

In Blake's opinion, Fezz got the better end of the deal. His Challenger for Fezz's truck. All so Blake could take a run across the bridge to BJ's Wholesale to pick up four additional metal shelving units for the bunker. That was the plan, anyway.

When Haeli had found out he was going out, she tacked on several more items. Laundry detergent. Bulk paper towels. A mammoth tub of vitamin-C gummies.

It didn't end there. Khat and Ima had gotten in on the action, too. Before Blake knew it, he had been signed up for a full-on shopping spree.

Even if he did a little faux complaining, he'd been fine with it. It had given him a chance to get out and run a couple of other errands he'd had been meaning to get to. Rounding off the morning, he'd stopped at West Marine for the petcock he needed for the boat, and then at Starbucks for a pick-me-up.

Any of it could have waited, but he wanted to make himself scarce. Before he left, Blake had turned over the thumb drive to Ima and Griff and issued them a challenge—get the new system fired up and break the encryption. Assuming there was any.

Every member of the team was the same in at least one regard—when a gauntlet was thrown, they were up for the challenge. Even when the stakes were low and the reward amounted to nothing but a few minutes of bragging rights, they would expend considerable energy in the pursuit. Never as much as when there were real-world implications.

When Blake had relayed the backstory behind the device to Griff and Ima, their eyes lit up like kids on Christmas morning. Blake understood. Like them, he'd once lived for that kind of thing. Truth be told, he still enjoyed it. But this was a good opportunity for Griff and Ima to work together and do a little professional bonding of their own.

In the few hours since Griff and Ima had raced each other down the stairs to the lab, it was unlikely they would have completed the configuration of the GPU array, never mind get the process running. Even with Ima's tweaks to the algorithms recovered from a legacy CIA file server, it could take days to get in.

Blake gave a wave toward the neighbors' house, in case they were spying out the window, then split off from the shared driveway. He made the loop around the circle so that the bed of the truck faced the front entrance of the house.

He could have backed into the garage and brought the shelves underground through the back way, but most of the items would stay inside the house. A few shelving units were nothing to hide from prying eyes.

Blake reached into the bed of the truck and pulled out the giant pack of paper towels and two gallons of milk bound together by a plastic carrying strap. He left the rest for when someone else could give him a hand.

Stopping only to toss the paper towels on the counter and put the milk in the fridge, Blake headed straight for the pantry. He swung open the hidden door and descended.

Downstairs, he found Griff and Ima right where he expected.

"How's it going so far?"

Chairs pushed together, they sat shoulder to shoulder, staring at the same screen. Griff used the mouse wheel to scroll through the text of what appeared to be a scanned document. Neither of them looked away at the sound of Blake's voice.

"Uh huh," Ima said, as if by reflex.

"Uh huh, what?" Blake chuckled. "Did you guys get anywhere with the decryption?"

Griff looked up. His face was drawn. "We're already in, Mick. You've got to look at this. You won't believe it."

"Wait, how? Was it not encrypted?"

"It was," Ima said, "but that's not important." She stood up and pushed her chair back. "Sit. Read."

Blake complied.

"Check this out, Mick. There's a ton of documents. Drawings. Provisioning reports. Maps." Griff scrolled through the file list. When he found the one he was looking for, he double clicked. "Here. This one will give the scope in a nutshell."

Blake read about Venezuela. The plan. The timeline.

The surrealness hit him.

In the past, Blake had been well-informed about foreign affairs. Once he'd retired, he no longer had access to the same amount of information, but still made it a point to consume some kind of news each day, even if the media rarely had the whole story.

Not so much anymore.

If he really thought about it, he could recall a few headlines on his news feed about protests in Caracas, but it hadn't meant much to him at the time. People were always getting hot and bothered about one thing or another. If it wasn't Venezuela, it'd be Jerusalem, Taiwan, Myanmar, Egypt, Portland. The world over, civil unrest and insurgency were far more common than foreign conflicts.

Often, these uprisings spawned plots to assassinate leaders to force regime change. While something like this could be expected in countries of, say, the Middle East, never in Blake's experience had he seen such a blatant cabal orchestrated by the United States. If he wasn't looking at it with his own eyes, no one could say anything to convince him this was real.

"Makes sense how this Robert Novak found himself full of holes," Griff said. "If this got out—"

"It would be the biggest government scandal in the history of the United States," Blake interjected. "Harrison said the thumb drive was meant for a reporter. That was why the victim was in Boston. To hand this off. Could you imagine? If he had lived long enough to make the drop, it'd be on the front page of every newspaper in the world."

"Shouldn't it be?" Ima asked. "Maybe I'm jaded—I mean, the government and I aren't exactly on good terms—but shouldn't the public know about this?"

"There's a lot the public doesn't know," Griff said. "And wouldn't want to."

Blake stood to allow Ima her seat back. She declined.

"I can't believe I'm saying this," Blake started, "but I agree with Ima. They've crossed the line. They killed one of our own in cold blood to cover their own asses. Someone has to pay."

"Who?" Griff asked. "The Army? Congress? The President? Who knows how deep this goes?"

"And how many more people will end up dead?" Ima added.

"Damn it," Blake said.

"What?"

Blake slapped his hand over his eyes and rubbed his temples. "The reporter."

By the look on Griff's and Ima's faces, they understood what Blake was getting at. Whoever Robert Novak was going to meet was a loose end. From the perspective of those responsible, Novak might have already passed information that could implicate them.

One thing was certain. If a member of an elite special forces unit stood no chance, the odds didn't look good for a member of the press.

"What do you want to do?" Griff asked.

"We need to find the reporter. Now."

"We don't have the first idea who Novak was supposed to meet," Ima said.

"We don't. But Harrison might." Blake took out his phone. "Griff, do me a favor. Round everybody up while I make this call. If we're going to do this, we'll have to move quick." He pressed Harrison's name in his contact list and brought the phone to his ear. "Let's just hope it isn't too late."

# CHAPTER 28

FIFTY-SIX MINUTES AFTER BLAKE, Kook, Griff, and Haeli loaded into Fezz's truck, Blake exited I-95 onto South Main St in Sharon, Massachusetts.

It had been easy enough to track down an address. The hard part had been getting a name in the first place.

On Blake's initial call, Harrison had confirmed that his contact mentioned the reporter's name. Only he couldn't remember what it was. "Archer something," Harrison said with confidence, only to second guess himself a second later. Eventually, after he'd reached his source, Harrison came through. "Archer Wade with the Boston Globe," Harrison reported, right before he gave himself a pat on the back for being close.

Once they had the information they needed, it only took a few minutes to put a loose plan in place and get on the road. Blake would have liked to have Fezz and Khat along as well, but the others all agreed they couldn't wait on this. Still in Westerly, it would have been another forty-five minutes before Fezz and Khat arrived back at the house. Forty-five minutes Archer Wade might not have had.

Besides, if all went well, they wouldn't need the extra muscle. As long as Wade was cooperative, the team would help him temporarily relocate to buy some time until they could develop a more comprehensive plan.

They intended to use Fezz's "cover apartment" in Newport as the safehouse.

There was one other benefit to traveling light. Everyone, including Wade, would fit into Fezz's truck. If they'd added two more people to the mix, they would've had to take Kook's van, which wouldn't have been pleasant for anyone. "The Mystery Machine," as they called it, had exactly one seat and a permanent odor, which could only be described as a combination of weed and surfboard wax.

"Seven minutes out," Blake said.

In the passenger seat, Kook sat with one foot resting on the dashboard. "I hope this dude's not the kind who goes to work on Saturday."

"I hope he is," Haeli said.

Griff responded with a snicker and a single clap.

Haeli shoved him. "I'm serious. Boston's a half hour away. If we knew for sure he was at the paper, we could call ahead and set up a meeting. All we'd have to do is tell him we have information about his story. He'd probably be more receptive if he felt like he's in control. Imagine if a group of people with guns showed up at our house. Wouldn't go over too well, would it?"

"She's got a point," Blake said.

Kook leaned to the left and tilted his head back between the seats. His blond hair dangled onto Haeli's knee, beneath his upside-down face. "At least here, if he doesn't listen to reason, we can just kidnap his ass," he laughed.

Wearing a mischievous grin, Haeli reached over and stuck her pinky finger into one of Kook's nostrils.

"Jesus!" Kook jerked his head and retreated to the safety of his bucket seat. "Mick, I told you your girlfriend was a gold digger."

"You're lucky she didn't get you with the wet willy." Griff plugged his left ear with his index finger. "Trust me."

"You kids! I will turn this car around. I swear to God." Blake swung at the air behind his seat as if trying to swat someone he couldn't seem to reach.

Laughter filled the truck again.

After it died down, a lull hung in the air. Blake's mind drifted to the documents he'd skimmed an hour earlier. He wondered what the outcome of the mission had been. There was nothing on the news about Maduro. Had they called it off at the last minute? Had the Venezuelan President eluded them?

It was possible the documents held more answers. Later, they would spend more time combing through them, line by line. Right now, their priority was keeping Archer Wade out of harm's way.

No one knew how much information Wade had received before the murder. Having viewed the contents of the thumb drive, the team likely possessed far more knowledge than the reporter. Still, even the slightest bit extra could help fill in the gaps.

Blake wasn't sure where all of this would lead. But he felt like they were on the right path. The facility they were building, the expertise they had gathered—it was all pushing them in a direction.

The computer lab was a prime example. Without it, or without Blake or Griff or Ima, they wouldn't have had a path to begin with.

It reminded Blake of a question he meant to ask. He broke the moment of silence. "You never told me what happened with the encryption, Griff."

Griff gave a flip of the wrist. "That was all Ima."

"And?"

"Should I explain it now?" Griff asked.

"That's why I'm asking."

"You want the short version or what?"

"The short version sounds good," Kook interrupted.

Blake looked in his rear view. "I'm almost sorry I asked."

"Fine. After we got the array running, we made a copy and started the regular brute force process on it, just using the password lists you and I compiled. For the other copy, Ima wanted to use a neural network. We chose a bunch of relevant data sources—mostly public government documents, some news feeds, stuff like that."

"Smart," Blake said.

"Right? Still, Ima looked at the performance graphs on the brute force and realized there was a bottleneck with the amount of time it took to hash the password candidates. She came up with the idea of running a script to copy the entire image over and over. As many as the system could do in parallel. Whenever one would finish duplicating itself, the AI would attach and go to work on it. By the time the neural network suggested a password that matched the hash, we had sixteen terabytes' worth of copies being processed."

"Even still, I wouldn't have expected it to be cracked so fast." Blake chimed in.

"It shouldn't have been. We got lucky. The guy set a stupid-simple password. If not, it would have easily taken a day or two. And if it had been random, the AI would have been no use at all."

"What did the password end up being?" Haeli asked.

"BobWoodward1!"

Kook twisted around. "Who the hell is Bob Woodward?"

Haeli just shook her head.

"Look alive." Blake took the turn off the main road onto the quiet dead-end.

There was a time for banter and a time for focus. All of them knew the difference.

Before leaving Jamestown, they had all examined the map of the Sharon, Massachusetts, neighborhood. Blake had a good understanding of the general layout. Wade's house was on the left side, two before the end. The back of the property extended to the backyard of a house in a separate neighborhood. Just as it had appeared from the overhead satellite image, the acre-sized lots were heavily treed, providing a measure of privacy.

As they passed the third house on the right, Kook returned a wave from a man on a riding lawn mower. It was the only activity they noticed.

Taking advantage of the cover of a tall hedgerow fifty-feet short of Wade's address, Blake veered to the left and parked.

As he stepped out, Blake reached toward the small of his back and felt for the handle of his Glock. Given the choice, he preferred to conceal inside a jacket for easier access. Or a drop holster if he wasn't concerned about concealing. It wasn't jacket weather, and a bulky rig strapped to his leg was out of the question.

"I'll go around back," Griff said in a hushed tone.

# DETACHMENT

Haeli joined Griff near the edge of the hedges. "I'll go with him. Text if you make contact."

Blake nodded and the two disappeared around the corner.

Compared to many of the other situations the group had found themselves in over the past several years, this one wasn't particularly risky. This didn't mean any of them would let their guard down.

*Hope for the best. Expect the worst.*

They were there for a reason. One man was already dead and more would likely follow. There was also a chance that one thing had nothing to do with the other. That Robert Novak was the victim of a random act of violence—robbery gone bad, stray bullet; the list goes on. The thumb drive, the cover up, the clandestine meet—a complete coincidence. It was possible, but in Blake's experience, there was no such thing as coincidence.

Blake ran through his mental checklist as a matter of habit. He considered the scenarios they might be faced with. Wade was home, Wade was in hiding, Wade was oblivious, Wade was dead.

"There's a car in the driveway, Mick," Kook said.

"Let's hope it's his," Blake chuckled. "We'll just go up and knock. The faster we can all get away from here the better."

"Lead the way."

Blake and Kook rounded the corner into the driveway, then cut across the front lawn. The main door was set into a stone facade, in front of which was a matching stone platform that spanned half the length of the house.

Kook stepped up onto the patio riser and reached for the doorbell.

"Hang on," Blake said. "Let me take a quick peek."

To the right of the door was a bank of three windows. There were no shades or curtains drawn.

Blake leaned in from the edge of the leftmost window, moving further away as he gained confidence no one looked back at him.

"No movement," Blake said.

Kook nodded. Just as he was about to press the doorbell, Blake saw something. A flash of movement at the edge of what looked like the kitchen door.

"Hold up." Blake stretched his left hand toward Kook and pressed his right against his brow to shield the glare.

He saw it again. This time, the sliver of black fabric protruding from the edge of the doorway grew into an elbow and then into an entire man. Dressed all in black from head to toe, the six-foot-something figure turned in Blake's direction. Blake retreated, but not before he caught a glimpse of the pistol in the man's right gloved hand.

"Shit." Blake drew his firearm from the small of his back. "They're here. One straight ahead. Armed. Go, go, go."

Without hesitation, Kook drew his own pistol, rocked backward, then exploded forward, foot first. The door flew open, sending splinters of the frame flying. Before Kook crossed the threshold, his silenced pistol cycled twice.

Blake followed him inside. On the floor a few feet away, the man in black laid in a heap.

Stopping only to pluck the pistol from the man's limp hand, Blake and Kook pushed forward to the kitchen. When it was cleared, they opened the rear door just as Haeli was lining up to kick it open.

"One down," Blake said as Haeli and Griff entered. "House isn't cleared."

Haeli put her index finger to her lips. "Listen."

From above, they could hear footsteps. Then the timbre and cadence changed, sharpening and echoing. "The stairs."

Blake darted toward the living room. He emerged just in time to see a figure disappearing through the front door.

By the time Blake reached the front patio, the fleeing man was already cutting through the side yard of the house across the street.

On pure instinct, Blake took off running. After only a few strides, he realized it wasn't worth leaving the others, and stopped in his tracks. The man had too much of a head start, and Blake didn't know the area well enough to anticipate where he would head next. On a Saturday afternoon, in broad daylight, the chances that someone would call the police on him were higher than him catching the man.

When Blake turned around, Haeli was in the doorway. Her Glock at the low ready.

"He's gone," Blake said. "Let's find Wade and get the hell out of here."

"Kook and Griff went down into the basement," Haeli said. "You and I should go upstairs."

Blake agreed. He took the lead. Haeli followed with her left hand on his back.

When they reached the top of the stairs, they could see straight to the end of the hallway. There were four doors, two on each side.

With a quick hand motion, Blake communicated that he would break right. Haeli took the room on the opposite side.

They each burst into their respective rooms and found no one. After a cursory search of the closets, they met in the hallway and moved on to the second set.

At the end of a silent three-count, they repeated the process. Blake right. Haeli left.

As Blake swung his sights around the room, he heard a thud from across the hall. It was followed by a flurry of commotion. "Haeli?"

Sprinting in, Blake found Haeli struggling with a large man dressed all in black, like the rest. Haeli's Glock lay on the floor. She had two hands around the man's wrists, controlling the direction of his muzzle while she stomped his ankle and tried to knee him in the groin.

Pistol in hand, Blake's first reaction was to shoot the man. But Haeli was bound up with him, twisting and turning in a combative dance. He couldn't risk hitting her.

Blake tucked his gun into his waistband and jumped into the fight.

As an extra set of hands, Blake was able to twist the man's pistol free of his grasp. He tossed it through the door. It slid across the hall and into the other bedroom.

Haeli let go and delivered a palm strike to the man's sternum. Blake hooked his arm around the man's neck and used his other hand to apply pressure.

In a few seconds, the lack of blood flow to the man's brain would render him unconscious.

The big man had other plans.

With speed and agility that Blake wasn't expecting, the combatant delivered a swift front kick into Haeli's abdomen and snapped his head back into the bridge of Blake's nose. The move loosened Blake's grip just enough to allow the man to twist and deliver an elbow with the force of a freight train.

Blake let go and dipped to the right. The elbow connected with Blake's ear, but his parry had reduced the impact.

In one final display of agility, the man threw himself backward, crashing through the bedroom window and into an irreversible commitment to a two story fall.

Both Blake and Haeli staggered to the window to confirm what they already knew. Torn up by shards of glass and broken by the fall, the man was surely dead.

Only, it wasn't the case.

They found the brooding man, climbing to his feet.

Blake pulled his pistol and trained his sights on the man's face.

The man looked back at Blake with a defiance he shouldn't have possessed. His hands were balled into fists at his side.

"Hands up where I can see them."

The man reluctantly complied.

Beyond the blurry post of the front sight, Blake got a good look at his features. A prominent scar defined the shape of one cheek.

How had he not noticed such a glaring anomaly during the struggle? This was the nature of tunnel vision. The honing of the senses to register only what matters to survival.

There was another thing Blake didn't notice. More than deformed, the man's face was familiar. He had seen it before?

Yes, he had.

He remembered.

*Piper Gaudet.*

Many years before, Piper's name had been on the lips of almost everyone in the special forces and intelligence communities. In a high-profile case, Piper was arrested and convicted after he and his team had reportedly gone rogue, killing over two dozen innocent civilians in a Panamanian Village. Blake had assumed he was still in prison.

What Piper Gaudet had to do with any of this, Blake couldn't begin to guess. But he intended to find out.

"Don't move. I will shoot you." Keeping his Glock on his target, Blake twisted his body to face his back to Haeli. "I have a pair of cuffs in my back pocket. Take them. Grab Kook and Griff and secure this guy."

Haeli slipped the handcuffs from his pants and hurried out of the room.

"You're not going to shoot an unarmed man, are you?" Piper asked.

"Apparently, you don't know me."

"That's true. I don't." Piper slowly lowered his hands. "Who are you?"

"Don't worry about it," Blake said. "I know you."

"Mmm," Piper grunted. "Of course you do. Because you *are* me, aren't you?"

"Lay down on the ground," Blake barked. "Interlace your fingers behind your head."

"Not today," Piper said. "Maybe next time."

As if stuck in slow motion, Piper's feet began carrying his bulky frame backward. Then he slowly turned and walked away.

From the second story window, Blake blurted out a few desperate commands. "Stop. Don't make me kill you." But it was too late.

Sauntering around the side of the shed and into the woods, Piper had called his bluff. No, Blake wasn't going to shoot an unarmed man. Somehow, Piper could sense it. It was a gamble, but it paid off.

By the time Haeli, Griff and Kook arrived, Piper was gone.

## CHAPTER 29

"YEAH, I REMEMBER HIM." Kook dumped the contents of the dresser drawer onto the bed. "I remember the House Armed Services Committee threatening to kill SOCOM after what went down. Not that it would have affected us."

"I imagine that was just posturing," Griff said. "Whenever the public shows outrage, everyone overreacts. It's all about virtual signaling, right?"

Haeli pawed through the clothing in the closet. "I don't know about that, but I feel like I know a few things about this Piper person. He's crazy, he's ugly, and he's indestructible."

Blake chuckled. "I'd agree with most of that, but 'indestructible' might be a stretch. Not that I have a better explanation. I have no idea how he survived that. He was bloodied up a bit, but nothing serious. If that were me, I'd have lost an arm, shattered my skull, and had four pieces of glass sticking out of my chest. This guy gets up and winks at me."

"Indestructible," Haeli repeated.

No one talked about how Blake let Piper walk away. He appreciated that. Normally, they'd at least break his stones a bit. But they would all have done the same thing in his position.

A few years earlier, Blake had given into his rage. Anja's death had changed him. Misaligned his moral compass. It was the one and only time he had killed someone in cold blood. And he had yet to forgive himself.

The rules were simple. In the heat of battle, anything goes. Kill or be killed. But when it's over, when the threat has been mitigated, lethal force is off the table.

To be fair, when it came to Blake's former work with the Agency's Special Activities Division, the rule was more of a suggestion. Based not in morality, but in practicality. A dead man isn't a useful one.

It made sense. It harkened back to childhood lessons. Lose with humility, win with humility. In little league, when one team had run away with the game, the umpires would call it. They'd called it the Mercy rule back then, and it wasn't much different today. Only now, it wasn't the other guy he'd spared. It was his own humanity.

Kook dumped another drawer.

"Knock it off, Kook," Blake said. "We're not trying to destroy the place."

"What *are* we doing?" Griff asked. "What exactly are we looking for?"

"Anything that can give us a—" Blake froze. "Shhhh."

"What?"

"Listen. Did you hear that?" Blake whispered.

The group listened.

"No," Griff admitted. "What is it?"

Blake looked at the ceiling. "Someone's up there," he whispered.

After another few seconds of listening to nothing but birds chirping and the distant lawn mower, Blake moved out of the bedroom to the hallway. The rest followed.

Above their heads was a pull-down door. Blake pointed in case anyone was unclear what he had in mind.

"How did we not check the attic?" Haeli whispered.

Kook pulled his pistol, and without further discussion, grabbed the cord hanging from the trap door. He yanked. "Archer. You up there, bud?"

There was no response.

Haeli tried her hand. "We're not here to hurt you. We're here to help. The other guys are gone, okay? Come on down."

No response again.

Blake reached over and pushed on Kook's gun. Kook responded by hiding it behind his back. With a flicking hand motion, Blake shooed him out of view.

"Archer. My name is Blake. We're here to make sure you're safe." Blake unfolded the wooden stairs and put his foot on the first rung. "Those men were after you because of Robert Novak, and they won't stop coming. We need to get you out of here."

Blake looked at Haeli and lifted his eyebrows. She seemed to understand the unspoken question. Should he go up? Haeli responded with a shrug.

Before Blake took another step, a head emerged from the opening above. A head and a mess of hair that suggested he could have been Kook's long-lost cousin. "Archer Wade?"

Wade nodded.

"It's all right. Come down and grab your things. We have to go," Blake said.

"How—how do I know you're not here to kill me? I don't know anything, I swear."

"I'll put it to you this way," Blake said. "You have two choices. Come with us and we'll help you. Or stay here and wait for those guys to come back with a dozen more friends. It's up to you."

Wade shifted his body around and let his legs drop onto the steps.

"There ya go," Kook said from behind the stairs.

"Who are you?" Wade took one careful step at a time.

"It's a long story." Blake held out his hand. Wade shook it. "Pack a bag. We'll fill you in once we're on the road."

"How do I know you're not with them?"

"Easy," Blake said. "Follow me."

Wade looked through the rungs of the steps at Kook, Haeli, and Griff. Haeli nodded, as if giving her approval. It seemed to work because Wade turned and followed Blake down the stairs.

In the living room, just inside the splintered front door, the body of a home invader lay lifeless. His blood saturated the area rug.

"Oh my god, is he—"

"He is," Blake said. "If this isn't proof that we're here to help you, I don't know what is."

"There's a dead body in my living room," Archer stuttered.

"A dead body that's not yours."

Wade's pale face slackened. Blake's comment had hit home.

"This is crazy," Wade said. "I'm just a reporter. What am I supposed to do with this? We need to call the police."

"No, we don't." Kook glided down the stairs. "That shed out back, is it locked?"

Wade nodded.

"Get the key," Kook said. "Then you can help me roll the guy up in that carpet and move him out back. My colleagues will wipe down the floor real quick. When there's time, we'll come back and arrange a more permanent solution. Okay?"

Wade didn't say anything. He stood completely still.

Kook clapped. "Go. Chop, chop. I need that key."

Wade hustled off to the kitchen.

"We could be floating in the pool right now, ya know," Haeli said from the top of the stairs.

Blake chuckled. "What fun would that be?"

## CHAPTER 30

BLAKE PULLED in front of Fezz's assigned garage. One of three in a row, the garage housed an old stake-bed that Fezz found on Facebook Marketplace. The idea was to build an armored box on the back. A street-legal MRAP of sorts. The problem was, it wasn't street legal. It wasn't even registered or insured.

After Fezz had made the deal, Blake had followed him back to the garage in case he got pulled over. To this day, Blake wasn't clear about what good it would have done. Was he supposed to intervene? "Officer, this is my friend. I know his vehicle is a heap of junk and it's not registered or insured, but I was following him, so it's okay."

Next to the garages were three separate units. Clad in weathered wood shake, the Catherine Street building was typical Newport construction.

Out of everyone's, Fezz's cover-apartment was Blake's favorite. A short walk to Thames Street and Bowen's Wharf, most people would give their eyeteeth for such a prime location. Fezz only stopped in two or three times a week to keep up appearances.

The good news was, Blake was driving Fezz's truck. The neighbors wouldn't think twice about it being parked in Fezz's spot.

"This is where you'll stay," Blake said. "It's safe. No one could possibly know you're here."

# DETACHMENT

"Whose place is this?" Wade unbuckled his seatbelt.

"A friend of ours. He's out of town for a few weeks. He's letting us use it while he's gone."

Everyone climbed out and regrouped at the back of the truck. Haeli carried the bag of sandwiches they'd picked up on the way through Bristol.

The food was her idea. It wasn't so much for them, but for Wade. This was a tactic they had learned through experience. Offering food to detainees worked wonders. Especially when the goal was to interrogate. In this case, they hoped it would lessen the shock of the trauma and build a sense of trust and normalcy.

Blake unlocked the door and the group filtered in. Haeli dumped the butcher paper wrapped sandwiches out of the bag and onto the kitchen table.

"Take your pick. Roast beef, turkey, or ham," Haeli said.

Wade took a seat at the table, selected the packet closest to him and started unwrapping it. He hadn't so much as glanced around the rest of the apartment, as if he hadn't registered that it would be his home for at least the next few days. Maybe more.

Not that there was much to see. A few pieces of used furniture, a few essentials. It was devoid of decoration except for the large sea-scape oil painting hanging in the living room.

When Fezz had first rented the place, it was empty, save three items. A bucket, a mop, and that painting. The owner had told him the previous tenant had left it behind and asked Fezz if he wanted to keep it. Fezz said he did. Not because he liked it—the thing was hideous—but because it represented a new identity, with new tastes, wholly unrelated to his own.

Kook and Griff joined Wade at the table and dug into their lunch.

"Want to sit?" Haeli asked.

"You go ahead." Blake grabbed one of the two remaining sandwiches and hopped on the kitchen counter.

Haeli took the empty seat next to Wade. She reached over and rubbed his shoulder blade. "I know this is a lot to take in, but we're going to help get to the bottom of this."

Wade looked around the table. "Are you with the government?"

"No," Griff said. "We operate outside of any formal structure."

"What he means," Kook added, "is we help people like you, who find themselves in situations like this."

"But no one—I mean, how did you—"

"We have our sources," Blake said. "You were supposed to meet Robert Novak, and correct me if I'm wrong, but he was going to give you a thumb drive containing secret documents. Only, he was killed before he could get to you."

"That's right. I never got the documents. After the murder, the police found the drive and kept it as evidence. There's no way to know what was on it."

"Well—" Kook said with singsong inflection.

"We have it," Griff said. "We've seen the documents."

"How?" Wade looked around the table and then over his shoulder at Blake. "Ya know what? I don't want to know."

"The specifics don't matter," Blake said. "The point is, we know about Venezuela. We know about the mission. And we know, just as you do, that the people involved will stop at nothing to keep it quiet."

"Venezuela?" Wade's brow furrowed. His jaw stopped, as if he forgot he was chewing a mouthful of bread and meat.

"Hold up," Kook said. "You really didn't know what you were meeting about?"

"I knew it was about an impropriety within the federal government. My editor put me in contact with Novak. Said to 'Look into it.' I spoke with Robert on the phone, but we only talked about where and when to meet. He wouldn't say anything else over the phone. Seemed real paranoid. I figured he was worried about getting arrested or losing his job." Wade paused. "What about Venezuela?"

Blake hopped down off the countertop. His boots landed on the linoleum with a *thump*. "Let's start by getting you up to speed."

For the next fifteen or twenty minutes, the crew explained what they knew and how they knew it. Of course, they sanitized the narrative to avoid revealing anything about themselves. They left out Harrison completely.

# DETACHMENT

They also learned more about Wade. His professional backstory. Why his editor had chosen him.

By the end of the discussion, Wade was like a different person. The group saw a spark in him that wasn't there before. A journalistic drive. Wade was a shark, and they had just chummed the water.

"I need those documents," Wade said. "This is a big story. The biggest of my career."

"Hold your horses," Kook said. The expression garnered funny looks all around. Not because they didn't know what it meant, but because he was the first person to use it since nineteen forty-two.

Blake paced. "Kook's right. It's not safe. You need to lay low."

It was a flimsy excuse. Publishing the story would all but ensure his safety. Once all the dirty details went public, killing Wade would only exacerbate the government's problems.

The truth was, Blake didn't know how he felt about the story getting out. The men and women involved in the mission would be sucked into the controversy. Tarnished for no reason. For simply doing their jobs.

Anyway, it wasn't the mission that Blake found reprehensible. The United States had sent troops to depose world leaders before. Like Manuel Noriega, some were widely known. Others, not as much. What stuck in Blake's craw was Robert Novak's murder.

Somehow, they needed to find a way to root out those who would stoop so low to cover their own asses without throwing innocents under the bus. If they played their cards right, Wade might prove an asset toward doing just that.

"I know you want to run with this," Haeli said, "but think about it. We don't know yet what transpired. You need more information."

Blake wagged his finger. "What you need is a living, breathing source. As soon as you release those documents, the government will claim them as forgeries. The media at large won't be able to verify, so they'll latch onto the only story left. You. A hack who tried to invent a conspiracy to boost your career. Now, it'd be different if someone on the inside could help back you up."

Wade sat in silence for a moment of assumed introspection. "There is something."

"What's that?"

"I think Robert Novak was just a courier," Wade said. "I mean, I don't think he's the actual source."

"Why do you say that?" Haeli asked.

"It was something Clint said."

"Clint?" Blake asked.

"My editor. When he first asked me to set up the meeting, I questioned whether the source was trustworthy. Clint said he'd known the guy for thirty years. Robert Novak wouldn't have been born yet."

"Fantastic," Griff said. "Call Clint and find out who the real source is."

"I'll try," Wade said. "He might not want to divulge. In fact, I'm pretty sure he won't."

"It's worth a shot," Blake said. "In the meantime, we'll go do a little digging on our own."

"What am I supposed to do, just sit around here?" Wade asked.

"Yes." Blake knew Wade was looking for more. He didn't offer it.

"What about the thumb drive? Can I see it?"

"I'll have another friend bring it to you. Her name is—" Blake caught himself before he uttered Ima's real name. "Olivia. She'll look after you while we're gone. In case you need anything."

"You're sending a babysitter?"

"Not a babysitter, an assistant. She'll bring a couple of laptops and she'll help you try to dig up more information."

"I'm capable of doing my own research."

"I'm sure," Blake said. "But not the way she can. Trust me."

"What is she, some kind of investigator?"

"No. She's some kind of genius."

## CHAPTER 31

BLAKE UNLOCKED THE DOOR. "Remember, your name's Olivia."

"Right," Ima said.

Inside, Blake and Ima found Wade sitting on the couch, playing with his new phone.

Wade had thrown a fit when Blake told him he had to leave his phone behind in Sharon. But after promising to replace it when they got to the safehouse and allowing Wade time to write down some of the numbers he had stored in his contacts, Wade let it go.

"Archer, meet Olivia," Blake said.

Wade took one glance at Ima, sprang to his feet, and offered his hand. "Nice to meet you, I'm Olivia—I mean, I'm Archer. You're Olivia." The following awkward pause was abbreviated by an equally awkward, nervous laugh. "Get yourself together, Archer."

Ima flashed a coy smile. "Do you always refer to yourself in the third person?"

"Not usually, no."

Blake wondered if he had made a mistake putting Ima on Archer duty. Ima hadn't been there ten seconds and Wade was already undressing her with his eyes. Then again, judging by Ima's permanent grin, maybe it wasn't Wade he should've been worried about. "All right, introductions made. What'd you find out?"

"I got ahold of Clint," Wade said.

"Did he give you a name?"

"It took some begging, but he did. John Novak, Robert's father. Clint's going to reach out to him to see if John will speak with me. I gave Clint this number. He said he'd get back to me."

"Oh my god, that's terrible." The corners of Ima's mouth drew downward. "His own father sent him to deliver the documents and it got him killed?"

"Hold up a minute. John Novak is the source? General Novak was the one who cut the order. He's the top guy at SOCOM. Olivia, let me see that laptop," Blake said.

Ima reached into her canvas bag, took out one of the two laptops, and handed it to Blake. She reached back in to retrieve the mobile internet hotspot, switched it on, and placed it on the side table.

While Blake was in Massachusetts, Ima had concatenated all the files into a single PDF document. Already loaded up, Blake only had to search for 'Novak' to find the document in question. When he did, he passed the laptop to Wade. "I noticed the last name and wondered if there was a connection between him and the victim. I was thinking maybe, if Robert was related to John, it could explain how he got ahold of the information. I wouldn't have guessed John Novak was the one to drop a dime on this whole thing. Actually, I'd pegged him as the ringleader."

"It doesn't mean he's not," Wade said. "Other than me, Robert, and Clint, he would have been the only other person who knew about the meeting."

Ima shook her head. "He wouldn't have set up his own son just to cover himself. Who would do that? And why would he hook up Robert with the Globe if he didn't want it getting out?"

"So he could control it," Blake said. "Because he and Clint are friends. It's possible. Let's say Robert found out what's going on, then confronted his father and threatened to go to the media. The best thing John could've done was act like he was on board, even offer to make the introduction."

Wade got up and grabbed the pencil and pad he left on the kitchen table. "If that were the case, I bet there would be a connection between

John and this Piper guy." He returned to his spot on the couch and picked up the laptop. "Can I use this?"

"Of course, that one's for you," Blake said. "Olivia, give Archer a hand. Go through all the old affidavits from Piper's court-martial. See if Novak's name pops up anywhere in there."

Ima nodded.

The sound of a marimba emanated from Wade's pocket.

"This could be Clint." Wade glanced at the number and then answered the phone. "Hello?"

Wade listened. A second later, his eyes widened, and he began waving his hand as if his wrist were possessed. "General, yes, of course." He pointed at the phone and mouthed the words, "It's him."

It was an unexpected turn of events. Wade had only put the feelers out a short time ago and Novak had cut out the middleman and was already making contact. Did this mean he was anxious to get his story on the record, or to lure Wade in to stop him?

"I will absolutely meet you. Oh, where? Um, let me see—"

Blake grabbed the pad and pencil and scribbled down an address. He stuck it in Wade's face.

Wade nodded and relayed what Blake wrote, verbatim.

"Tomorrow morning. Eight A.M. I'll be there." Wade hung up the phone.

"What the heck just happened?" Ima said.

"This is huge." Wade ran his hands through his hair. His excitement was palpable. "This is going to blow this story wide open. There's not much time. I have to prepare."

"No you don't," Blake said. "You're not going."

# CHAPTER 32

PIPER ROUNDED the side of the house to find Ron Phillips in his regular spot.

"Piper," Phillips said from behind his newspaper. "Tequila?"

Piper thought about it. Under the circumstances, he could probably justify one drink. The fact that it was seven-thirty in the morning helped him keep his resolve. "No, I'm good."

Phillip peered above the newsprint. "What the hell happened to you?"

"It looks worse than it is." Piper wasn't minimizing. Despite the contusion on his forehead, four stitches in his eyebrow, a black eye, and one chipped tooth, he'd been in worse shape after a friendly Jujitsu match.

"I'm assuming all went well?"

Piper sat. "No. All did not go well. Schriever's dead."

"What? How?"

"We were ambushed at the reporter's house."

"Ambushed by who? Are you telling me some reporter took out Schriever and messed up your face like that?" Phillips gritted his teeth. "He better be in the ground."

"This wasn't Wade. We didn't find him."

A low, ominous laugh escaped Phillips' parted lips. "You didn't find him." With un-telegraphed intensity, Phillips swiped the glass of tequila off the table. It smashed on the concrete deck. "Then who did you find?"

"I don't know. I think Wade hired protection. When we got to his house, Wade wasn't there. Next thing you know, Schriever's taking a couple rounds to the chest and the place is swarming with armed men. These were professionals. They used silencers. Tactics. These guys were SF, I'd bet anything."

"Where did they come from?"

"How am I supposed to know? Once Wade realized what happened to Novak's kid, he must have got spooked. Got himself a bunch of bodyguards. We got caught with our pants down. I accept responsibility for that. We weren't supposed to have any opposition."

"Where's Schriever now?"

"I had to leave him."

"And Charlie?"

"He's fine."

Phillips folded the paper into quarters. "I'll call the contracting firms. When I find out which one took the job, I'll have them pull the detail. I want you to draw the reporter out and clean this up. I don't care how you do it, just make him and his associates go away. Is that clear?"

"Clear."

"Good. Don't come back here 'til it's done."

Piper nodded. "There's one other thing that may help. They had a woman with them."

"What do you mean *with* them?"

"Just what I said. One of them was a woman. But this wasn't an ordinary woman. She was as capable as any of my guys. Better, actually. Can't be too many of those around, right? And one of the guys was a ginger, if that helps. As far as the others, I never got a good look at them."

"Fine. A woman and a ginger. Got it."

Piper stood, intending to leave. But there was one other loose end they didn't discuss. "What about Novak?"

"Ah, Novak." Phillips' mouth tightened in the slightest of smiles. "I'll take care of Novak myself."

# CHAPTER 33

BLAKE STOOD inside the main entrance of the abandoned Aerosol factory. He wore a ball cap, a pair of jeans, and a blazer. He'd put a gaiter around his neck to later pull up and cover the lower half of his face. If Novak held true to his word.

When Novak had pressed Wade to pick a place to meet, one location had come to Blake's mind. He had visited the Connecticut factory before, more than a decade ago, under similar circumstances.

What occurred there stuck with him. So much so that he never forgot the address.

*Two Hundred Sixty Old Gate Lane.*

The way he remembered it, the abandoned building was the perfect setup. Amid a commercial area, it offered easy entry and complete seclusion. Railroad tracks behind the facility provided an escape route inaccessible to vehicles, and the sheer expansiveness made it easy to stay hidden if necessary.

The reality was, it was an abandoned building like any other. In much worse condition than the last time he was there, it smelled of dead animals and mold. The abundance of graffiti indicated it wasn't as desolate as he had remembered.

In retrospect, there were probably better and closer options. He also

# DETACHMENT

could have done worse. He could have picked Starbucks. He had a solid hunch the ski-masks wouldn't have gone over well there.

"You read me, Mick?" Fezz said over the comms.

Blake adjusted his earpiece. "I've got you. Everyone in place?"

"We're set up. F.Y.I, you got two bogies headed in your direction. Looks like kids. They're carrying skateboards."

*Great. Shoulda just said Starbucks.*

The chain-link fence that once secured the property had all but rusted away. Some sections had no fence at all. Blake was able to walk right in. Why shouldn't everyone else?

"They're walking toward the main entrance," Fezz said.

"I figured."

There was a reason Blake set up where he did. The giant doorless opening was the easiest and most visible entry into the building. It was where anyone would go. Novak, or a couple of teen skaters.

Blake stepped in front of the doorless opening. The kids stopped in their tracks.

"Where we going, boys?"

"Nowhere," the shorter of the two said. He had silver braces on his teeth.

"You wouldn't be the ones vandalizing this place, would you?"

"No. We were just—"

"We got lost," the other interrupted.

The two boys were no more than thirteen years old. They seemed like decent kids. Blake wanted to laugh at their flimsy excuses, but he kept a stern face. "I can take you down to the station and call your parents, if that'll help."

"No. That's okay," the shorter one said. "We'll just go back that way." He pointed in the direction they'd come.

"Okay. I'll buy it this time. But if I see you here again—"

"You won't." The shorter kid bolted, leaving his buddy behind. When the taller kid realized he was alone, he took off, catching up to his friend before the two disappeared beyond the gates.

Blake returned to his post.

It was funny how the mere suggestion of authority would cause the guilty to jump to conclusions. Kids or adults, it didn't matter. Blake never said he was a cop or showed them a badge.

A few years back, Blake had a conversation with a DC Metro cop at Kelley's Irish Times about the very same thing. He couldn't remember the cop's name but could picture the man's face, plain as day. The guy had told a story about how he was off duty one day and saw a couple of crackheads fleeing a home with armfuls of cut copper pipes. He'd jumped out, ordered them to drop the copper, and put their hands on the vehicle. The guys had complied. It wasn't til he'd patted them down that he realized he was unarmed, wearing shorts and flip flops and driving his old beat-up pickup truck. He'd never identified himself, and they'd never asked. The guy had to call for a patrol car to scoop up the two burglars.

"Heads up, someone's coming in from the road," Fezz said.

"I've got eyes," Griff added. "Could be the target. Adult male. Appears to be alone."

It was good news. There were only five of them. Blake, Fezz, Khat, Griff, and Kook. Haeli had stayed behind to look after Ian while Ima was working with Wade to dig up whatever dirt they could find on Novak and Piper.

As long as Novak didn't have half the Seventy-Fifth Ranger Regiment staged down the block, five would be plenty. Fezz and Griff had both taken perimeter positions. Kook and Khat were situated further in the building. The idea was to lure Novak in and then pinch him from four sides.

From what they could gather, Novak had been a highly capable operator in his day. The last thing they wanted was to be caught sleeping on him.

"Contact in thirty seconds," Fezz said.

Blake keyed the mic. "Fezz, Griff. Move in as soon as he's inside. Give Kook and Khat the go-ahead when you're close."

Pulling his ball cap onto his brow, Blake found a spot next to a support beam, just far enough away from the door to be cast in shadow. He leaned against the beam and waited.

"Archer?" Novak's voice echoed through the cavernous room.

"Are you alone?" Blake kept his head tilted downward.

# DETACHMENT

"I am." As Novak navigated a path around puddles and debris, his gait was sporadic and measured. Each click of his heels melded with the echoey plinking of dripping water. "What are we doing here?"

Blake didn't respond. He held still.

When Novak got within twenty feet, he stopped. His body tensed. "This isn't right," he muttered under his breath.

Novak was spooked. Blake could see the coil in his stance. He was about to run.

Blake reached up and pulled his neck gaiter over his mouth and nose.

"You're not him." Novak reached for his waistband.

From out of the darkness over Blake's shoulder, Kook's voice boomed. "Don't do it."

Frozen from the neck down, Novak's head swiveled side to side. Khat and Kook flanked Blake, their rifles pointed at Novak's head.

"Put your hands above your head and turn around," Blake said.

Novak raised his arms and spun around, coming face to face with Fezz and Griff. Fezz reached into Novak's waistband and removed the Kimber Nineteen-Eleven.

Fezz nodded to Griff, who slung his rifle and searched Novak. All he found were his wallet and set of keys.

"This is what it comes down to?" Novak's voice was low and wispy. The sound of a broken and defeated man. "After everything I've done for this country?"

"We know all about what you're done for this country," Blake said. "And so does Robert."

Novak spun around. Like a switch, the fiery fortitude of a life-long soldier replaced the vulnerable demeanor. "Don't you say his name! He never did anything but try to live up to the patches on his sleeve. He was loyal to the core. Not like you. You all think you're tough. But not tough enough to stand up for what's right. Well, you can tell him I'll see him in hell."

"Who?"

Novak scoffed. "You know who. Phillips. Or Moore. Whoever has you doing their bidding. You should be disgusted with yourselves. Those are your brothers over there. And you're just going to let them rot? Without even trying? You'll be next, when they're done with you. You get that? To them, you're expendable."

*Let them rot?*

What was Novak implying? Were there men left behind? Was that what this was all about? It would make more sense. The cover-up. The lengths they had gone to in order to keep it quiet.

Before they'd met Novak, Blake wasn't sure who they were going to meet. An evil mastermind? An unwitting patsy? Now, he was sure 'evil mastermind' was off the table.

Blake pulled his mask down and approached. "What do you mean 'brothers over there'? Are you talking about Venezuela?"

Novak bowed his head and laughed. "Oh, that's perfect. You don't even know." He raised his head to look Blake in the eye and bared his teeth. "You killed my son, and you don't even know why!"

Before Blake knew what hit him, a wad of saliva and phlegm was running down his cheek. He used his sleeve to wipe it off. "We didn't kill your son."

"It doesn't matter. You or someone like you. Blindly following the orders of a maniac. How can you call yourself soldiers?"

"We don't," Blake said. "Because we're not."

"Then who the hell are you?"

Blake turned to Kook and motioned for him to lower his rifle. Khat followed suit. "We're not here to kill you. Believe it or not, we're here to help."

"Help." Novak laughed. "Unless you're going to bring my son back, you can keep your help."

"I'm sorry about Robert. I am. I know you'd do anything to bring him back. But he's gone. The only thing we can do is make sure the people responsible are held accountable."

"Not Robbie," Novak said. "Jackson. Jesus, you really don't know anything, do you? My other son Jackson, he was on the team that was captured. He's still there and no one cares."

Blake, Fezz, and the others all shot each other the same look of horror and disgust. Blake felt a pit inside him. It was filled with anger. Sympathy. Solidarity.

# DETACHMENT

This man in front of Blake was cut from the same cloth. Still, Blake couldn't begin to understand how he was feeling. If one of Blake's crew was in need, he would go to the ends of the earth to bring them home in one piece. He already had. He could only imagine how much worse it was for a father and his sons.

"When I said we were here to help, I meant it. Even if we have to go to Venezuela and get your son ourselves."

Novak jeered. "Don't be ridiculous."

It was a ridiculous notion, he would get no argument from Blake. But Blake was serious.

Fezz moved to face Novak and removed his balaclava. "Listen. This is going to require a leap of faith on your part, but you need to come with us. There are some very determined men out there who want to eradicate everything and everyone connected to Venezuela. It's not safe to go home. Or to work. Let's go sit down like civilized men and talk."

"And I should just trust you? I have no idea who you people are."

Khat spoke up. "You should trust us because if we wanted to make you disappear, we already would have done it. Look around you. No better place, right? We know it, you know it."

"We have a place that you can stay for the time being," Blake added. "The real Archer Wade is there now. You can have your opportunity to tell him your story."

"And if I want to leave. Right now, if I want to walk out that door, then what?"

"Then you walk out that door," Blake said. "But I hope you don't. I hope we can work together to fix this."

"Give me my gun back," Novak said. "Start with that."

Fezz pulled the Kimber from his waistband, removed the magazine, and ejected the round in the chamber. He handed the gun to Novak, handle first.

Novak looked at Blake.

Blake shrugged. "You're a little edgy. Better safe than sorry."

"Fair enough," Novak smirked. His shoulders dropped and he looked around, making a point to look each of them in the eye. "Screw it. Lead the way."

# CHAPTER 34

BLAKE DROPPED his gear bag on the kitchen island. The rest of the crew filtered in through the front door.

Haeli opened the slider but stayed outside. The landscape lights rimmed her hair, separating her from the inky backdrop. "How'd it go?"

"It was interesting," Khat said.

Griff sat on the couch and unlaced his boots. "Not what we expected, for sure."

"You gonna come in?" Kook asked.

"I'm keeping an eye on Ian in the pool."

Kook nodded, satisfied with the answer.

"Turns out Novak isn't a bad guy," Blake said. "He filled in some major holes. Ya know how we were wondering why they were so freaked out about the Maduro thing getting out? Didn't fit, right? Because it wasn't the assassination they were trying to cover up."

Haeli looked toward the pool and then at Blake. "What was it then?"

"They sent a Delta team on short notice. The team got ambushed and were captured. Instead of negotiating or sending a rescue team, they cut their losses."

"No way," Haeli said.

Fezz peeled off his black long-sleeved shirt. "He's right. They denied the whole thing and refused to even acknowledge the mission, never mind provide support." He slipped on a Tommy Bahama short sleeve button-down. "It gets worse. You know that Robert Novak was John Novak's son, right? Well, his other son is one of the Delta guys."

"No!" Haeli's mouth hung open. "That's some bad luck."

"It's a mess," Blake said.

"Where's Novak?"

"We took him over to Newport. He's with Ima and Wade," Blake replied.

"Olivia and Wade," Khat said.

"Right. Them, too."

"We got a lot more of the story on the way back," Griff said. "Robbie was Delta as well. That's how he was able to get his hands on the documents. Novak admitted he set up the meeting with Wade through the editor, Clint. They were hoping that by leaking the story, it would put pressure on Moore to organize a rescue. Apparently, Moore had his people keep a close eye on Novak."

Haeli scowled. "Piper. He's Moore's dog?"

"We're guessing." Blake opened the fridge and selected a lime seltzer.

"So what do we do now?" Haeli asked.

"Why don't you get Ian out of the pool and we'll all sit down and discuss."

Haeli nodded and closed the sliding door.

"Are we seriously considering taking this on?" Khat asked.

Blake smiled. "You're the ones who wanted to see some action. Here ya have it."

"I don't think invading a sovereign nation was what everyone had in mind," Griff said.

"Oh, sure." Blake laughed. "That's where you draw the line? Infiltrate a sadistic cult, sign me up. Helicopter dogfight, piece of cake. Steal a three hundred-fifty-million-dollar jet and intentionally crash it into the ocean, all in a day's work. But sneaking into a country to rescue American servicemen, now we're going too far."

Griff pursed his lips. "Point taken."

"I want to jump in the shower before we get into it," Kook said. "I feel like I've still got rat shit in my hair."

"Sounds good." Blake walked to the slider, opened it, and called out to Haeli. "We're gonna put this stuff away and get cleaned up. We'll meet in the dining room in twenty, okay?"

Sitting on the edge of the lounge chair with her elbows on her knees, she gave an unenthusiastic wave of acknowledgement.

Blake leaned further out until he could see Ian around the shrub, planted outside the door. "Hi, Ian."

"Five more minutes," Ian said. "Please."

"What did Haeli say?"

"She said I have to get out right now."

"Then you have to ask her, not me. Right?"

With raised eyebrows, he turned and stared at Haeli.

"Five more minutes," she said.

"Yes!"

Ian dipped under the water. Haeli fell back into the chair. Flat on her back, she let her arms fall to the concrete. "I'm never having kids."

---

"WHERE'S FEZZ?" Kook asked. "Let's get this show on the road."

The entire team, except Fezz, sat around the dining room table. A weird silence filled the room. Not because they were uncomfortable, but because they didn't want to start discussing until everyone was there. They'd only have to repeat everything over again.

"Fezz!" Khat yelled. "Come on ya big oaf."

"Hold your horses!"

"Oh, great," Blake said. "Good job, Kook. Now you've got Fezz saying it."

Fezz came into the room and stood as if he were about to perform. "Listen up. I have an announcement."

Khat leaned toward Griff. "This outta be good."

"You all know I've been working on something special."

"Oh, we know," Haeli said. "Can't miss the power tools at seven A.M."

Fezz smiled. "Even though you've been breaking my stones about it, I know you're gonna love it. Still needs a few finishing touches, but I think it's time to unveil it."

Kook tilted his chair back on two legs and folded his arms across his chest. "Right now? Aren't we supposed to have a meeting?"

"We can't have the meeting in here," Fezz said. "It doesn't feel right." He turned and walked through the door. "Come on. Trust me."

The crew got up and lumbered after him. They regrouped in the hallway next to the mudroom just inside the side door. The sheets were still hanging along one entire wall.

"Wow," Khat said. "Still looks like a bunch of sheets."

"Ladies and Gentlemen—"

The group groaned.

"Fine." Fezz grabbed two handfuls of fabric, and with one big yank, pulled them off their clips and let them fall to the floor.

Blake stood stunned.

Behind the sheets was varnished wood and frosted glass. Applied to the glass was a familiar decal. Maroon lettering bordered in white that read, "Artie's."

Blake could feel the lump in his throat growing. And he wasn't the only one. As much as Khat tried to hide it, his eyes were glassy and an uncharacteristic smile took over his face.

"Inside," Blake said. "Is it...?"

Fezz showed a quiet, gentle grin and swung open the door.

"Oh my god," Griff blurted. "It's beautiful."

And it was.

A complete replica, down to the last detail. The pictures on the wall, the rickety old bar stools, even the brass ring game on the wall inside the door. All well-worn, like it had always been there. Like it used to be.

"I'm speechless," Blake said. "How did you do this?"

"It wasn't easy."

Khat ran his hand over their usual high-top table. "You did this from memory?"

"Not exactly," Fezz said. "I paid a guy to go down to Artie's and take a thousand pictures. His only instruction was to not get caught." Fezz laughed.

"This is above and beyond. Come 'ere." Blake grabbed Fezz and embraced him.

Blake was going to say, 'you don't know what this means to me,' but the truth was, Fezz did. It was why he had spent so much time and energy working on it. Not just for Blake, but for everyone. Having to leave their homes, routines, entire pasts behind took a toll. This room was about reclaiming a little piece of it. Comfort, Blake would say. Grounding.

"Sit," Fezz said. "I'll get us some beers."

The crew pulled a couple extra stools around 'their' table and Fezz headed behind the bar.

"Playing the part of Artie tonight—" Griff joked.

"You even have working taps," Khat noticed. "How'd you get the kegs in here? I can usually smell 'em."

"Don't you worry. I ordered cheap, crappy beer. I wanted you to have an authentic experience. And don't worry Mick, we're stocked with plenty of cheap, crappy whiskey too."

"Just when you think you've seen it all," Haeli looked around. "There's even crushed peanut shells on the floor."

"Yeah, don't remind me." Fezz topped off a pint. "I never want to see another peanut as long as I live."

Blake realized that Kook was quiet. He wasn't part of the original Artie's crew. "Hey, Kook. You know what this is?"

"It's Artie's bar in Virginia," Kook said. "I've been there once or twice. Always preferred the Gallery over Artie's though."

"Well, you'll learn to love it my friend."

Fezz dropped four beers on the table. "I only wish Ima was here for this. Every day she asked what I was doing in here. I told her she'd be the first to know." He returned to the bar for the other two pints. When he came back, he proposed a toast. "To the good 'ol days."

The group clinked glasses and sipped.

Blake smacked his lips. "This is incredible. I feel like I was sitting in this very spot when we found the diamonds Haeli sent."

"Or the last drink we had with Bonzo," Khat added.

Fezz put his glass on the table and pulled up a stool. "I figured since we can't ever go back to D.C, we'd bring it to us. Still, it's not the same without Artie himself."

"I'll drink to that." Khat downed his beer, then hopped off his stool and walked to the bar to refill.

"Now that we're here," Fezz said, "let's talk business. What are we thinkin'?"

Blake started. "First thing is, we're gonna need a ride. Kook?"

"I've got us covered. Just have to get out to Henderson and you'll have your pick."

"Great," Blake continued. "Has to be something we can set down in a field or on a road. Airports are out of the question."

"Like I said, I've got us covered. What we should worry about is what we're gonna do once we're in."

"We don't know where they are yet, do we?" Haeli asked.

"Yes, we do." Blake reached into his back pocket and pulled out a folded piece of paper. "Novak drew this. It's the layout of the compound. The same one from the thumb drive. He says they're still holding the team in one of the buildings." Blake pointed to a rectangle labeled 'Barn.' "It's offset from the house, maybe three hundred yards."

Khat grabbed the paper and slid it toward the middle of the table. "It's perfect. We come in from behind, here." Khat used his index finger to illustrate their proposed position. "We're out of view of the main house. If we can get the guys out and into this line of trees, we can work our way down here, or up here, depending on where the extraction point is."

"And if they sound the alarm?" Griff asked. "Novak said there were over thirty soldiers, maybe more."

"I was thinking explosives," Blake said.

Fezz looked at him cross-eyed.

"As a diversion. And only if needed."

"We'll talk about it," Fezz said.

Haeli chimed in. "What about Novak? Is he coming along?"

Kook shook his head. "I don't think that's a good idea. I mean, the extra body would be nice, but he's the only link to this thing. If something happens to us, he and Wade can still expose the whole story."

"How about Ima?" Griff asked. "Is there a place for her in this?"

"We need her to stay and keep tabs on Wade and Novak," Blake said.

"Hold on," Fezz said. "I don't think we want to leave her alone with Wade and Novak while we're gone."

Khat laughed. "No, *you* don't want her alone with Wade 'cause you're sweet on her and she's gettin' cozy with him."

"You're a child." Fezz sighed. "I'm just saying, she has to take care of Ian. Here."

Blake waved his hand while finishing his last sip of beer. "Not a problem. I'll call Christa. I'm sure they'd be happy to take Ian for a couple of days. Lucy can look after him. I'll triple her rate just to see Fezz squirm."

Haeli patted Fezz on the back. "Alright, alright, leave Fezz alone. If we're going to do this, we have to move fast. Let's hash this thing out for real. Step by step, from the beginning. Y'all with me?"

Nods all around.

"Okay. Step one. Get to Henderson."

# CHAPTER 35

"HOME SWEET HOME." Kook passed the driver a twenty-dollar bill. "Thanks. Tell your kid good luck today."

For the whole ride from Las Vegas, Kook and the van driver, Ravi, had chatted up a storm. As a result, everyone had learned more about the middle-aged Indian immigrant and his soccer playing son than they'd bargained for. It was okay with Blake. Ravi was a nice guy, and it passed the time.

Kook hopped out of the passenger seat and popped the side door. The rest of the crew climbed out.

Once everyone was clear, Kook slammed the door shut, slapped the roof, and waved Ravi on his way.

"Brings back memories." Griff zombie-walked toward the familiar hangar building, as if an invisible force pulled on him.

Kook fell in next to him and slapped Griff on the back. "I bet."

"How long till we can get underway?" Blake asked.

"As soon as we're loaded up. My guys should have her fueled up and ready to go."

Kook was visibly pleased with himself. Blake figured it was because he won the argument last night over which aircraft they would take.

Maybe they had all been high on nostalgia, sitting in Artie's bar, but their rough draft of the plan had seemed so simple. They'd fly a small aircraft in, take care of business, and get out. As they got into the logistics, it became a lot more complicated.

Kook owned a Beechcraft B55 that would fit all six of them, and Kook was ready to offer it up. The problem was that the twin engine prop plane was relatively slow and had limited range before refueling would be necessary.

On top of the figuring out the timing and hassle of multiple stops, they faced a bigger issue. How would they get the prisoners out?

Khat was adamant about ditching the original idea, taking a commercial flight directly to Columbia and procure a few vehicles to drive into Venezuela.

The group wasn't opposed. It would be much faster, and several vehicles could provide enough room to transport everyone back across the border. But there were a few major flaws in this plan as well. The biggest being equipment.

If they flew a commercial airline, they would have to gear up after they arrived. Fezz had a Columbian contact involved in some of the shadier areas of commerce, but it was probably too short notice, even if they could reach him. And according to Fezz, he wasn't the most trustworthy individual.

Ultimately, the team liked Griff's idea the most. A hybrid of the other two, he'd suggested flying Kook's recently purchased Dassault Falcon. The twelve-seat luxury jet had plenty of range to reach Columbia without refueling and could store all the weapons and equipment they could get their hands on.

But Kook wasn't having it. As part of the recent expansion, he'd financed the six-million-dollar aircraft to capitalize on the expanding market for high-end business charters to Las Vegas. His main clients were based in Silicon Valley, San Francisco, and Los Angeles, but they'd take the occasional flight from Kansas City or even Chicago.

An operating cost of over one hundred thousand a month, including the loan payment and millions of dollars of liability, Blake understood why Kook was reluctant.

Kook had also voiced his concerns with leaving the plane unattended

# DETACHMENT

in Columbia but seemed most averse to canceling two days of bookings, which would no doubt upset otherwise loyal clients.

To combat the growing pressure toward Griff's idea, Kook worked overtime to convince everyone that the small plane was the way to go. Armed with an iPad and a calculator, Kook drew up a detailed itinerary. They would stop in Torreón, Mexico, Villahermosa, Mexico, Buenos Aires, Costa Rica, and finally Arauca, Columbia. He'd even found a suitable landing strip in Venezuela. Based on elevation measurements and satellite imagery, the remote clearing was wide enough, long enough, and flat enough to put the Beechcraft down safely. The best part—it was less than a mile from the compound.

In the end, the group gave in.

The agreed upon plan ended up being as simplistic as it had started. After they freed the captives, they would load the wounded and feeble into the plane and Kook would fly them out. The team would hike the ten-plus miles to the border with the other, able-bodied rescues. From there, they'd figure out transportation back to the States.

Though he didn't bring it up, Blake did have one reservation. What if they were all wounded? There was a good possibility the men were being tortured, subjected to sleep deprivation, malnutrition, or worse.

When it came to the high-octane, seat-of-your-pants kind of mission they were about to embark on, there were some things they couldn't plan for. As a team, they had always been good at adjusting on the fly. At this point, the most Blake could do was trust it would still hold true.

"Why does he insist on locking this door?" Kook complained. "I told him. When he's here, we're open."

"The new manager?"

Kook pulled out his keyring and unlocked the glass doors. "Yeah. Doug. That's his car right there." He pointed to the blue Nissan Xterra parked cockeyed against the building.

The group followed Kook through the small, darkened classroom, back toward the main hangar.

Off the hallway, light streamed from Kook's office. As they moved by the doorway, a head popped up from behind a computer screen. "Kip. Hi, you're already here? How was Acapulco?"

"Relaxing," Kook said. "Doug, don't lock the door during business hours."

"Sorry. 'Cause I'm here all alone, ya know? I'd hear someone knocking."

"Just don't." Kook shook his head. "I'll be in a meeting for a bit. Is the Beechcraft ready?"

"Yes. Manny got her set up and put her in the hanger before he left, like you asked."

"Okay. Thanks."

Blake followed, nodding to Doug as he passed by.

Inside the hangar, Kook flipped on four circuit breakers. Fluorescent lights flickered to life.

The oversized garage was barren except for a small twin-prop aircraft facing the doors in the dead-center of the space.

Kook locked the door behind them. "He's pretty good. A little weird, but dependable." His keys still in hand, Kook selected one and used it to remove the padlock from the giant plywood cabinet on the right wall. He swung the doors open to reveal his considerable collection of "things that go boom."

"What do we all want?" Kook asked.

"All of it," Blake answered.

Kook laughed as if Blake were joking.

"We'll need to be light," Fezz said.

"Just remember," Blake added, "we'll have to arm all the Delta guys. Anyone who can hold a weapon."

Khat reached into the cabinet to grab one of the three MP-5's. "I can tell you exactly what we need—"

"Hold on," Haeli interrupted. "Is everyone going to carry on like they didn't just hear that?"

"What?" Kook asked.

"Kip? Your real name is Kip?" Haeli laughed.

"Oh yeah," Fezz said. "Kook's real name is Kip. In case you were wondering."

"How did I not know that?"

"You never asked," Kook said.

Khat bumped Haeli. "You never asked me either."

"You're right. Okay, what's your real name, Khat?"

"Bartholomew Ignatius Danforth-Duncan, the third."

For a moment, it looked as though Khat had her going, but Fezz wasn't able to keep it together.

"Queen of the Nile and keeper of the seven stones," Fezz laughed.

"Ha. Ha." Expressionless, Haeli took a Desert Eagle fifty caliber pistol off its mount and racked the slide.

"Here, we may need this." Kook handed Blake a tan canvas bag. Inside were stacks of cash bound by elastic bands. "Forty K. Just in case. I expect that to come back to me."

"All expenses will be reimbursed in full." Blake slung the bag over his shoulder. "As far as the weapons, same thing as last time we were here. Let's keep it to one or two types of ammunition. The fifty-cal is out. Five-five-six and nine-millimeter only. Throw in whatever body armor and night vision we have. If we're in the air in the next few minutes, we can make it to the compound before dawn."

"Not with the time change," Fezz said. "We gained three hours comin' out here. We'll lose it again on the way back east."

"Actually, we'll lose four all together," Kook said. "But I'd throw the night vision in just in case you guys have got to hunker down past nightfall."

Blake didn't like the thought of it. If they were still in Venezuela by nightfall, something would have gone very, very wrong.

Kook lifted a wooden ammo box from a stack in the corner and carried it to the rear of the plane. "Don't just stand there, load it up."

The crew went to work. A little of this, a little extra of that.

Having the right gear for the job was half the battle. The other half was purely mental. A laser focus, zeroed in on nothing but winning at all costs.

None of them were in the right frame of mind quite yet. But Blake wasn't worried. They had nineteen long hours to work it out.

# CHAPTER 36

"DID YOU GET IN?" Wade sat down next to Ima, curled up on the couch with her laptop.

Ima nodded. "I did. I'm running a query. In the meantime, I had to take care of something for the guys. They needed me to file an ICAO flight plan and a customs entry request for Torreón, Mexico."

"You know how to do that?"

"Not really, no." Ima giggled. "I think it's all right, though. I copied what others submitted. Kook gave me the tail number and some info about the route and aircraft, the rest I gave my best guess."

"You never cease to amaze, Olivia."

From the bathroom came the sound of a flushing toilet.

"Ya know," Wade said, "you can sleep in the bed tonight."

Ima swallowed hard. She didn't know how to respond. It wasn't that she was repulsed by the idea. Quite the contrary. She just wasn't expecting him to be so forward.

"No, no. I mean, I'll sleep on the floor. You can have the bed. This way crusty-pants in there can still have the couch and you can get some rest."

"Oh." Ima blushed. "That's okay. I don't mind the floor. I can sleep anywhere."

"So what's the verdict?" Novak burst out of the bathroom, drying his

# DETACHMENT

hands with a paper towel. "Find anything on Piper?" He tossed the towel in the trash next to the counter.

"Let me see if it had any hits." Ima smiled at Wade.

He smiled back.

"Wow. Yeah, a bunch. Look at this. Personnel files. Court documents."

Wade leaned over to see the screen. Ima could feel his hair brush against her ear.

Novak moved behind the couch and leaned over to better see the screen. "Pull up that charge summary. Third one down."

Ima did.

All three read in silence.

"What's wrong with these guys?" Ima asked. "They went house to house. Just massacring people. Why?"

"Hell if I know," Novak said. "Word was, they were pissed off about losing men at an airstrip out there. But that's just speculation. I don't think Piper ever testified. To be honest, I wasn't paying close attention. It was talk around the barracks, ya know?"

"How is this guy not in prison?" Ima asked.

"Do me a favor, bring up that personnel record," Novak said.

Ima clicked and opened the pages-long document.

"Right there. SEAL Team Four. Who was his superior?"

"Hold on, I'll have to cross-reference."

After a search and a few more clicks, Ima brought up the classified roster. "A guy named Ronald Phillips."

Novak slapped the back of the couch.

"Robert Phillips, as in the Secretary of State?" Wade asked.

"You better believe it," Novak said. "I should've known. The guy's a snake."

Ima touched Wade on the knee. "This is who tried to kill you."

"That's who *did* kill Robbie!" Novak seethed. He stomped a path around the kitchen table and back.

This wasn't definitive proof, but Ima had to admit, it all fit. The court documents never mentioned Phillips as one would expect. Then, as Phillips had moved up in the ranks, Piper and his cohorts had been quietly released. A reward for keeping their mouths shut, perhaps.

Ima had no experience in the military, but this was as plain as day. Phillips was pulling the strings.

"I'm going for a walk." Novak threw open the front door and stormed out of the apartment, without shutting it behind him.

Ima was going to protest. Blake did say that no one should leave. But Novak was hot and could have used some space. Besides, there was no way anyone was looking for him in Newport, of all places.

Wade fidgeted. "Phillips is the key to this whole thing. He's the story. The President might not have even known about it."

Ima got up and handed Wade the laptop. "Here. Maybe there's more here you can work with. I'm going to make sure Novak doesn't get himself into any trouble."

"Okay." Wade all but ignored her. He tapped at the keyboard and stared at the screen.

"Don't let it go to sleep, we'll lose the connection." She opened the front door. "And, hey, we can always share if you want."

Wade looked up from the laptop.

"Share?"

"The bed. It's big enough for both of us. Don't you think?"

# CHAPTER 37

"WAKE UP." Griff shook Kook by the shoulders.

His eyes snapped open.

At the eight-hour mark, Griff had taken the controls so Kook could get some rest. Griff was comfortable enough following the chart plotter and keeping them on track with speed and elevation, but that was about the extent of his willingness to share in the piloting duties. Flying a plane was easy compared to the helicopters Griff was used to. Landing was the hard part. Especially in the dark.

"We're a couple miles out," Griff said. "Time for you to take over."

Kook didn't hear any of it, but he seemed to get the gist. He picked up the headset from his lap and put it on. He keyed the mic for internal transmission. "I've got it from here."

After flicking a few switches on the dashboard, Kook radioed to the tower in preparation for their arrival. He switched frequencies and stated his intention to take on fuel. Just as in Torreón, they were directed to the private plane area with self-service pumps.

In Torreón, the ground crew had instructed that only the pilot exit the plane and operate the fuel pump. They were not to interact with any other individuals, nor were the passengers allowed to disembark. Otherwise, they would need to comply with regular customs procedures.

These procedures were why Kook had wanted to stay with small regional and municipal airfields. For example, instead of the International Airport in Villahermosa, he hoped to stop at the Aerodromo in neighboring Cucuyulapa. The problem was, it was the middle of the night. The tiny airstrip in the middle of a banana plantation didn't have runway lights or a night staff. Carlos Rovirosa Pérez International would have to do.

Over the past few hours, the others had dozed off here and there. Blake had found himself fighting it—getting his bearings every half hour or so and then settling back into a state of twilight.

Now, approaching the end of the second leg, everyone was awake and attentive.

Blake put his headset on. "We made pretty good time. Ten hours, twenty-five minutes total, with the stop."

"Only another nine to go," Kook said.

Another couple of switches and Blake could feel the landing gear rattle its way into position.

Kook got clearance, and after a few turbulent dips, they were on the ground and rolling from the runway to the taxiway system. They followed the instructions to the refueling station.

Once stopped, Kook climbed out. Blake thought of nothing else but stretching his legs. The four seats in the passenger compartment were made of overstuffed leather and were comfortable enough, but in Blake's estimation, four were two too many.

At least with the engines turned off, they would have a ten-minute reprieve from the incessant buzzing of the propellers. If anyone wanted to have a normal conversation, without the use of electronic devices, now was the time to do it. Blake, for one, had nothing to say. No one else seemed to be interested in small talk either.

The sound of the nozzle clattering against the port meant Kook was already hooked up. Unlike the last stop, where they had to wait in line, they would be in and out in no time.

Blake looked out one of the oval windows. Kook stood by the wing. To Blake's surprise, Kook wasn't alone.

Three men surrounded him. Each carrying Galil rifles.

"We've got company!" Blake unbuckled and squeezed next to Griff. "Open the door."

Griff did as Blake asked and then hopped out onto the tarmac. Blake followed right behind.

"What's this?" Blake moved toward Kook and the three-armed men. Griff hung back.

"They say they're customs. They want to search the plane." Kook shot Blake a sharp glance.

Blake nodded. He and Kook were thinking the same thing. These men weren't with customs. They weren't Federales either. If Blake had to guess, these were Cartel henchmen. Based on the locale, most likely Jalisco Nueva Generación.

"We're just stopping for fuel and we're carrying on," Blake explained as if Kook hadn't already tried. "We filed the paperwork and have already been through customs up north."

Two of the men looked to the third, a grumpy fellow with leathery skin who stood about five foot two. Either he was the only one of the three who spoke English, or he was in charge.

"We bring aeroplano in and we check." The man spoke in broken English. He was motioning to a nearby hangar. "You push." He pointed again.

Blake got the idea. He wanted them to physically push the plane into the hangar. With a couple of guys, it wouldn't be difficult. In fact, they had pushed it onto the tarmac in Henderson earlier that day. The issue was why they wanted it done.

It was no mystery. They wanted to get out of the open. Away from the scrutiny of any actual authorities. At least the ones who weren't on their payroll—if there were any such thing.

"Yeah, that's not gonna happen," Kook said.

The little man raised his rifle. His sidekicks followed his lead.

"Okay, okay." Blake held his hands at shoulder level. "Look, if we've done something wrong, I'm sure there's probably a fine, right?" He turned to Griff. "Have Fezz pass you the bundle."

Blake made it a point not to say *a* bundle. English wasn't these guys' strong suit, but the distinction wouldn't have been lost.

Fezz leaned over the cockpit seat and handed Griff a stack of hundred-dollar bills. He tossed it to Blake.

"Here is ten thousand dollars. Everything we have. This should cover any inconvenience, yes?"

The short man looked at Blake and then at the stack of money. He nodded and held out his hand.

"Deal?" Blake asked.

"Si."

Blake handed the cash to the eager recipient. He passed it back to the man on the right, who stuffed it in his vest pocket.

"You have more?"

Kook gritted his teeth. "No. No more. You have your money and we're moving on."

"No. I no think. You push. You push, now."

"You want more money?" Kook said. "Fine. Griff, tell Fezz it's time to give them everything we've got."

Blake knew what Kook was getting at, and he also knew the message would be properly received. Things were about to get hairy.

"We'll give you everything we have. A hundred thousand dollars. But you have to agree to let us leave."

"A hundred thousand dolares?" The man bared his crooked yellow teeth and looked back at the man to his right. "Cien mil dolares."

When he turned back to Kook and Blake, Fezz was already in the open cockpit doorway, his rifle pointed at the leader's chest. At the same time, Blake and Kook pulled their pistols, each taking a target on their respective sides. The two sidekicks froze, leaving the muzzles of their weapons pointed at the ground.

From behind Fezz, Haeli hopped out, a tech-nine submachine gun in hand. Khat climbed into the copilot seat and swung his legs toward the door. He reached back, grabbed an M4, and passed it to Griff. He pointed his weapon down to avoid lasering Fezz, Blake, and Kook.

"Pon tus armas en el suelo," Blake commanded. He wasn't sure the sentence was grammatically correct, but he was confident it contained all the key words.

The three men laid their weapons on the ground.

"Griff." Blake didn't need to say any more. Griff hustled over and collected the three Israeli-designed rifles from the ground.

"The dinero." Kook held his left palm up and waggled four fingers.

With a sneer, the man in the vest withdrew the bundle and handed it over.

"You should have just taken the money," Kook said. "You got greedy. Never be greedy."

"Lay down on the ground and put your hands on the back of your head."

The men looked at each other but didn't comply.

"On the ground," Fezz yelled.

"The floor," Blake pointed to the asphalt. For some reason, the word ground never seemed to translate. 'Floor,' they understood.

The men complied.

"Pon las manos en la cabeza tuos."

Again, they did as they were told.

"Griff, hold 'em here. Everyone else, get in."

Kook holstered his pistol and ran over to pull the gas nozzle.

Khat retreated into the rear of the plane and Haeli climbed in after him. Next Fezz, then Blake.

Griff stood over the three men while Kook fired up the engines. He stepped to the side as Kook backed up the plane a few feet to get the clearance he'd need to swing around. The right wing passed over the three prone men.

Kook waved Griff in.

As soon as Griff's feet were off the ground, Kook gunned the throttle. He pressed the left pedal, swiveling the front wheel. The aircraft turned toward the taxiway.

Kook threw his headset on. Not to talk to the tower, but to communicate with the others. They wouldn't be asking for clearance this time.

As Kook straightened the plane out and headed for the runway, Blake peered through the window. Given the angle, he could just barely see the three men getting to their feet.

The little guy reached toward his beltline. Blake couldn't see the pistol from that distance, but he recognized the motion. "Look out," he yelled, loud enough to be heard without the comms.

A second later, the whap of a slug penetrating the fuselage sent all of them ducking, head to knees. It left a hole in one side and a dent in the other. They braced for another that didn't come.

Kook hit the runway, a quarter of the way from the starting end. A four-engine aircraft had just turned onto the hashes and accelerated at full throttle.

As they made the corner and pointed down the runway, the big four-prop bore down on them. Kook pinned the levers. The engines growled.

There was no use looking, they could no longer see behind them. Blake held his breath and visualized the big plane braking hard. Willing it to stop in time.

He closed his eyes.

Then it came. Not a crash, but the weightless feeling of the wheels leaving the ground.

They were airborne, intact, and back on their way to far worse peril.

## CHAPTER 38

RON PHILLIPS CLIMBED the stairs in lockstep with the assistant butler in charge of escorting him to the President's private gym.

The White House contained a full-fledged physical fitness center. But Moore had a few pieces of equipment moved into what was a bedroom, next to the solarium on the top floor. As far as Phillips knew, Moore never used the full facility. Phillips understood why.

Early that morning, like every other workday, Phillips arrived at the Pentagon Athletic Center at four-thirty sharp for his morning workout.

The PAC, located on the Mezzanine level, Corridor 7, was an impressive establishment. Swimming pool, squash, basketball, and an indoor running track were some of its more extraordinary offerings. Not to mention the world class training staff.

It opened at five, but Phillips had been granted special privileges. He counted the arrangement as one of the more gratifying perks of his office.

Phillips didn't know what it was about the gym. There, people who would normally pass you in the corridor with their heads down, would speak freely, always about the same subject. What might Phillips be able to do for them? Not that he didn't understand and respect ambition, but he wasn't interested in being a horse for every flunky with a political aspiration.

"The President has requested you go right in." The attendant opened the door and stepped back.

From inside, an odd mixture of grunting, breathing, and whirring noises foreshadowed what Phillips was about to walk into.

He trudged ahead. The door closed behind him.

Facing the window with earbuds in his ears, Moore was unaware of Phillips' presence.

As Moore pumped the pedals of the Peloton stationary bike, the scantily clad woman on the attached display clapped her hands over her head. Her hair bounced from side to side.

Slowing his cadence, Moore grabbed his towel from the handlebars, wiped his face, then stood out of the saddle. He picked up his speed again.

For a moment, Phillips saw Moore for what he really was. Vulnerable.

This was a testament to the true level of access Phillips had. Unguarded, unattended admittance. It triggered a dark but fleeting thought. With one swift motion, he could take out the leader of the free world, forever changing the geopolitical landscape of the entire planet. And Moore would never have seen it coming.

"Sir," Phillips shouted.

Moore snapped his head toward Phillips and removed one earbud. He continued to pedal. "Ron, come in. I've got five minutes left 'til cooldown."

"Sure," Phillips said. "I'll come back."

"No need," Moore panted. "We can talk now. I've got a full morning." He turned his attention to the screen and, as if following instructions, turned the single knob under the screen. "My god, she's relentless."

"I assume you're looking for an update on our little problem," Phillips said. If they were going to get into it, they might as well jump right in. Rip the bandaid off, as they say.

Between every other word, Moore gasped for air. "Has—everything—been taken care of?"

"Not by a long shot."

Moore slowed his stride, almost to a stop, and removed the other earbud. "Don't screw with me, Ron. The story—it's dead right?"

"The reporter Rob Novak planned to meet has gone underground. My people are working on it, but they haven't come up with him yet."

"How is that possible? With the resources at your disposal—"

"I know what it looks like, but we believe he's had significant help."

"Help? What kind of help?"

Phillips tread lightly. "According to my sources, a group of individuals may be providing support."

Moore unclipped his shoes from the pedals. "Jesus Christ, Ron. What does that even mean? A group of individuals? Who? His God-damned book club?"

"The good news is, we recovered the documents before the kid could to pass them off. We're confident no one else has seen them."

Grabbing his towel and water bottle, Moore dismounted. "So, this reporter—what's his name?"

"Wade."

"So even if Wade stays hidden, he's got nothing. No paper will publish a farfetched conspiracy theory without the slightest bit of proof."

"Probably not, but there's one other factor." Phillips was a straight shooter and, unlike most of the other members of the cabinet, Moore didn't intimidate him. But even he was reluctant to tell Moore what he was about to tell him. "Our people set up surveillance on the Boston Globe offices, some of Wade's coworkers and Wade's personal phone and internet accounts. Wade must have ditched his phone, but we were able to intercept a call from Wade to his boss at the Globe. It was made from an untraceable line."

"There's no way to find out his location from the call?"

"No. And there's a worse problem. It looks like he might be trying to get in touch with Buck Novak." Phillips realized he was sugar coating a little too much. "Let me rephrase. He has probably already linked up with Novak."

"I knew it," Moore barked. "Didn't I tell you Novak was going to be a problem. Where is he now? Bring him in."

"He's AWOL, sir. At this point, he might already be with Wade and whoever's protecting him. We found out he took a flight to Hartford,

Connecticut. From there, we don't know. We have to assume he headed to Boston."

Moore's face contorted, and he twisted his towel as if trying to strangle it. "This is an absolute debacle!" Spittle flew from Moore's quivering lips. "We need to get ahead of this. Novak is the guy. He was acting alone. Went insane and—"

"Let's not get ahead of ourselves. I get the thinking, but without Novak in hand, it's a risky option. Look, my people are very good at what they do. They're in Boston, and I'm flying there this afternoon to ensure that this thing gets done right. You're going to need to trust me. We'll take care of it."

Whether or not Phillips could back up his own bravado, he had every intention of seeing it through. Not for Moore's sake—he was the one who insisted on the ill-advised plan in the first place. As far as Phillips was concerned, Moore deserved whatever was coming to him. In fact, Phillips would have loved to see him dragged through the muck. But like it or not, his own fate was inextricably tied to Moore's. The moment Phillips took the appointment, he had hitched his wagon to Moore's legacy. If Moore went down, he and everyone associated with him were done. Forever.

"This is out of control," Moore said. "You keep telling me you're handling it. Just get it done."

Phillips nodded and took the cue to excuse himself. He exited with headstrong determination and unwavering confidence that he didn't have the slightest idea how he was going to make good on his promise.

# CHAPTER 39

A HALF HOUR AGO, Kook got back on the yoke.

The sun had been out for some time. Since then, Blake had settled his head against the small window, allowing him to watch the ground. He found himself zoning out to the lush green images scrolling by some five thousand feet below.

Every so often, there was a farmhouse, a small ranch, or a cluster of houses. At one point, he saw what looked like cowboys on horseback, moving a herd of a few dozen cattle across a flooded plain.

In between the smattering of tiny pockets of civilization were huge expanses of open land. Rolling hills, dotted with patches of dense trees. The landscape would offer some freedom of movement without encountering many locals.

Of course, they were not without challenges. By flying in, they were hardly inconspicuous. Even if the landing site was secluded, everyone within miles of their path would know they were there. Blake didn't believe it would be much of an issue. In remote places like this, small planes would be a common fixture. Unlikely to garner a second look. Plus, Blake found that sometimes, the more brazen one was, the less suspicious they became.

"We're coming up on it," Kook announced over the intercom.

Blake bumped Haeli's leg to get her attention. He made a downward pointing motion to let her know they were about to land. Haeli gave a thumbs up, then put her headset on.

"How many times have you done this, Kook?" Khat asked.

"Land? Let me see, uh, every time."

"We know that's not true," Haeli interjected.

Blake chuckled. Haeli was right. The last time Haeli had flown with Kook, he bailed out midair. Technically, the plane landed. Nose first. But Kook couldn't count it as a landing if he wasn't there when it happened.

"Fine," Kook said. "Every time but one."

"That's not what I meant," Khat said. "I'm talking about this kind of landing."

Kook turned around. "Don't worry about it."

"That's a 'never,'" Fezz said.

"I have every confidence in our captain," Griff keyed in. "On a completely unrelated side note, this would be a good time to check that your belts are fastened. Really, really snug."

Griff was trying to be funny, but it was sound advice, nonetheless. Blake sat up straight and pulled the nylon strap over his lap, then glanced over at Haeli to make sure she was also strapped in. Behind him, Fezz and Khat were on their own.

Outside the window, the tops of the trees drew closer until it seemed the landing gear would scrape the highest branches.

Kook banked a hard left and performed a slip maneuver, bleeding off altitude in preparation for the short landing. Normally, as the plane was about to touch down, they would use the extra lift from ground effect to float the wheels down for a soft landing. In this case, there wasn't enough space. Kook had to push, touching down with a teeth-clattering thump.

In a cloud of dust, they rolled to a stop on a slight incline.

Blake let out the breath he didn't realize he was holding. "Hell of a job, Kook."

"Thanks." His head swiveled back and forth. "Looking at this now, I'm thinkin' landing was the easy part. Might be a trick getting off the ground. Depends if the wind cooperates. Hang on, I'm gonna put us in position."

Kook pushed the throttle, and the plane rolled. He got as close to the tree line as he could before turning to face the opposite direction.

It was smart. Not only would they be less out in the open, but they were also set up to take off. Depending on how things went down, even a few extra seconds could mean the difference between life and death.

The engines cut out and the two propellers wound down.

Everyone unbuckled and filed out, one after the other.

The air was muggy but not unbearable. If Blake had to guess, he'd say it was in the high eighties.

Khat bent at the waist. With his arms dangling toward his toes, he bounced. "I feel like a pretzel."

"We should get moving," Fezz said. "You can work out the creaks and squeaks on the way."

Blake had to agree. On the ground, the landscape wasn't as flat as it had appeared from the air. There were hilltops all around. Not dramatic, but high enough to provide an overlooking vantage point on their position. From a tactical standpoint, this was a bad place to hang out. "Grab your gear. We'll regroup once we're out of sight."

Haeli unloaded a camouflage rucksack. She handed it to Griff. "You mind taking the med bag?"

Griff slung it over his shoulder without protest.

Aside from the weapons, the medical gear would likely prove to be the most important equipment they had. It contained the essentials needed to patch up the wounded enough to get them moving. Stitches, splints, morphine, ephedrine, a cauterizing element, quick clot. The usual assortment. What they didn't have were stretchers. If anyone was in that bad of shape, they'd have to employ a fireman's carry. Blake nominated Fezz for the first shift, whether Fezz knew it or not.

Kook locked the doors. The chintzy latches weren't much of a security measure, but Blake was hopeful they would serve as a deterrent if some curious rancher came poking around. With the amount of weapons and cash on board, it would be like hitting the third-world lottery.

After the group agreed on a distant landmark as a waypoint, they started walking. Blake and Haeli stayed together. For the most part, they didn't speak.

Blake's senses were heightened. His body buzzed. He wasn't nervous, but the absurdity of the task was beginning to set in.

In general, they were people of action. Rarely hesitant to convert ideas into deeds. But even for them, this was reckless. They had no support. No safety net. In fact, they had no business being there in the first place. It was only when Blake thought about the alternative did those reservations melt away.

When they reached the cover of the canopy, they huddled up. Griff took out his handheld GPS and held it so the others could see.

"Three quarters of a mile, over that hump." Griff pointed west-northwest.

"Let's do it." Without a consensus, Khat walked off in the direction of the target.

Kook shrugged, then peeled away to catch up with him. The rest followed, not far behind. They walked at a comfortable pace.

"I wonder how Ima's doing with Wade and Novak," Griff said.

Haeli smiled. "I'm sure she's schooling both of them."

"I still don't understand why Ima had to stay with them," Fezz said. "She should be with Ian."

"Ian's fine," Blake said. "He loves hanging out with Lucy. It's the only reason he wasn't throwing a fit about not being able to come with us. The boy's got some guts, I'll give him that."

Fezz sighed. "You've got to stop doing that, Mick."

"What?"

"Treating Ian like he's part of this."

"Come on, Fezz. He's a kid. He just wants to feel included."

"He takes it seriously," Fezz said. "He looks up to us. He thinks this is his future."

"And what if it is?" Blake asked. "Is that so bad? He's a brilliant kid with a lot of potential."

"Exactly!" Fezz growled. "He has the potential to go have a real life. But you all insist on clouding his mind with promises of training and cool missions and catching bad guys. It's messed up." Fezz threw up his hands. "Ya know what, I don't want to talk about it." He stomped off to join Khat and Kook.

"What was that about?" Griff said.

"He's just looking out for the kid," Haeli suggested. "I think it's sweet."

Blake wondered if Fezz's outburst was really about Ian, or himself. It was clear that Fezz had become close with Ima and Ian alike. Was he envisioning an alternative future of his own? Whatever the case, Blake decided to be more conscious of how he handled Ian's enthusiasm.

Griff pulled the sack from his right shoulder, swung his rifle over, and hoisted the bag onto his left side. "Call me crazy, but Ian's chances of being a normal, average kid are about the same as me being a popstar. Look at what he's been through already. I mean, have you met the kid? He's a freak of nature." Griff paused. "Don't get me wrong. I love the kid. I'm just saying he's got more baggage than all of us combined. If there was ever a place he'd fit in, it's with the rest of us rejects."

"I don't agree," Haeli said. "He's got something none of us have. Actual family. Ima's a great mom. She'd do anything for Ian. How many of us could say that?"

Blake knew where Haeli was coming from. She never knew her mother. Most of them didn't have any family, aside from each other. Griff, Fezz, Khat—no one to write home to. Blake didn't know if Kook had anyone other than his ex-wife, who he was pretty sure Kook considered more a combatant than a relative. None of them had any children—that they knew about.

Out of all of them, Blake was the only one who had living parents. Blood relatives, only a phone call away. Only, it had been a long time since any such phone call had occurred.

When Blake gave in and told Haeli the whole story, she had called him stubborn. Maybe she was right. He had broken off contact, not because he didn't care, but because he cared too much. He couldn't bear to see the people he'd loved and respected become brainwashed shells of their former selves.

For the most part, he had made peace with his decision. But it was times like these that he second guessed himself, when faced with the very real possibility that he wouldn't make it back. Fezz may have longed for a family of his own, but unlike him and the rest, Blake had one. All he had to do was forgive.

Blake put his arm around Haeli. "What would you say about taking a trip to Florida when we get back?"

"That sounds nice about now," Haeli said. "A little beach, a little dancing. I've been wanting to check out Miami."

"Miami's overrated. I was thinking, maybe it's time I introduced you to my parents."

"Really?" Haeli stopped walking.

Blake stopped as well. "I thought about what you said. That night at dinner. About biting the bullet, and all that."

"Oh my god, yes, that would be great."

Haeli started moving again. Blake followed her lead.

"I don't want to make a big thing about it, and I don't even know if they'd be willing. But I think I'm ready."

Haeli rubbed Blake's back. "That makes me so happy. I'm so proud of you. When we get back, we'll work it out. Can't wait to meet them."

"You have parents?" Griff fell back a few feet to join them. "How did I not know that?"

"Everyone has parents, Griff." Blake cringed as soon as the words left his mouth. He intended the comment to be sarcastic. He hoped Haeli didn't take it the wrong way. She was the one exception. Luckily, she didn't seem to key in on it, so he left it alone.

Ahead, Khat, Fezz, and Kook stopped and crouched down on the crest of a mound. Khat turned back to Blake, Haeli, and Griff, and pointed at something Blake couldn't see. But Blake knew what he meant. They had reached their destination.

Linking up with the others, Blake looked down at the corrugated metal building. Beyond, he could see the main house in the distance.

"I don't see anyone, do you?" Khat asked.

The answer was no. There was no sign of movement anywhere on the sprawling property.

"That's the barn," Kook said. "For sure."

"Let's get over there while we've got the chance," Fezz said. "If we get behind the building, we'll have good cover."

"I don't like this," Haeli said. "There's no one around. What if they've moved the prisoners?"

"We'll find out." Blake gripped his rifle. "Everyone ready?"

"Ready," Kook said.

"Let's move."

The group rushed down the hill, through the swath of sparse trees, and regrouped at the back of the barn.

"We're too late," Griff said. "This place is a ghost town."

Fezz shook his head. "Novak was sure. The intelligence says they haven't moved them."

"Shhh," Blake cupped his ear and pressed it against the cold metal siding. If there were people inside, they should be able to hear something.

Kook paced along the exterior. "Of course there's no door."

"We'll have to go around to the front." Blake knew it was risky. In full view of the main house, they would have to move fast and hope no one was paying attention. "Kook, Griff, hold the exterior. Haeli, Fezz, Khat, are you with me?"

"We came this far," Khat said.

Blake walked to the corner of the building and peered around the edge. He focused on the house for any sign of movement. There was none.

Fezz, Khat, and Haeli stacked up behind him, their rifles at the low ready.

"All clear." Blake looked over his shoulder. "See ya on the other side, yeah?"

Fezz nodded and put his hand on Blake's shoulder.

Blake took one last look.

"Go!"

## CHAPTER 40

THE TOASTER POPPED. To avoid burning her fingers, Ima speared the slices with a butterknife and dragged them onto the plate. "Anyone else want toast?"

Novak ignored her.

"You made the eggs. I can handle making my own toast." Wade walked over to the counter, a sly smile on his face. As he reached around Ima for the bagged loaf, he pressed his body against hers.

Ima pulled away and ducked under his extended arm. Wade's expression slackened.

"You okay?"

Although she dismissed the question, she was asking herself the same thing. There was nothing wrong—nothing she could put her finger on. Although she couldn't help but wonder if spending the night with Wade was a mistake.

Not that she didn't enjoy it. She did. Very much. But the whole business with Wade and Novak was messy, and she feared they had only made it more complicated.

It had been a long time since she'd been physical with a man. After all, the fugitive lifestyle wasn't exactly compatible with dating.

Her seclusion wasn't the only reason, just the most convenient excuse. She also had to consider Ian. And, truth be told, relationships made her uncomfortable. She worried that Wade might expect more than she was willing to offer.

Of course, none of this was Wade's fault. He was a nice guy. Handsome. Had a decent job. Besides being tracked by a homicidal maniac, there didn't seem to be many negatives. Still, she wasn't sure if she wanted this to be an ongoing thing.

Ima set her plate on the table and sat. "Buck, your eggs are getting cold."

After a dozen requests, Ima gave in to Novak's pleas to call him by his nickname. "John was my father," he'd say each time. It was finally beginning to roll off her tongue.

A peculiar character, Novak was. Aloof, stoic. Ima still suspected there was a big heart beating in that barrel chest. He was dealing with a lot. As far as Ima was concerned, he had earned the right to be withdrawn.

Novak put down the paper and hoisted himself off the couch with a groan. Reaching the table at the same time as Wade, they sat on either side of her.

Wade slapped his phone on the table. "Is it possible to switch numbers on this?"

"Switch numbers? Why?" Ima took a bite of her toast.

"I have an idea. A friend of mine works in the White House press corps. I was thinking I could call her and see if she could pass a message to someone in the Press Secretary's office. Or anyone who might be able to get it to Phillips."

"I don't think that's a good idea," Ima said.

"Why not? It can't hurt, right? It's a long shot, sure, but he might want to get ahead of the story. If he has my number, it gives him a chance to tell his side. Maybe there's a better explanation. I just don't want to use the same number in case it links back to Clint."

"It's a VOIP tunnel routed through rotating proxies," Ima said. "You can have a new number every thirty seconds if you wanted, that's not the issue. I just think you should wait until the others get back."

"No need to pass any messages," Novak said. "I know Phillips' cell number."

"You do? Wait." Wade hopped out of his seat and went for the notepad on the side table next to the couch. "Why didn't you say so earlier?" He held his pencil at the ready. "Shoot."

---

AS SOON AS he said it, Novak had a feeling he shouldn't have mentioned having Phillips' phone number.

Phillips wouldn't provide anything of value. At least, not to Wade. Calling Phillips directly was like poking the bear.

But Wade wouldn't take no for an answer. It was worth it to give to him, if only to keep him occupied for a few minutes.

Over the past day and a half, Novak struggled to get his head together. He lay awake most of the night, recalling little moments from the past. Robbie's sixth birthday, when he got his first bicycle. Jackson's hearty laugh. The time both boys had broken the same arm in the span of a single week.

He missed them. Almost more than he could bear.

People talked about the seven stages of grief as if they were a progression. Novak felt them all at once. Shock, anger, depression, bargaining. All except hope.

To make matters worse, he was pent up in this small apartment with people he didn't know from Adam. People with their own motives. Their own secrets.

Watching and listening, he'd tried to gauge how far he could trust any of them. Were Olivia's people really in Venezuela, or was it all part of some scam? Or was it all just a bad dream? Never mind anyone else, he couldn't trust his own mind to tell him what was real anymore.

"You hardly ate anything." Ima appeared from the bedroom.

"Not hungry," Buck said. "Did he call?"

"He's trying, but Phillips won't pick up. Can I get you anything? I can take a walk to the store if you need."

"Thanks, no. I was going to take a walk myself. I can't stand being in this room any longer."

Ima sat next to him and put her hand on his. "I know I've said this before, but I'm going to say it again until you believe it. If there's anyone who can bring Jackson home, it's these guys. What they did for me was beyond anything you can imagine. They're a special breed. I've seen it with my own eyes."

There was something about Olivia that Novak couldn't pin down. By all appearances, genuine and empathic, but he got the feeling she had a darker side. Then again, didn't they all?

"Can I ask you something?" Novak asked.

"Of course."

"Why do you care? I mean, why go out of your way to help me? You don't know me. You have nothing to gain and everything to lose. Help me understand."

Ima squeezed his hand and then let go. "We do it because we can. Because no one else will. It's not about gaining anything. It's about not losing any more. Every one of us has felt that loss. But I'm here to tell you —look at me, Buck—I'm here to tell you that you will survive if you have the will."

"I—" Tears welled in his eyes. He tried to fight them back, but it was no use. Before he knew it, he was sobbing like a fool.

"It's okay." Ima leaned over and wrapped her arms around him. "This is good."

Hating himself for his weakness, for losing control, he wanted to lash out at her. To say, "leave me alone, I'm fine." But he didn't.

Instead, he did the only thing that felt right. He buried his face in her shoulder and cried.

---

WADE PICKED up his phone and hit the button to redial the last number. He would call every hour on the hour if needed. He held it to his ear.

It rang. And rang.

There could have been a multitude of reasons why Phillips wouldn't answer. He was in an area without service. His battery died. Or, like many people, he didn't answer numbers he didn't recognize. Not that Wade would have left a record of his call, but Phillips' line didn't seem to have voicemail. It simply rang for eternity.

The possibility crossed Wade's mind that Novak had made up a random number. But why would he bother? Novak was the one who offered it in the first place.

"Who's this?" The gruff voice blared in Wade's ear. Startled, he pulled the phone away so fast, he almost tossed it across the room.

"Mister Phillips?"

"Who is this?"

"Sir, my name is Archer Wade. I'm a reporter with the Boston Globe. I was hoping to speak with you, if you have a minute."

Based on everything they had learned, Wade was certain Phillips knew who he was.

"What is this about? How did you get this number?"

*What is this about?* Did he actually not know?

Wade dropped the bomb and then waited for the explosion. "Venezuela."

It didn't come.

"If you're referring to the uprising, the Department does not have an official stance. I can direct you to Public Affairs for any comment."

*Public Affairs.*

This was not the reaction Wade had expected. Either Phillips was doing a fantastic job of keeping cool, or he was in the dark. In which case, Novak was lying. There was only one way to find out.

"Sir, I know about the mission. I know about how it ended. And I'll be honest with you, everything I have right now implicates you."

"Implicates me?" Phillips sounded surprised. "Listen, you don't know the first thing about it. Implicates me. That's ridiculous. I had nothing to do with it."

"So you do know what I'm referring to?"

"Yes, I know. But I have nothing to do with it. The person you're looking for is a senior commander who just happens to have gone AWOL. And that's all I'm going to say about that."

Wade knew it. It was Novak all along.

"Mister Phillips, it's important I get your side of the story. If what you're saying is true, the best thing you can do is help clear your own name."

## DETACHMENT

"Not over the phone," Phillips said. "We'll meet in person."

"Great." Wade flipped the page of his pad. "It'll be a day or two before I can get to you."

"You said Boston Globe, right?"

"Yes."

"I happen to be at Logan airport as we speak. Can I meet you somewhere?"

It wasn't a question Wade was expecting. Should he tell Phillips he wasn't in Boston? He couldn't have Phillips come to Newport.

Then it occurred to him. He went to the wastepaper basket next to the dresser and pulled out the crumpled piece of paper Blake had handed him when they had set up the meeting with Novak. If Blake had deemed it an appropriate spot, it would work just as well for this.

"I'm going to give you an address. It's in Connecticut, is that alright?"

"That's fine."

Wade relayed the address and they agreed on a time, accounting for travel.

When they hung up, Wade gave himself a fist pump. Novak was a fool for giving him the number. He was about to blow the entire story out of the water.

As soon as he figured out how to get to Connecticut.

---

"—AND he just looked at me with chocolate all over his face and hands." Novak laughed.

Ima couldn't help but laugh along with him.

After Novak had pulled himself together, she asked about his sons and his family. They spoke for a good hour or two, trading funny stories. It was the first time she had seen Novak smile since they'd met.

When she'd walked in the room, she never intended to be a shoulder to cry on. But it was what he needed.

"I'm sorry about the divorce," she said.

"Don't be. That was all my fault."

Ima's phone rang. It was Ian. "Do you mind?"

"Please." He stood up. "Take your call. I'm going to go get some air."

Ima picked up. "Hi, honey."

"Hi, Mom. Guess what?

"What?"

"I went to Mackerel Cove and used a boogie board."

"You did? I wish I could have seen that."

"When are you coming back?"

"Soon."

After a few seconds, Ian responded. "Okay, I'll accept that."

Ima chuckled. "Well, I'm glad. What do you two have planned for the rest of the day?"

"Lucy said I can help her study for her tests."

"That sounds fun."

"Yeah. Okay, I just wanted to say Hi."

"Call me anytime you want. I love you."

"Love you too, Mom. Bye."

Ima hung up and turned to Novak. He was already gone.

---

WADE OPENED the kitchen drawer closest to the fridge. There was nothing but a plastic tray and four sets of silverware.

He moved on.

"Nothing yet, huh?" Ima opened her laptop to pick up where she left off earlier.

"No. I doubt that's even the right number."

"Novak wouldn't lie to you."

"I know, I just mean, maybe he mixed it up or something. He gave it to me from memory. I wouldn't blame him. I can barely remember my own phone number."

"You're better off anyway. Once we hear back from Venezuela, we can figure out our next steps. All we have to do until then is just lay low."

Wade opened the drawer next to the sink. Towels.

"What are you looking for?" Ima asked.

"Uh. Tweezers. I think I've got a little splinter."

"Did you check the bathroom?"

"I did."

"Then come here," Ima said. "Let me see if I can get it with my nails."

"No. Thanks." There was no need to have Olivia digging around for a non-existent splinter.

In the garage was an old Chevy 2500. Somewhere in the apartment was the key. All he needed to do was find it.

"Suit yourself." Ima shifted her focus back to her screen.

Wade continued his hunt.

The last drawer under the microwave was empty. Except for a single item. A metal, double sided key. He picked it up and slid it into his pocket.

He had no doubt it belonged to the Chevy. Now he only hoped that it still ran.

"I don't like that Buck's still not back," Ima said. "I hope he didn't do anything stupid."

"He's fine."

Little did Olivia know they might be rooming with the enemy. If Novak was the one who ordered the attempt on his life, it didn't matter if Novak stayed or left. The safehouse was burned, and they both needed to get out.

Wade considered telling her as much. She wouldn't believe it. And the last thing he needed was for her to try and interfere with his plan.

He would tell her as soon as things were in motion. He owed her that much.

Ima leaned over the back of the couch. "Hey, about earlier. Me pulling away like that. I didn't mean to be rude. It's just—I needed a little time to process, ya know?"

"No worries," Wade said. "I shouldn't have assumed—"

"No, you should have. I was being stupid."

"Look, Olivia, last night was great. That's all it was. One night. No need to overthink it."

"You never know, one could turn into two."

Wade smiled and nodded, knowing full well it was probably never going to happen. "That's true, you never know."

NOVAK CLOSED the door behind him.

Ima popped her head out from the bedroom. "Oh good, you're back. I was getting worried. Where'd you go?"

"Just walked. Needed to clear my head."

"It's been hours. Archer just left to go look for you."

"Jesus. I'm not a child. I'm a General for God's sake. I think I can manage to take a walk by myself without getting lost."

"That's not fair," Ima said. "I'm just saying, we need to stick together."

"I know. I'm just tired. I'm going to take a shower. Do you need the bathroom before I go in?"

"No. I'm gonna try to catch Archer before he gets too far."

Ima stepped outside. She looked down the street in both directions. He was already out of sight.

She took out her phone and dialed. No answer.

From around the side of the units, she heard a motor rev and then saw the nose of a white truck peek out from behind the corner. The bumper was rusted and had one broken headlight. It took a second to register, but she recognized it. It was Fezz's truck.

As it started pulling into the street, Ima saw Wade in the driver's seat. She sprinted into the roadway.

Wade slammed on the brakes, just in time to avoid hitting her.

"What are you doing?" she yelled.

Wade poked his head out the window. "Get out of the way, Olivia. I've got to go."

"Where?"

"To meet Phillips."

"Phillips? I thought you couldn't reach him."

"Please, Olivia. Move."

"You can't go to meet Phillips by yourself. It's not safe."

"It'll be fine. Safer than being here. Trust me, you need to get out of here. Novak can't be trusted."

"You were going to leave without telling me?"

"I'm telling you now. And I'm telling you that you have to go now."

"If I do, then I'm coming with you."

Wade grunted. "Fine, get in."

Ima started to move but caught herself. She knew what came next. As soon as she got to the passenger side, he would take off without her. "No, no. You get out and open my door."

Holding her ground, she could tell that he was weighing his options. There were only three. Stay there, let her come, or run her over. She banked the assumption he didn't have it in him to opt for the third.

Wade got out, ran around to the passenger side, and opened the door. Ima met him there and hopped into the truck.

When Wade got back into the driver's seat, Ima flashed him an innocent smile.

He shook his head and shifted into drive.

"So, are you going to fill me in or what?"

# CHAPTER 41

BLAKE TOOK OFF, his rifle pointed at the main house.

Behind him, Fezz, Haeli, and Khat packed in tight.

As they reached the large sliding door, they were as vulnerable as they'd ever been. In full view of the main house, lightly armed, and on foreign soil, there was nothing about the situation that sat well with Blake.

"Get the door," Fezz said.

Khat stepped up and grabbed the handle.

In every other case Blake could remember, the entry posed the most danger. In this instant, it felt the opposite.

Fingers on the trigger, they pushed forward through the widening gap into the relative darkness.

Then it hit Blake.

Not bullets or fists, or even shouts. But the smell.

It was unmistakable. Ammonia, sulfur, garlic, and mothballs. The odor of decomposition.

At first glance, the place was empty. But as Blake's eyes adjusted, the magnitude of the scene came into focus. There, along the main support beam, were a dozen men. Stripped nude and hanging by their necks.

Haeli froze. She slung her rifle and stared up at the macabre display.

As Khat entered, he began to pull the door closed behind him.

"Leave it," Blake said.

Khat turned to Blake. His expression turned from confusion to horror. "Jesus Christ almighty."

"We're too late," Fezz said.

Haeli lifted her shirt over her nose and moved forward. "Oh, my god. How long have they been dead?"

Blake moved in next to her, put his arm around her and pulled her close to his chest. "Long enough that there was never a chance."

Fezz balled his fists. Blake knew that look. If there were anything in arm's length, Fezz would have destroyed it. "They were never hostages. It was all bullshit. They just executed them."

"Anything showing?" Griff asked over the comms.

Blake responded. "No hostages. Hold your positions."

"Are we sure these are our guys?" Haeli asked. "Maybe these were the captors. Maybe our guys already escaped."

Blake switched on the flashlight, attached to the rail of his rifle. He walked under one of the corpses and shined the light at his torso. Despite the heavy decay, one of the man's tattoos was still visible. Blake could make out the telltale arrowhead shape. "No. These are Americans."

It explained a lot. The compound looked abandoned because it was. Probably on the same day the team was captured and killed. The intelligence said the soldiers were still in the barn. That much was true. But it said nothing about anyone coming or going.

"Which one is Jackson?" Khat asked. Of course, he wouldn't have expected anyone to know the answer.

"Poor Novak. He had such hope Jackson was still alive. What do we do now?" Haeli pulled her shirt off her face. "We can't leave them here."

"Well, we can't take them with us," Fezz said.

"Do me a favor," Blake said. "Shine your lights while I take pictures."

Blake zoomed in his smartphone camera to get a decent upper body shot. Bloated, with their tongues swelling out of their mouths, identification would be difficult. But not impossible. He worked his way down the line, taking multiple pictures of each.

"We could bury them," Haeli suggested.

"We don't have time for that," Khat said. "If we can find some fuel, we can just light the whole place up."

"Heads up," Kook's voice came over their earpieces. "Two armed bogies headed your way."

"Damn it," Fezz growled. "It's a trap."

Without hesitation, Blake lunged toward the open door. In one swift motion, he pulled the handle and plunged the team into complete darkness.

Now they'd wait.

---

KOOK HUGGED THE WALL. A hundred feet away, two men strolled the perimeter. They were close enough that Kook could hear them laughing and speaking in Spanish. Kook keyed his mic and whispered, "I don't think they know we're here. Let 'em pass, then get your asses back here."

As the two men worked their way across the grass in front of the barn, Kook poked his head around the corner. They were out of sight. There was no way to know if they would go inside. He gave an update. "Hold steady. They're right out front."

Kook turned toward Griff who was peeking around the far side of the barn. From the looks of it, they hadn't yet cleared the front. He waited for Griff to give a signal.

In a sudden, jerky movement, Griff scrambled from the corner and barreled toward Kook. He raised his arms and made a pushing motion. By the time Kook realized he was mouthing the word "Go," it was too late.

Griff looked over his shoulder and froze.

Twenty feet away and in plain view, one of the men had made his way to the back corner of the barn. He stood facing the trees, oblivious to Kook and Griff, a stone's throw to his right. Kook pressed his back against the corrugated steel and held his breath.

The man put the butt of his rifle on the ground and rested the barrel against his leg. He unzipped his fly and began urinating, whistling as he went.

Griff looked at Kook with wide eyes.

# DETACHMENT

When the man was finished, after what seemed like an eternity, he zipped up and lifted his rifle. As he turned, his eyes locked with Kook's. Both stood frozen for half a second. Then, as expected, the man shouted and raised his rifle.

Both Kook and Griff let off two rounds, striking the man at center mass before he could get a shot off.

"Where's the other one?" Kook asked.

"I don't know."

Kook keyed the mic. "Get out of there. We gotta go. Right now!"

## CHAPTER 42

"TURN HERE." Ima watched her phone's mapping application. "Stay to the left and go all the way back."

Wade followed her directions. Initially, he had planned to park on the street and walk in. But after Olivia examined the map's satellite view, she came up with a plan of her own.

Next to the defunct factory was a recycle center. At the rear of the yard, there appeared to be a cut-through, leading to the back of the abandoned building.

As she made her pitch, Olivia shoved a close-up view of the dirt path in his face. Despite nearly veering into a guardrail, he had to admit, it wasn't a bad idea. It looked plenty wide enough for a vehicle, and there was no visible fence.

Now, seeing it from ground level, the idea had lost its luster. "This place is still open. Isn't this going to look conspicuous?"

"Look at this truck," Ima said. "If we don't fit in here…"

Olivia was right about that. As they moved toward the back of the expansive lot, past the piles of shredded metal and rows of forty-foot containers, they had only seen one other person. A grizzled looking fella, unloading a truck not unlike their own. It was a little older, and green, but on par with the amount of rust and bondo patches it boasted.

When they made it to the end of the row, the cut-through was visible.

Without stopping, Wade made a wide turn around the last container and slipped through the break in the bordering tree line. He turned right and looped around to the back of the enormous factory building, taking care to avoid any major potholes and several small trees that had forced their way through the crumbling asphalt.

"This place is huge. Do you know where you're supposed to meet him?"

Wade put the truck in park and shut off the motor. "I have no idea. I figured it would be obvious."

"I don't like this. Couldn't you have just met at a Starbucks or something?"

"It was the spur of the moment, all right? When Blake picked this place, he said it gave him an advantage. And that it was private."

"An advantage for him because he knows what he's doing." Ima huffed. "I told you, you should have waited until they got back. We don't even have any way to protect ourselves. If you had waited a minute, we could have at least brought a couple of guns."

Wade laughed. "What would I do with a gun? I wouldn't even know how to load the thing."

"Then I should have brought one for me."

"Oh, and you're an expert? Is that why you were left to keep tabs on me? I didn't see you at my house or going to nab Novak. Or were you just saving your skills?" Wade caught himself. He decided to dial back on the sarcasm. Olivia had done nothing wrong. He was nervous and taking it out on her. Besides, how much did he really know about her? She very well could have been an expert. "I'm sorry, that came out wrong."

"No. You're right. I'm not like the others. But I can handle myself. You'd be surprised what I've learned in the past eight months. I'm actually a pretty good shot."

"Of course you are." The truth was, he wouldn't be surprised if Olivia could do a whole lot that he wasn't aware of. She was brilliant. And brilliant people often possessed an aptitude for anything they set their minds to. Maybe that was why he found himself doing everything he could to push her away. He was a simple man, and she was out of his league.

Ima unbuckled. "What are we waiting for? If we're going in, let's get it over with."

"Oh, no. Not *we*. Me. You're staying right here."

"What if this is a trick?"

"That's why I need you to stay. If I'm not back in one hour, I want you to call nine-one-one. If I need more than that, I'll come back and let you know everything's okay. Anyway, Phillips is expecting me to be alone. I don't want to spook him. He has to feel comfortable talking to me. The only way that happens is if he trusts that I'll protect his anonymity."

She crossed her arms over her chest. "One hour."

"Promise." Wade opened the door. "If you see anyone, duck down and call me."

"Be careful."

Wade smiled and shut the door.

In search of an entrance, he worked his way along the side of the building. He kept his eyes peeled for anyone lurking in the brush. With each step, he became more uneasy.

He had to ask himself. If he was so scared, what was he doing there in the first place? Maybe he should have waited, like Olivia had insisted. Maybe he should have given her more credit.

In most aspects of his life, Wade considered himself measured. He'd make decisions in an analytical way. But when it came to his job, all of it seemed to fly out the window.

As soon as he smelled a story, he became like a rabid dog. Rushing at it headfirst. He didn't know why. He had always been that way. In his estimation, it was the one thing that allowed him to excel.

Then again, if he used his logical brain, he'd realize that expecting the boogieman to pop out from every nook was the definition of irrationality. Ron Phillips was the Secretary of State, not some two-bit criminal. Even more so than Wade, it was in Phillips' best interest to get in and get out without any complications. The last thing Phillips would want was for anyone to know they were meeting. Once the story came out, any evidence that he and Phillips were together would pose enormous problems for the Secretary.

Around front, Wade saw the gaping opening that he assumed had

# DETACHMENT

been the main entrance. He headed for it.

Looking at the expansiveness of the facility, Wade realized that even if Phillips showed up, they could spend several hours roaming the building, never running into one another.

Lucky for him, that wouldn't be the case.

As soon as Wade entered, he saw Phillips, pacing with his head bowed and his hands in his pockets.

"Mister Secretary," Wade said.

Phillips startled. "Wade?"

Wade approached with a smile and an extended hand.

Wearing a white button down shirt with the sleeves rolled to his elbows and a loosened tie, Phillips looked as though he had just closed a wedding reception.

With a quick handshake and a furtive look around, Phillips spoke. "Did anyone see you come in?"

"No," Wade said. "We're alone. You can speak freely."

"You're not recording this are you?"

"I'm not. Here, you can search me." Wade held his arms out to the side, inviting Phillips to give him a pat down.

Phillips checked his pockets. He found Wade's cell phone. "I'm just going to shut this off, if that's alright."

"Of course." What else was Wade going to say? There was no viable excuse for needing to keep it on. He would have to keep an eye on his watch to make sure he got to Olivia before she called for help.

"Let's get away from the door. In case anyone wanders in here."

Wade nodded and followed Phillips across the open floor and through one of several openings along the back wall. As they passed into a smaller room, Wade could feel drops of liquid hitting his hair and ears.

"This is good enough," Phillips said. "We've got to be careful. If anyone found out I was talking to you—"

"I understand. I assume you looked me up after our conversation. If so, you already know that protecting my sources is my highest priority."

"You're right, I did. I was having second thoughts about coming out here, but once I saw your record—let's just say I was impressed. You're the real deal."

"Thank you. I appreciate that. So what can you tell me about Venezuela?"

"I can tell you a lot. I have full access to the investigation into General Novak. I can tell you he's a very unstable man. He's liable to do something crazy to weasel out of this whole mess. He hasn't tried to contact you, has he?"

"No."

"Because you could be in danger. If you know where he is, we need to know. It's important that we put a stop to this before anyone else gets hurt."

So far, Phillips had more questions for him than vice versa. Wade didn't like it. He'd consider telling Phillips where to find Novak, if he'd ponied up with some information. But it was a card he'd hold on to for the moment. "I don't know where he is. He hasn't reached out to me. Do you think he'll try?"

Phillips shook his head, ignoring the question. "That's too bad. If you don't know where Novak is, you've diminished your usefulness. If that's the case, do you know what that makes you?"

It was an odd question, but Wade played along by taking a stab at it. "Useless?"

"Disposable."

From the right, three large men appeared.

Wade's stomach dropped.

"I want you to meet a few people." Phillips turned to one of the men. "Come, say hello to my new friend Archer Wade."

The big man approached. Wade could see he had a deep scar across his face. There was no question who it was, and what his presence meant.

*Piper.*

Without a word, Piper hauled off and struck Wade in the jaw.

Pain radiated through his teeth and the world spun. He felt himself falling backwards.

Piper grabbed him by the hair and lifted him to his knees. Spots floated in front of Wade's eyes.

"Does that jog your memory?" Phillips said. "Where is Novak?"

Wade started to regain his wits. "Novak doesn't have anything to do

# DETACHMENT

with this, does he? It was all you." He tilted his head back to look at Piper looming behind him. "I know who you are."

Phillips nodded to Piper.

Piper hauled off and kicked Wade in the ribs.

Wade gasped and hunched over. "Any minute—" He wheezed. "Any minute, my people are going to come through that door."

Phillips crouched down. "Your people, huh? You mean that little girl sitting in the truck out back? Hey Piper, is that the girl who kicked your ass?"

Piper laughed. "No. Different girl."

Wade should have known. They were watching the whole time. He needed to warn Olivia.

In a stroke of genius, an idea occurred to him. He called out as loud as he could, hoping his voice would register through the fabric of his khakis. "Siri, call Olivia."

Phillips burst out laughing. "That's your plan, eh? You do realize your phone is off? Don't worry, we'll be paying Olivia a little visit."

"You bastards. What do you want from me?"

"Just a location."

Wade knew there was only one option left. He would have to burn Novak. Unless he could string them out for another forty-five or fifty minutes. If he could hold out that long, Olivia would call the police. There might still be a chance for them. The bad news was, there was a lot of pain to be had between now and then.

"So how about it, Archer? Protect Novak or save yourself. Which will it be?"

"Can I choose both?"

One of the two quiet men behind Phillips snickered.

Phillips turned and sneered. "Funny, huh?" He stood up straight. "This is a waste of time. The girl will tell us. Piper." With a flick of his wrist, he summoned Piper. Then turned to walk away.

Piper came around to face Wade, pulled his pistol and jammed it into Wade's eye.

"Okay, okay—" Wade managed to say, before the back of his head exploded.

# CHAPTER 43

KOOK DARTED TO THE CORNER. In the distance, halfway to the main house, the second guard ran full bore, yelling his head off. Kook lined up his sights, but it was too long of a shot.

From around the front of the barn, Blake, Fezz, Khat, and Haeli came sprinting. Behind them, Kook could see more men piling out of the house. The original squealer had turned around and headed back with the growing group.

Shots rang out. Bullets rustled the leaves behind Kook.

Without slowing, Blake and the crew rounded the corner and headed up the embankment behind the barn. Kook and Griff filed in.

"Not abandoned," Blake said through heavy breaths.

"What do we do?" Haeli asked.

Kook's arms swung, his rifle bounced wildly. "Get to the plane."

Fezz panted. "It's too open between here and there. We need a defendable position."

"We'll get bogged down," Kook said. "This is our one chance."

"We'll never keep this pace," Fezz argued.

Kook looked over his shoulder. Griff was already falling behind. "Drop the bag, Griff."

With a pained look on his face, Griff dumped the medical rucksack and picked up his speed.

To the right, was a small, dense patch of trees. Blake pointed it at. "There. Get to the trees."

The crew sprinted.

More shots rang out from behind them. No one turned to look.

When they hit the wood line, they each found a trunk to use as cover.

Blake leaned out and fired several shots.

Down the hill, at least twenty men dotted the open field. They scrambled to get low.

"Keep suppressing!" Fezz fired several shots of his own.

It was working. Out in the open, the advancing men had no choice but to get down in the grass. The problem was, they would start to move laterally, eventually overtaking their position from all angles.

"We can't stay here," Blake said.

Khat fired a barrage. "Hot damn, I think I got one."

"I have an idea," Haeli said. "I'll cut south to the end of this patch. You all pop out the back, and head north toward the plane. If I lay down fire, I can draw them in the wrong direction. They'll think we're headed that way. Then I can loop around and head to you. If you're all ready to take off, I just jump in and we go."

"That just might work," Blake said. "I'm coming with you."

"It'll be faster if only one of us has to get on the plane," Haeli said.

Blake fired. "Yep. Still going with you."

"If that's the plan, we should go now," Kook said.

"Right," Blake said. "Then why are you still standing here?"

# CHAPTER 44

IMA PULLED out her phone and checked the time.

*Forty-two minutes.*

She was getting jumpy. A few minutes prior, a loud bang rang out from the recycling center or somewhere nearby. A dump truck or one of the metal containers being dropped. Nonetheless, she dove for cover under the dashboard as if she were taking fire.

It was one of the reasons she looked up to Haeli. Cool and calm under pressure, Haeli was a machine. Ima knew that no matter how much they taught her about guns or tactics, she would never be able to do what they do. She just didn't have it in her.

Anyway, she was perfectly content staying behind the keyboard. There was a lot she could do to help from there. And for Ian's sake, it kept her relatively safe.

She checked her phone again.

*Forty-three.*

In a way, it was a good sign that Wade wasn't back yet. It meant Phillips probably showed up. Ima wasn't sure if Wade had meant it when he said to call the police if he wasn't back in an hour, but she intended to take him at his word. As soon as the last minute elapsed, she would dial.

Until then, she'd wait.

She wished she could turn on the radio to pass the time, but Wade had taken the keys. No doubt afraid she'd get scared and ditch him there. Luckily, the truck was equipped with all the premium features, like manual crank windows. Otherwise, she'd already have boiled alive.

Stowing her phone in her pocket, she kicked her legs up onto the bench seat and leaned her back against the door. The breeze felt good against her neck.

Out of the corner of her eye, she caught something moving in the side mirror.

Before she could blink, a man stood at her window. His pistol pointed at her throat.

Ima raised her hands.

At the driver's side, a second man peered in through the open window.

"Are you the police?" Ima asked. They didn't look like it, but it was still a possibility. She *was* trespassing, after all.

The one on the passenger side reached in and pulled the manual lock, then popped open the door. With a hand around her bicep, he yanked her to her feet. "Let's go."

"Get off of me!" Ima tried to pull away, but the man's grip was too tight.

"Shut up and walk."

"No!" Ima struggled.

The second man came around the front of the truck to help.

"Grab her legs," the first said.

He bent down to scoop them, but Ima kicked as hard as she could. The man backed off, then shot in again. This time, he was able to grab hold.

With his arms under Ima's armpits, the first man held her weight while the second lifted her legs off the ground.

"Help!" Ima screamed. "Somebody! Help me!"

Her abductor smashed his hand over her mouth and squeezed.

She tried to bite, but couldn't get any meat in between her teeth.

They carried her around the building. Despite her squirming, they had little trouble getting her inside.

Once into the dank interior, the man let go of her mouth.

"Help! Help!" Her cries reverberated off the towering concrete walls.

"Scream all you want now," the man holding her legs said. "No one can hear you."

They took her through a doorway into a darker room. There, they dropped her on the floor.

Ima's heart raced. Of all the situations she had found herself in over the years, she had never been in a position like this. She was terrified. More than that, in shock.

*This is really happening.*

A million thoughts rushed through her head but settled only on one. Ian.

The two men rifled through Ima's pockets and removed her phone.

"Olivia, is it?" Another man asked.

Ima had been so caught up in the shock of what was happening, she hadn't noticed there were more people in the room. She looked at her surroundings.

To her right, a body lay on the floor. She recognized the clothing. "Archer!" She scrambled to him and pulled on his shoulder. He was heavy and lifeless. She pulled harder. As his torso tipped, his head flopped toward her. Staring into his mangled face, she screamed.

"Shhhh."

Ima stared up at the man standing over her. It was Phillips himself. "You killed him!"

"Not technically," Phillips said. "Anyway, he did it to himself. All he had to do was answer a simple question. Don't worry, I'll give you the same opportunity. I hope you choose more wisely than he did."

"What do you want?"

"Easy. Tell me where Buck Novak is."

"Why, so you can kill him too? Hasn't he suffered enough?"

From behind Phillips a fourth man stepped forward. Phillips put out his arm as if holding him back. Ima knew exactly who he was.

"Piper Gaudet. You should be in prison where you belong."

"Feisty one," Piper said. "I might just take my time with you." He moved forward.

Ima shimmied backward. "Get away from me, you filthy animal."

Piper stopped and laughed.

"Just tell us where Novak is," Phillips said. "We don't want to hurt you."

"Right. As soon as I tell you, you'll kill me anyway. I'm not stupid."

Without warning, Piper launched himself at Ima. Landing his knee into her abdomen, he grabbed her by the throat. "By then, honey, you'll be begging for death."

Ima struggled for a breath. Panic set in. She reached up and dug her nails into his rutty cheek, dragging them across the hardened scar tissue.

Letting go of her throat, he knocked her arm away with such force, she thought her forearm might shatter. He pulled his pistol and shoved it under her chin.

"Stop," Phillips shouted. "Not this time."

Piper looked over his shoulder.

"Get off her," Phillips said.

The pressure on Ima's lungs released and Piper receded. Ima took a long, deep breath.

The four men spoke, disregarding the fact that she could hear every word. She lay still and tried to formulate some sort of plan. Her next move, at least. She drew a blank. The only thing she could think of was her son, waiting for her to get home.

"What, did you grow a conscience all of a sudden?" Piper asked.

"God, I hope not." Phillips chuckled. "Did you hear how she talked about Novak? I think this woman cares about him. Which means, the feeling might be mutual. If she's not going to tell us where he is, she can help bring him to us."

"Hell of a good idea," one of the other two men said.

Phillips shook his head. "I have to do everything."

"You think he knows where she is?" Piper asked.

"Doesn't matter. I have a plan. Piper, tie her up and find a spot deep in this place to stash her. You two, I have a job for you. I'm going back to Washington. Try not to screw it up this time."

Ima breathed a sigh of relief. Their idiotic plan had bought her some time. Maybe it would work. Maybe Novak would come. But if he did, he'd better bring an army with him.

# CHAPTER 45

IAN'S left arm swung in an exaggerated arc. His right was held stationary by Lucy's interlaced grip.

It had been Ian's idea to take a walk, but no one else complained. On the contrary, they had all jumped at the chance to get out for some air. Christa, Gwyn, Lucy, and Ian, together.

As they strolled down the hill toward the wharf, Chief limped out from his side yard.

"Look at you," Chief said. "Wanderin' about, side by each."

"How ya doin,' Chief?" Christa and Gwyn stopped to talk with him.

Lucy squeezed Ian's hand, holding him back. Against his will, he might add.

"I'm good. I tell ya though, you better watch out, the cars come flyin down here," Chief said. But Ian heard, "you bettuh watch out, the cauhs come flyin down heuh."

Christa and Gwyn eyed each other and smiled. It was probably the hundredth time he'd told them that.

"Who's this now?" Chief hobbled over toward Ian. "What's your name, young man?"

"Ian," he responded. "You talk funny."

"Ian!" Lucy turned a light shade of red.

"I was gonna say the same thing about you." Chief smiled and

# DETACHMENT

winked. "Welp, I've gotta go run to Cumbies. The old lady ran out of Autocrat."

"Nice seeing you, Chief." Gwyn said.

"Same here."

Lucy waited for Christa and Gwyn to start moving before Ian felt her pull slacken.

*Finally.*

At the bottom of the hill, beyond the timber lip of the pier, a sailboat motored in toward the pump-out dock. Two people stood along gunnels, looped lines in hand.

"Look at that beautiful boat," Lucy said.

Ian glanced ahead. "That's a Pacific Seacraft. Sloop configuration. Excellent bluewater boat."

"Really?" Lucy looked over her shoulder to see if Christa or Gwyn heard what had just come out of his mouth. They were engrossed in their own conversation. "How do you know that?"

"Blake wants a sailboat. I told him I'd help him find a good one. Pacific Seacraft would be a solid choice, but the closest one for sale right now is in Newport News."

"You mean Newport?"

"Newport News. Virginia. Not Newport, silly."

"Whatever.," Lucy said. "I want to get a laser."

"For what? Like a laser pointer or like, a killer death ray?"

"No, like a tiny sailboat. A dinghy. Look who's silly now." Lucy tickled him on his ribs. He didn't flinch.

As they walked along, Ian wore a permanent smile. Even though his hand was sweaty, he wouldn't let go of Lucy's grasp. "It must be nice having two moms."

Lucy laughed. "It's the best."

"I miss my mom," Ian said. "I don't understand why I can't be with her. She says she's working. But I've always been there when she's working. I bet she's done with work and now she's on a romantic getaway with Fezz."

"What? With Fezz? Why do you say that?"

"Cause they like each other. I think he loves her. All the signs are there."

Lucy chuckled. "What signs? And what do you know about love?"

"I've started puberty, you know. And I'm not an ignoramus. I know when a man is attracted to a woman, dopamine is released in the brain. Then the man acts funny and says things he wouldn't normally say. And the woman too. They become irrational. They look at each other funny and act like they want to kiss each other, but then they don't. That's what Fezz and my mom do. Like I said, all the signs are there."

"You've got an overactive imagination. That's what I think. Your mom and Fezz? I don't think so."

"You'll see. He asked her out on a date. I bet that's what they're doing. After Fezz and my mom kicked some ass—"

"What kind of language is that?" Christa interrupted.

Ian hadn't realized the adults were listening. "Sorry. I sometimes forget I'm in mixed company."

Christa suppressed her smile.

Lucy shrugged. "Well, if Fezz likes your mom, and your mom likes Fezz, then I think that's great."

"It is," Ian said. "But since I already know, she should just come home. I don't like not being able to see her."

"I know. She'll be home soon. Anyway, we never get to hang out this much, right? And you get to stay up late and play my guitar. Hey, I don't let just anyone in my room, ya know."

"Yeah, I like sleeping over. Maybe you can come sleep over in my room next time."

"Maybe."

"Hey Ian," Gwyn called from a few feet back, "Have you ever skipped rocks before?"

Ian slowed to think about it. Skip rocks? He didn't think so.

Christa and Gwyn caught up so that all four were side by side. Or, as Chief would say, side by each.

"It's one of my favorite things," Christa said.

"Come on guys." Gwyn took Christa's hand and jogged toward the north side of the narrow boat yard. "I bet I get the most hops."

Ian let go of Lucy's hand and hustled after them.

Down a path through the thicket, they emerged onto a small, rocky beach.

"This is perfect," Gwyn said. "The water's so calm, we should be able to get some good distance. The trick is finding the right stone. It has to be flat and smooth. Not too heavy and not too light."

All four traipsed around with their heads down, scouring the beach for the holy grail of skipping rocks.

"Look at this one," Ian said.

"Nice." Lucy held up her own. "But this one is the winner."

Gwyn went first, then Christa. Ian followed their lead.

Four skips. Respectable for his first try, he thought.

He set out to find another. This time with a better weight distribution and more aerodynamic shape. "When we get back, we need to go over everything again." Ian's eyes remained focused in front of his feet. "You're not ready for the exam."

"Hey, I've been studying hard."

"Yeah, but you're not ready yet."

Christa laughed. "You heard him, Luce. Not ready. Looks like you know how you're spending the rest of your evening."

Ian plucked a stone from the sand. Pinching it between his fingers, he crouched low and flung the flat rock at the water. It skipped at least nine times. "Don't worry. I'm going to make sure you ace your test. I've got a few more tricks you can use."

"You know what?" Gwyn said. "We might not give you back."

## CHAPTER 46

BLAKE LEAP-FROGGED past Haeli's position and ducked behind the next tree trunk he could find. He fired three shots.

A barrage of bullets came in response.

As they had done for the past five minutes, when the incoming fire died down, Haeli took her turn jumping beyond Blake.

Overall, the strategy seemed to be working. The small hoard of enemy combatants listed left along the hillside. More importantly, no one appeared to have headed toward the landing site.

"How long should we give them?" Haeli asked.

"A couple more minutes," Blake said. "We're almost at the end, anyway."

Blake peered around the trunk. Most of the men were crouching, and slowly moving toward them. Rats, mesmerized by the piper's song. To the right, another small group had gathered and was moving toward the trees near where Blake and Haeli had started.

It made sense from a tactical standpoint. If the enemy got into the trees further down, or even cut through to the other side of the grove, they could attack Blake and Haeli from the rear. Worse, they'd cut off access in the direction of the landing site. If that happened, Blake and Haeli would be cooked.

"On second thought," Blake said, "it's time." He fired a few more rounds at the main group. Then a few more toward the far group, hoping to slow them down. "Follow me."

Trekking east through the width of the grove, Blake led Haeli in a zigzag pattern. Within half a minute, they were emerging into the clearing. They turned north and sprinted as fast as they could.

On the left, trees ticked by, one by one, until there were none. Blake didn't have to look over his shoulder to know the enemy could see them, should anyone happen to turn their attention north.

In another minute, they would reach the crest of the slope. Five seconds after, they would be completely out of view. It was within reach. But as it turned out, they wouldn't make it.

Shots crackled in the distance. First a couple, then more. Like popcorn on a stovetop.

"Damn," Haeli muttered.

She put on the afterburners, pulling away with ease. Blake dug deep and pushed himself to keep up. It had been a while since he'd seen Haeli run at full speed. Since that day in Zurich, she seemed to have only gotten faster. Or he'd just gotten older.

Unable to resist the urge, Blake looked back. The troops were advancing like medieval infantry on a battle pitch. Their collective war cry filled the plain. They were still too far away to make their shots count.

Over the next hump, they raced neck and neck. Ahead, they could see the airplane. Blake tried to make out the shape of the propellers. He was happy to find he couldn't. It meant they were spinning.

Blake's legs burned, but his feet no longer felt like they were touching the ground. They were on the verge of giving out.

Behind them, the group had spread out further. The runners up front and the donut brigade all the way at the back. While half of them were too far away to be of any threat, the runners seemed to gain on them. Even if they could make it to the plane without getting hit, they still had to take off. By then, there was a good chance one of them would be close enough for an effective shot.

"You get on first," Blake said. "You're more nimble."

It was an understatement.

Haeli broke away, leading Blake by two, then three, then four strides.

The crackling of rifles didn't let up.

As they approached the plane, Blake could see that the cargo door was swung open. Under the windows on the starboard side, a wide but slender half-door was meant for loading and unloading cargo when the rear seats weren't installed. In this case, it was clearly meant for loading them.

Blake waved his arms. Kook got the message.

The aircraft began to move. Like a gazelle, Haeli ran alongside, then slipped through the slot and into the interior.

Blake pumped his legs. The plane picked up more speed.

*Now or never.*

With every last bit of energy, Blake launched himself toward the cargo door. He caught one leg of an interior seat with his left hand, his own legs still running beneath him.

As the plane accelerated, Blake could no longer keep up. His left shoulder and pectoral bulged as his boots dragged through the dirt.

The crackling turned into booms. As if matters weren't bad enough, a bullet skimmed off the bottom of the fuselage, next to his hip.

Blake pulled his head inside, and lifting his leg, hooked his heel on the door frame.

The aircraft jostled, causing his boot to slide out and sending his legs dragging once more.

Bullets whizzed, a few piercing the skin of the airframe. There was no way to know if anyone had been hit.

Then, in an instant, the vibration traveling from his feet to his fingers stopped.

His handhold wobbled.

They were airborne.

Blake hooked his heel again and twisted until his shoulder was through the slot.

He felt Fezz's meaty hands under his arms. He heard the cacophony of panicked voices mix with the blaring hum of the twin props.

Just like that, he was onboard. In one piece. And on his way home.

If only they all were.

# CHAPTER 47

CLINT TAYLOR TOOK the napkin from his lap, wiped his mouth, and tossed it onto the table in a heap. "I should be going. John, Linda. Thank you again."

"Absolutely."

Clint stood. The stuffed veal chops felt like a ton of bricks in his stomach—in a good way, he decided. One thing was for certain. He never left Strega unsatisfied.

To his right, Steven Tyler sat with three other people. During the meal, Clint and Tyler had shared a few pleasant words. As a big Aerosmith fan, he wanted to spark one more interaction. Say "Enjoy the rest of your night," or something to that effect. Maybe shake his hand. But his better judgment told him not to be *that* guy. Instead, he graciously took his exit.

Outside, Hanover St was bustling. He fished his keys from his pocket and set off to find his car somewhere on Salem St.

Crossing Hanover, he cut up Tileston Street.

Barely wide enough for one car, Tileston was one of many North Boston remnants that brought with it an instant sense of history. It was impossible to not imagine horses plodding through the narrow streets hundreds of years before.

In the modern sense, it was just eerie. Like being trapped in a maze.

As he passed Unity St, he noticed two men in black hoodies leaning against a brick building between Tileston and the back side of the Paul Revere mall.

For some reason, the sight of them sent a shiver down Clint's spine. He didn't know why. Vagrants and the homeless were a fixture in every part of the city. Nothing out of the ordinary. He wouldn't have even noticed the men if they weren't the only people around.

But he did notice, and it didn't seem right. The two looked similar, leaning with the same posture, but not close together. Hoods cinched to their cheeks.

Maybe they weren't vagrants at all, but bar-goers waiting for a ride, or addicts waiting for a delivery.

All of these would have been fleeting thoughts chalked up to an overactive imagination, if he hadn't glanced behind him. Now, the two men were together, walking side-by-side up Tileston in his direction.

Clint picked up his pace. He didn't run, just pushed his normal stride to its upper limits.

Another glance confirmed his fear. The men had sped up, closing the gap between them.

The reality had clicked. There were no two ways about it. They were going to mug him.

Heart pounding, Clint ran through his options. One, try to get to his car and hope there were enough pedestrians and motorists to scare off the muggers. Two—There was no 'two.'

He looked over his shoulder again. It was too late.

Now ten feet away, both men barreled toward him in a full run.

Then he felt the impact.

One of the men laid an elbow into his chest, sending him stumbling backward, toward the building. His shoulder blades slammed into the wrought iron bars covering one of the windows.

The next thing Clint knew, one of the attackers had his forearm jammed against his throat. The faceted iron bars dug into the back of his head.

Clint didn't fight back. It would only make things worse. He would let them empty his pockets, take his watch, whatever they wanted. If he didn't resist, he thought, there would be no need to hurt him.

While the first attacker kept him pinned, Clint could feel the other's hand brushing against his ribs. He reached into Clint's inside blazer pocket.

Hot breath washed over Clint's face. It smelled of peppermint. He focused on the man's features—the little he could see through the puckered opening in the hood. Light skin. Prominent nose. Five o'clock shadow.

If he could speak, Clint would have told them which pocket his wallet was in. Helped to speed up the process. To get it over with.

Then something else happened. Clint didn't know what, and he didn't care. Whatever his attackers had seen or heard had scared them. The pressure on his throat released, the peppermint subsided, and as fast as they were on him, they were gone.

Clint crouched and rubbed his neck. He looked around. There was no one. No one, except for the two shadowy figures removing their hoods as they disappeared around the corner onto Wiggin Street.

He tapped his right pocket to check for his keys. As he expected, they weren't there. It took a few seconds for his rattled mind to realize he was still holding them in his left hand.

In the next moment, he was climbing into the driver's seat of his Lexus, with no recollection of how he got there. As he pulled the door shut, the world outside the metal cocoon silenced. He took a breath. He was alive.

Closing his eyes, he sat still, letting the adrenaline dissipate. Disbelief turned to relief. Relief turned to anger. He had to call the police. Did he still have his phone?

In his left pocket, he found it. And that wasn't all. His wallet, his watch, it was all there. Had they not taken anything? He checked all his pockets again. As if it couldn't get any weirder, he found something he didn't have before. In the inside pocket of his blazer was an envelope.

The attackers hadn't taken anything, they *left* something. As unbelievable as might have seemed, there was no other explanation. It wasn't a mugging. It was a delivery.

Clint tore open the envelope and turned on the overhead light. Inside was a piece of paper and two glossy photographs.

Holding one of the photographs in the light, he tried to discern what he was looking at. It was a person. No, a body.

Then it hit him.

*No, no, no, no.*

There was no doubt about it, it was Archer Wade. Dead. Very, very dead.

*Oh my god.*

A lump formed in his throat. Was this image real? Was Wade murdered? Why was this given to him? Was it some kind of threat?

He was reluctant to look at the second picture, but there was no real choice. He flipped it over.

It was a woman. Bound and gagged. He racked his brain but couldn't place the face.

Last, there was the piece of paper. On it were written two words. "For Novak."

## CHAPTER 48

BLAKE TRIED THE DOOR. It was locked.

"I've got it." Fezz took out his key.

Shortly after crossing into Columbia, Blake had tried to call Ima. Over the next twenty-four hours, they all had. Repeatedly. She never answered.

From Green airport, Fezz wanted to drive straight to Newport. Kook, Griff, and Haeli asked to be dropped off at the house on the way through Jamestown. As far as Blake was concerned, it was understandable. The last few days had been grueling, on the body and the soul. But Blake also figured there was another reason. They didn't want to be there when Novak got the news.

With a little badgering, Fezz gave in. He stopped at the house but hadn't allowed time for anyone to grab their bags from the back before he was off again.

Fezz swung the door open. Blake followed him in.

Novak sat alone at the kitchen table.

"Where's Ima?" Fezz popped his head into the bedroom, then the bathroom.

Blake stopped at the far side of the table. "He means Olivia."

Novak stared into space as if he wasn't even aware of their presence.

"Hey, are you okay?" Blake asked.

"He's dead, isn't he?"

Blake was taken off guard by the question. On the trip back, he had prepared a speech and run through it over and over in his mind. A tactful and empathetic way to tell Novak that he no longer had any sons. Now, it was all out the window. A direct question deserved a direct answer.

"I'm sorry." Blake walked to Novak and put his hand on his shoulder. "He's gone."

Novak's head nodded but his eyes were blank.

"When you're ready, I'll tell you anything you want to know. Just say the word."

"I knew he was gone. I could feel it. An emptiness, ya know? Just tell me one thing. How did it happen?"

Blake winced. He didn't want to say the word, but there was no delicate way to put it. "Hanged."

Novak let out a breathy laugh and pinched the bridge of his nose. "Hanged." He tilted his head back and then brought it level again, as if there were a reset switch built into his neck. "This is my fault. I could have stopped this before any of it happened. I could have forbidden Robbie from getting involved. I could have ordered that Jackson be cut from the team from the outset. Everything I did was wrong. Everything."

Out of the corner of his eye, Blake could see Fezz standing off to the side, his impatience bubbling over. Blake held up his index finger in hopes that Fezz could contain himself for just another minute or two.

Blake pulled out the chair next to Novak and sat. "How many times have you looked back at an operation, or anything really, and not said 'I could've done things differently?' Hindsight has nothing to do with the decisions you make in the spur of the moment. You did the best you could at the time. You may blame yourself, but no one else can. This isn't on you."

"Robbie is on me."

He had a point.

Blake thought about how Jackson and the others had been killed shortly after being captured. The efforts to leak the story to force a rescue wouldn't have made a bit of difference. To Novak, that fact only would mean that Robbie had lost his life for no reason. No purpose, whatsoever.

As a father and a soldier, it would be too much to bear. For that reason, Blake decided not to mention it.

"There's something you need to see." Novak took out his phone, opened it and placed it on the table.

Blake picked it up. On the screen was the image of Archer. He could feel his face warming. An intense anger surged up inside of him. "How did this happen?"

Fezz leaned in, trying to get a look. Blake showed him the screen.

"Where's I—Olivia?" Fezz asked.

"Swipe to the next picture," Novak said.

"No!" Fezz's skin blanched. His body shook. He grabbed the phone out of Blake's hands and swiped his finger across it. His squinted eyes opened wide. "She's alive?" He turned the screen toward Blake and then to Novak. "Tell me she's alive."

"I don't know," Novak said. "I was sent those pictures late last night. While you were gone, Archer was trying to contact Phillips. The next thing I knew, he and Olivia were gone. They just vanished."

Fezz growled. "They went to meet Phillips?"

"It's possible."

"Where was this picture taken?" Blake asked.

"I don't know any more than you do. Looks like an abandoned building to me. Like the place we met."

Blake examined the pictures again.

Fezz was already on his phone. "Griff, listen, Ima's in trouble. Find out her phone's last location. And get everyone geared up. We're going after her. Be ready to go in thirty."

"First my sons, all those brave men, and now Archer and Olivia, or Ima, or whatever her name is. This has to end. It's me they're after. I should just give them what they want."

Blake slapped the table. "You know what? That's exactly what we'll do."

# CHAPTER 49

KOOK PULLED over to the edge of Old Gate Lane, just past the main access road.

When they had rallied up, the group decided one person needed to stay behind and travel to Boston to deliver all the materials they'd compiled to Wade's editor at the Globe.

Everyone agreed it needed to be done as soon as possible, but no one wanted to be excluded. Haeli commented that they'd have to 'draw straws.' Fezz, who exempted himself, took it literally.

Gathering five of Ima's smoothie straws from the pantry, Fezz cut one a little shorter, mixed them up, and forced the rest of them to participate in the ridiculous game. Of course, Khat, the poorest sport of them all, chose the short straw. But Blake had to hand it to him, he took it like a man.

"This is you." Haeli opened one of the two opposing doors. Novak scooted around her, then stepped into the grass.

"Last checks." Griff activated his mic. "You read me?"

Novak reached into his ear and adjusted the volume. "Loud and clear."

"Hang tight," Blake said. "Wait for our signal."

With a nod, Novak slammed the door.

Kook pulled out and took the immediate right into the adjacent motel parking lot.

Behind the motel was a big box home improvement store. As seen on the overhead images, only a twenty-foot-wide strip of thick foliage separated the north side of the old aerosol factory from the narrow parking lot running alongside the store. This spot would serve as their insertion point.

The plan was simple. The team would try to get inside the facility without being detected. At the same time, Novak would present himself at the front, hopefully drawing the attention of whoever was inside. With luck, they could extract Ima before anyone realized she was gone.

It was one scenario, anyway.

No one had any doubt that Phillips was behind this. And Piper was handling the dirty work. Having confirmed that Ima's last ping was from this location, everyone fully expected Piper and his gang to be inside. If Blake had learned anything from their past encounters, Piper's people wouldn't give up without a fight.

Instead of pulling into a parking spot, Kook pulled over to the right, burying the side of the van in the leaves.

As expected, there were cameras mounted on the corners of the building. While his parking job was likely to draw some suspicion, it was better than the alternative. Geared up with tactical vests and automatic weapons, it wasn't as though they could go strolling across the lot. With the doors open, it was like a makeshift tunnel, allowing them to slip straight into the dense foliage. No one would be the wiser.

They had considered leaving someone behind to move the van once they were out, then swing back to pick them up after. But considering they were already missing Khat, they needed as many hands as they could get. The place was huge and there was a lot of ground to cover. On top of that, they had no idea how many combatants they might face. For all they knew, there was an entire shadow unit in there.

Griff went first, then Haeli and Blake. Fezz tossed the Halligan onto the dirt, jumped out, then picked it up and wiped it on his pants. Last, Kook climbed over the seat, hopped into the brush, and closed the doors behind him.

"We're on the property," Blake updated over the radio. "Standby. I'll give you the go once we find an entry point."

The team slogged through the growth along the north exterior wall. Within a few seconds, they came across a square piece of plywood screwed to what they assumed was a window frame or an old duct pass-through. If the opening was the size of the plywood, it was big enough to accommodate even Fezz.

After snapping a few branches and clearing a few vines, Fezz jammed the Halligan between the wood and the wall and pried. The old screws popped without much effort. Blake and Fezz each grabbed a corner and ripped it the rest of the way off.

From inside, Blake could smell the familiar dank odor. He hoisted himself up and in. "We're making entry. Start moving to the front."

"Roger," Novak acknowledged.

Each of them slipped inside with ease.

At the far side of the room was a doorless opening that led into a corridor. Sunlight streaming in from one of the many gaps and holes in the exterior illuminated it enough that flashlights wouldn't be necessary. At least not yet.

The team stacked up at the edge of the opening. From there, they went to work.

---

AS HE WALKED, Novak rested his arm against the handle of the loaned pistol. The silenced Glock 22 was given to him for his protection, he was told. Not to 'be a hero.'

The object was not to engage, but distract. Novak had his own objective—clear and concise.

Kill Piper Gaudet.

There was nothing he could do to bring his sons back, or correct the mistakes he'd made, and he wasn't trying to. What he wanted was pure revenge, plain and simple. To make Piper, Phillips, and even Moore pay for what they had done.

As the crumbling front facade of the factory building loomed larger, Novak whistled as loud as he could. "I got your message! Well, here I am!"

There was no response but the sound of birds and traffic.

He approached the front entrance, stepped over the threshold, and stopped.

"Hello."

His voice reverberated back at him.

"Ron?" *Ron—Ron—Ron.*

He whistled again and took a step forward.

"Piper. Show yourself!"

Reaching into his waistband, he withdrew the long pistol and hid it behind his back.

He took one more step.

Above, catwalks ran from one end of the plant to the other. He scanned for any sign of someone looking to get the drop from above. There was no one.

Then he saw something.

Movement in one of the dark openings.

"Who's there?"

Piper stepped out of the shadow. A pistol in his lowered right hand. "You created quite a mess, haven't you Novak?"

Novak squinted. Piper was too far away to risk a from-the-hip shot. If he missed, he'd lose him to the interior. He could move closer, but he liked his own position, two feet from the exit. If Piper's arm so much as flinched, he could be through the door before Piper got the shot off. The problem was, Piper had the same advantage.

So there they stood, in a long-distance standoff.

"Where's the woman?" Novak asked.

"Oh, Olivia? She's fine. Come in, I'll show you."

"Not a chance. Where's Phillips?"

"You've got a lot of questions. That's okay, I like this game. Phillips is gone. It's just me and my lonesome. And, of course, Olivia. Now, I have one for you. Who is this girl to you? You're here, so she means something to you."

"She's a decent person who has nothing to do with any of this. That should be enough. My turn. When did you decide to shit on everything this country stands for? Did Phillips have to work on you a while? Or were you just always an asshole?"

Piper laughed. "You know what your problem is? You're a joiner. A rule-follower. And look where that got you. Have some imagination, man. You know when I was on the teams, the bureaucrats would make all their little rules, pretend their hands were clean, but who went out there and got things done? We did. It was dirty, and it was effective. Fear is the only motivator. Violence is the only solution. I would have thought you knew that. But you've turned out to be quite a disappointment."

"You didn't have to kill him."

"Who's that? Your precious son? He was no different than you. Poisoned by the lie of honor. I did the country a favor."

Novak's blood boiled. His peripheral vision darkened. Nothing existed in the world but Piper Guadet. "I will kill you."

Piper stepped back into the shadow. "Maybe. But I doubt it. You can pull that pistol you're holding behind your back and we can have ourselves an old fashion high-noon, OK corral shootout. Or I can take one step behind this wall and be gone. Then it's a different game, isn't it? One called, 'Can you find me before I kill her?' It's a big place, Bucky boy. Lots of spots to hide."

"You're a big man, aren't ya? Threatening defenseless women. Why don't you drop your pistol and we'll go mano y mano, how 'bout that? Or is the only reason you don't believe in honor is because you don't have any?"

"Let's talk about honor. Here you stand, knowing that you could save this poor girl's life. But instead, all you want is revenge. Isn't it? I'll put it to ya straight. A test of honor. You drop that gun and accept your fate, and I'll let the girl go. It's a simple choice. You go out with honor, saving the young maiden. Or leave her to die and admit to yourself that honor is a fallacy."

For a moment, Novak considered the option. His life no longer had meaning. He had no children. No job. There was some truth in what Piper was saying. If he believed in sacrifice for the good of the innocent, like he always thought he did, why wouldn't he fall on the sword?

## DETACHMENT

The answer could only be answered in context. He wouldn't, because Piper couldn't be trusted. There was no way that Piper would spare Olivia once Buck was dead. That was how they operated. Erase anyone and anything posing a threat to their impunity.

"Okay," Novak said. "I'll do what you ask. But you have to promise to let her go. Unharmed."

"Pinky swear."

With a slow, deliberate movement, Novak brought the pistol out. "I'll put it down, but I want to see her leave before we settle our business."

Piper shrugged. "Deal."

Eyes fixed on Piper, Novak slowly crouched. As he brought the pistol toward the ground, he held his breath. With a flick of his wrist, he levered the muzzle in Piper's direction and mashed the trigger.

*Crack.* The echo amplified the suppressed report.

Across the room, the doorway was empty.

*Damn it.*

Novak sprang into motion.

As he reached the opening, he dove around the corner, gun first. Piper had disappeared.

---

"CLEAR." Haeli and Griff joined Blake, Fezz and Kook in the corridor.

"This is going to take too long," Kook said. "We should split up."

Blake nodded. "I agree. If we—"

*Crack.*

"Was that a gunshot?"

Blake got on the comms. "Buck, talk to me. What's going on?"

His earpiece crackled. "I took a shot at him. I think I missed. He's loose."

"Damn it, Buck," Blake said.

"We've gotta find her," Haeli said.

Blake keyed the mic. "Who'd you see, Piper? Phillips? How many are there?"

"Just Piper. I think he's alone. He may be going for Olivia."

"Okay," Haeli said. "Split up." She sprinted off down the corridor.

Blake ran through the logic. If Piper was really alone, then he'd left Ima. If she was in that corridor, Piper wouldn't be able to get to her without running into them. They could push forward without checking the rest of the rooms.

"I'm going to move to the main floor to see if I can head him off." Blake took off running. As he wound his way through various rooms, he paused every few seconds to listen. There was no sign of Piper or Novak.

*Boom.*

Another, much louder shot rang out. It was close.

Blake darted in the direction of the sound. "Buck, what's happening?"

"Wasn't me. Do you have him?"

"No." Blake dipped into a room. Then another. And another. It had to have come from somewhere close. He keyed up. "Anyone have anything showing?"

"Negative," Haeli responded.

Blake moved to the next opening. He stepped into the dark room, did a quick look around but saw no movement. As he was about to move on, something caught his eye in the corner. Amidst a pile of trash was a pair of sneakers. As he looked closer, he realized the sneakers were attached to legs.

He flipped his flashlight on and rushed toward the corner.

"Haeli! Fezz! Someone, come quick!"

Blake lifted Ima off the floor. Her white shirt was saturated with blood.

Carrying her into the corridor, he set her down on her back and felt for a pulse.

"Shit," Fezz bolted down the corridor and dropped to his knees. He grabbed her in his arms. "Stay with me Ima. Don't you die. Don't you do it."

Blake let go, stood up, and raised his rifle. What he knew, and what Fezz hadn't yet realized, was that she had no pulse. And she never would. She was shot through the heart.

"No! God, no!" Fezz's sobbing echoed in Blake's ears. Blake pushed

# DETACHMENT

forward with pure determination to destroy the evil that was Piper Guadet.

"Someone help Fezz," Blake yelled into his mic.

Room to room Blake went. Slamming and kicking and yelling. "Show yourself, you coward!"

As he turned into an adjoining corridor, he almost ran into Novak, traveling in the opposite direction.

"Not down this way," Novak said.

"You sure?"

"I'm sure."

Blake turned around, followed Novak for a few seconds, then broke off into another set of rooms.

Clicking on his flashlight, Blake checked every inch.

In the second of the four adjoining rooms, there were several rusted machines. He shined his light on each. Against the far wall, his light cast a shadow. A silhouette of a long since neglected hunk of metal. Only—for a split second, the shadow seemed to move.

Blake scanned again, then got down on all fours.

Thanks to a set of stubborn angle-iron legs, there was a two-foot gap between the floor and the underbelly of the dilapidated kettle. Through the gap, Blake saw legs. And boots.

He took aim. With pleasure, he squeezed off a shot.

Piper cried out as he crumpled to the ground. His pistol skittered into the corner. He clutched his leg and groaned.

Blake rushed in, grabbed his shattered shin, and dragged him out into the open.

"Please!" Piper writhed in pain.

"Please?" Blake trained the barrel of his rifle on Piper's skull.

From behind Blake, a giant hand swooped in and pushed his rifle downward.

"No." Fezz said, as calm as could be.

Blake took a breath. Fezz was right. The scumbag wasn't worth it.

He slung his rifle and squeezed Fezz's shoulder. "I'm sorry brotha."

Fezz tensed his lips and nodded. Then, without warning, he raised his rifle and fired a round into the center of Piper's chest.

Then another, and another. Until the magazine had run dry. When it did, he pulled out his pistol and emptied it into Piper's mangled corpse.

Blake stood stunned.

Fezz stared at the lifeless body.

"Feel better?" Blake asked.

"No."

## CHAPTER 50

THE KEURIG MACHINE gurgled and spat the final drops of Breakfast Blend. Blake grabbed the mug and returned to his laptop. The Boston Globe's website filled the screen.

In addition to the full article, the online edition of the paper provided extra content that couldn't be included in the hardcopy. Of course, Blake had already seen most of the materials. But there was something that caught his interest. Biographies for each of the men lost in Venezuela.

Jackson Novak's story was featured. Both online and in print.

Since the article hit the wire earlier that morning, it dominated every facet of the media. Morning news shows, radio broadcasts, and even social media platforms buzzed.

On the television mounted above the fireplace, Blake tuned in to one of the twenty-four-hour news stations. Although he had muted the volume, the captions and headline banners made it clear what the talking heads were relaying.

"Mornin'." Haeli shuffled down the stairs in a set of pink satin pajamas.

Blake was hunched over the kitchen island, swiping the trackpad to scroll the page as he read. "This kid, Ashton Furst, qualified for the Olympics in snowboarding but decided to go to basic training instead. Such a shame."

Haeli walked over and kissed Blake on the forehead. "Did you get any sleep?"

"Not really. I got up and came down here at about four-thirty. Didn't want to wake you with my tossing and turning."

"I was awake. Just didn't want to give up hope quite yet."

"Thinking about Ima?" Blake asked.

"Yeah."

"Me too."

"I just can't believe it," Haeli said. "After everything she went through. To finally be free. And then this. What was she thinking going there without us? She must have known the risk, right? Why would she put herself in that position?"

"I just don't know," Blake said.

"And what about Ian? How do we—ya know?"

"That's the other thing that kept me up. I haven't even told Christa yet. When I spoke to her last night, I only asked if she minded keeping Ian another day. I figured if I told her what happened, she'd be emotional, and Ian would key in on it."

Haeli's voice cracked. "We should all be with him when we tell him. He'll need the support. So he doesn't feel like he's abandoned."

"I agree. I'll call Christa this morning and see if she can bring him back later today."

"Okay." Haeli put her hand on Blake's shoulder and then moved past him. "I need a cup of coffee."

"Or two," Blake said. "You should check out the article. Incredible how fast they put it together."

"We handed them the whole thing," Haeli said.

"I know. Someone still had to write it up. And there are all these bios. You really should read some of this."

"I will." Haeli loaded a coffee pod into the machine. "Once I can see straight."

"Blake." Novak leaned over the railing on the second-floor landing.

Blake looked up at him. "Everything all right?"

"Would it be possible for someone to drive me to the airport?"

"Sure. Why? Did something happen?"

"Phillips was arrested." Novak smiled. "I just spoke with the Pentagon. They took him into custody at his home a half hour ago. They want me to come to Washington as soon as possible. Apparently, there's word that a resignation may be imminent."

"I hope so," Blake said. "Hard to make the cabinet meetings when you're in prison."

"No. Not Phillips. Moore."

"You're kidding," Haeli said.

"Wow. I thought for sure he'd try to hold out. Yeah, I'll shoot you up to the airport if you want."

"Thanks. I'm just going to jump in the shower, if that's all right."

"Of course. The guest bathroom should be stocked with whatever you need. And if you want a change of clothes, you're welcome to raid my closet."

"Great. Thanks again." Novak hurried off into the hallway.

Haeli rejoined Blake, her steaming mug of coffee in her hand. "Buck turned out to be a great guy."

*Yes, he did.*

By the time they'd left Connecticut, it was late. They'd contemplated returning Novak to the Newport apartment, but after everything they'd just been through, they agreed Novak was trustworthy enough to stay at the house. It wouldn't have been right to dump him off by himself.

The hours following Ima's death had been trying. Out of everyone, Fezz took it the worst. Inconsolable, Novak had helped him regain his composure.

Grieving himself, Novak understood what Fezz was going through—what they all were going through. The entire time they'd sat there in the factory, waiting for dark, Fezz never left Ima's side. And Novak never left Fezz's.

Although it was often overshadowed by the trauma of the event itself, Blake always found the aftermath equally distressing. In the past, he, Fezz, and Khat had taken part in assignments that required cleanup after the fact. Clandestine operations that needed to stay that way. It was never easy, but none had ever been as emotionally draining as this.

After the team had finished clearing the factory and were sure there were no other threats, Kook and Griff had gone back to the van to move it to a proper parking spot. They'd gone into the adjacent hardware store and purchased several tarps, a spool of cord, a couple of shovels, and a few cleaning supplies.

With as much reverence as could be observed, they'd wrapped Ima's body in the green plastic. The same went for Piper, only they'd handled his body with considerably less care, and even less compassion.

When it had gotten dark, the group carried both Ima and Piper to Fezz's truck behind the building and secured them to the flatbed with rope.

They had driven to Arcadia State Forest, in Exeter—Fezz and Novak in the truck, and the others following in the van.

In the woods, Fezz had insisted on digging two holes. Everyone agreed. The idea of Ima sharing a grave with the likes of that animal was sickening.

It had been bad enough that she wouldn't be afforded a proper funeral. But the reality was, Ima had already legally died almost a year before. And if anyone knew she hadn't, it would stand to reason that none of them had.

So, in lieu of a ceremonial burial, they'd held a service of their own—each taking turns saying something about Ima. About what she'd meant to them. In a way, it was more intimate and fitting than any funeral home could have ever provided.

"Fezz!" Haeli startled as Fezz burst through the front door. "I thought you were asleep upstairs."

"I went for a walk."

Blake moved to meet him. "In the middle of the night? How long have you been out there?"

"I don't know, a few hours." His voice cracked and he clenched his fists. "I'm so goddamn angry. I wish I could kill him again."

Maybe there was something appropriate to say. Something to convey how deeply sorry Blake was. If such words existed, Blake wished he had them to say. But he didn't. He reached up and wrapped his hand around the back of Fezz's neck.

Fezz embraced him.

After several seconds, he patted Blake on the back, pushed away, and ran his knuckles under his eyes. "Uh. What the hell is wrong with me?"

Blake laughed. "How do you want it, in alphabetical order, or?"

Almost imperceptibly, the corners of Fezz's mouth turned upward. "You're a jerk."

"I know."

Fezz ambled toward the kitchen.

"You really should get some rest, Fezz," Haeli said.

"I will." He sat on a stool at the opposite side of the island. "Ya know, I walked all the way down to the lighthouse. I climbed down onto the rocks and just sat there, listening to the waves crash. All I could think about was Ian. About how he would ever recover from this. It's crazy to think that after living most of his life in hiding, after being kidnapped and trafficked, it would turn out that we're the worst thing that ever happened to him."

Haeli sipped her coffee. "That's not true."

"It is true. We brought them into this life. This awful life. We think it's worthwhile because it's the only thing we've ever known. But Ima didn't belong here. Ian doesn't belong here."

"Maybe," Blake said. "But look at it this way. If Ima was in prison, where would he be? Or even if they were still on the run, what if something happened to her then? The one bright side is that Ian has a family now."

Fezz didn't respond. For a moment, he sat staring into oblivion, then stood up and walked toward the stairs. "I'm going to lie down."

"Good idea." Blake looked at Haeli and raised his eyebrows.

As Fezz climbed up, Novak came down. He was dressed in one of Blake's button downs and a pair of black slacks. Both were just a tad too big for him.

"Perfect," Blake said.

Novak looked down at his outfit and twisted his hips, as if trying to gauge the fit from various angles. "It'll work. I'll get you back. Next time."

"Don't worry about it." Blake placed his mug in the sink. "You ready?"

"Good to go."

"Great. Let me grab my keys."

## CHAPTER 51

BUCK NOVAK SHIFTED his weight and straightened one knee to relieve the ache emanating from the other. The activities of the previous twenty-four hours had taken a toll on his aging body.

Under the overhang, looking out into the White House rose garden, he found himself wedged between an older woman in a pink jacket, and a tall, slender gentleman with thick-framed glasses. He had never met either of them, and did not know their names.

While he knew few of the attendees personally, many were familiar faces. Chief Justice Abeleen, Speaker Branigan, and Secretary of State, Laurel Conway, to name a few.

Out of all of them, there was one man he considered an acquaintance. A friend, really. The man of the hour, Irving Oakley.

It was Oakley who had invited him to attend. His "personal guest," as he had put it on the phone. To Novak, there was no bigger honor. Especially because he knew he would be there to represent his boys. The true guests of honor.

Of course, he accepted without hesitation. It wasn't until afterward that he realized he had come to D.C. with nothing but the shirt on his back—a shirt that didn't even belong to him—and was in no way prepared to be seen at such a high-profile event. Not unless he was prepared to look like a fool.

While the short notice had sent him scrambling, it was the Vice-Chairman of the Joint Chiefs of Staff, Chris Davidson, who'd squared him away with a one-word suggestion. "Suitsupply," he said.

It turned out to be sage advice. What sounded to Novak like some place you'd go for department store seconds, ended up being an ultra-stylish establishment offering expert assistance, impressive selection, and most importantly, custom on-site alterations.

There was something about being well dressed. Despite his frayed nerves and lack of sleep, he had to admit, he felt good. For the first time in a while, he felt as though Jackson and Robbie would be proud of him. Proud for seeing it through. Proud for finding hope.

At the podium, Chief Justice Abeleen was quoting French Historian Alexis de Tocqueville. "'Society is endangered not by the great profligacy of a few,'" she recounted, "'but by the laxity of morals amongst all.' Today we recognize that the deeds of the charlatans and profiteers among us, do not define us. For we strive to be the beacon on which the righteous rely."

Novak thought of Ima, of Blake, and all those who'd sacrificed themselves for righteousness. He had known few people able to set aside personal motives, absent any mandate or oath to uphold. They were extraordinary people. He wished they could be there to bear witness to the fruits of their diligence.

"And now," Abeleen said, "please place your hand on the bible and repeat after me. I, Irving Lenard Oakley..."

Novak couldn't help but smile. "Do you see this?" he wanted to say to Jackson as if he were standing right next to him. "Whatta ya think, Robbie? You guys did it."

Moore was a scourge. And Phillips was worse still. Today the country would have a President they could look up to. Someone with the best interest of every American citizen in mind. Novak truly believed it.

The crowd broke into applause. Photographers' flashes popped all around. Novak put his hands together for Irving Oakley. The people's President.

"Thank you. It is my distinct honor to stand before you today as your humble servant. I vow to you to do my best to wash away the sins of the past as a stalwart defender of the Constitution of the United States and the ideals that all her people hold dear." He paused and looked around the crowd of reporters and dignitaries. "That is, we're going to clean this place up."

The remark garnered a laugh, as it was meant to do. But Novak knew that underneath the levity was real determination to do just that.

"As many of you know, the former Secretary of Defense, Ron Phillips, stands accused of a series of heinous crimes against this nation and its people. While I can't comment on the investigation, I can say that the allegations regarding the selling of information to foreign governments are some of the most egregious. I'm not going to sugar coat it folks. The lives of a dozen brave soldiers and sailors were lost as a direct result of these actions. Today, we pray for them and their families."

Oakley paused for applause.

"Ladies and Gentlemen, I want to introduce someone to you." He raised a hand toward Novak and smiled. "Retired SOCOM Commander General John 'Buck' Novak stands here today having lost both of his sons to the greed and corruption of the former administration—Jackson Novak and Robert Novak, both decorated members of the 1st Special Forces Operational Detachment-Delta."

A solemn silence filled the garden.

"Today we honor Jackson and Robbie, just as we honor all the men who were betrayed by the very people who were supposed to have their backs." Oakley leaned on the podium. "Ya know, I've known Buck Novak for a long time. Our children went to school together. Our families enjoyed each other's company. And when I spoke with him today and found out that he had filed for retirement, I thought to myself, 'what a shame.' Here is a man who embodies everything we value as a nation. Even after all he has lost personally, he hasn't lost his faith. His sense of patriotism. So Buck, thank you for being here, and thank you for your service."

The crowd clapped. Novak gave an embarrassed wave.

"Now, you all might be thinking, 'why is he giving a retirement speech at this historic inauguration?'" Oakley chuckled and pointed at a bald reporter holding a handheld voice recorder with an outstretched arm. "Bobby, I know you are."

The reporter smiled and nodded.

"Well, as a matter of record, I intend to execute my first order as President of the United States. As of this moment, I hereby appoint John Novak to my cabinet as the new Secretary of Defense. Buck, come on over here."

Novak's stomach sank. All eyes were on him. Was this for real? Oakley hadn't mentioned anything about it. Hadn't given him time to think about it. Then again, who was he kidding? The answer was, and would always have been, an unequivocal yes.

As Oakley waited for Novak to make his way over for the obligatory handshake and photo op, he leaned back toward the microphone. "I won't make him speak folks. He didn't know I was going to do this."

Novak stepped up and took the President's hand as the crowd laughed and applauded.

"Congratulations, Secretary."

"Thank you, Mister President. Thank you."

## CHAPTER 52

FEZZ SWUNG the hatch and pushed the rolling tool chest aside.

Through the side door of the garage, he loaded his truck.

It was a gorgeous day. The air was still. The birds were singing. Under Fezz's feet were twenty-four square miles of New England paradise.

All of that might have been true, but he couldn't see it. The only thing he could see was Ian's innocent face, engulfed by the putrid pestilence of reality.

Fezz was no stranger to death. Hell, he'd delivered more than a few to its icy clutches. Destroyed families. Orphaned children. And all without blinking an eye.

But it wasn't always a one-way street. He had lost. Held friends in his arms, promising them they would live, even though he knew it was a lie. Somewhere in the back of his mind, friend or foe alike, the dead lived on. Waiting for a trigger to spawn a momentary recollection.

Ima was no different. A casualty of a cruel and violent world. Collateral damage.

As horrible as Ima's death was, Fezz could already feel the shock and grief receding. Eventually, the memory of the tragedy would recede, leaving only ethereal images of a talented and unique woman he once knew.

## DETACHMENT

Even now, mere hours after she'd perished, it wasn't Ima he mourned. It was Ian. Or rather, who Ian might have been.

Fezz understood the intent behind the whole group giving Ian the news. "It takes a Village," and all that. But he worried it would be overwhelming.

Unless he imagined it, he and Ian had developed a bond far greater than anyone else understood. Greater than Fezz had expected. It was why he needed to be the one to tell him.

When he'd first asked himself why he was so compelled, the answer seemed simple. It was best for Ian. Wasn't it? If not, it was what Ima would have wanted. Right? Or was he only thinking of himself? Because, for some reason, he was affected in a way he had never experienced before.

The reason was moot. The decision had been made.

Fezz put the truck in gear and rolled into the shared driveway.

Next door, the neighbors were getting into their car. Cornelius waved. Fezz pretended not to see him. Ever since Blake had offered Fezz's services, he'd made an effort to avoid the couple. The last thing he needed was to get caught up in a conversation.

The drive to Christa's house was only a few miles, but it felt like a cross-country trip.

North on Beavertail Road, past the old Revolutionary War battery, the pastures of Fort Getty, and the Indian-head rock marking the edge of Mackerel Cove. Up Southwest Avenue with its smattering of civilization, and into the leafy canopy of Narragansett Avenue.

With each mile, came more anxiety.

Ian was a tough kid, he thought. He didn't need coddling. What he needed was help. Someone who could see the big picture. The path to the future.

By the time Fezz pulled in front of the little yellow cape, his nerves had hardened. He knew he would hold it together.

From the porch, he saw Lucy through the storm door. He rapped on the glass.

Lucy opened the door. "Fezz, hi."

"May I?"

"Uh, yeah. Of course," she said with sweet sarcasm, then stepped back to allow him in. "My mom's on the back deck with Ian."

Fezz made his way through the dining room and out onto the deck. Lucy followed him out.

"Fezz!" Ian jumped up from the table and administered the secret handshake the two had spent an hour perfecting the week before. "Is my mom here?"

"No, buddy. Just me. I came to pick you up."

"You didn't need to come out," Christa said. "I already talked to Blake, and was going to bring him home in a little bit."

"I was out and figured I might as well just swing by."

"I'm teaching Christa origami," Ian said. "We're making a swan."

With a childish grin, Christa held up a folded mess of paper. "It kind of looks like a swan, right? Or a hedgehog."

"Ian's been teaching us all kinds of things," Lucy said. "I learned how to solve a Rubik's Cube. Without taking the stickers off."

"He's good at that. Taught me a few things, too. Isn't that right?" He put his hand on Ian's head.

Ian flashed a proud smile.

"Why don't you go grab your stuff," Fezz said. "We should get going."

"Okay. My bag's upstairs."

Ian ran off to get it.

Fezz sighed. "Thank you. Both of you."

"Our pleasure," Christa said. "He was so easy."

"Well, I really appreciate it. I mean, we all appreciate it."

Christa waved off the heaviness of his tone. "Stop. It was nothing. Did you work out whatever you guys were dealing with?"

Fezz knew Christa had already talked to Blake, and no doubt asked the same question. She was fishing for more detail. He felt bad for keeping her in the dark about Ima, but now wasn't the time. He'd let Blake fill her in with whatever story he chose to provide. Still, he didn't want to outright lie.

"There were some complications. It's a long story. But it's been handled."

"Well, I'm glad."

# DETACHMENT

"Can we still come over and use the pool later?" Lucy asked.

"Sure can. Anytime you want. You never have to ask."

Lucy bounced on her toes, a huge grin on her face. "I'll go see if I can help Ian find everything."

"Thanks," Fezz said, as Lucy slid open the screen and closed it behind her.

"You and Gwyn and Lucy have been so good to him. He's been blessed." Fezz approached Christa and lifted his arms in an awkward pose. "Do you mind?"

Fezz didn't know Christa as well as Blake did. As far as he knew, she would think him too forward. But he would have regretted not making an effort.

Christa laughed. "No, Fezz, I don't mind." She walked up to him and graciously accepted the bear hug he offered. "Are you okay?"

"I'm good."

From inside, Fezz could hear Lucy and Ian talking as they came down the stairs.

"I'm gonna—" He pointed toward the screen door.

"Okay," Christa said. "I'll see you later."

"Sure thing." Fezz slid the screen and met Ian inside. "Say 'thank you.'"

Ian held his bag with both hands. "Thank you."

Lucy opened the storm door and Fezz followed Ian out.

Christa and Lucy gathered on the front porch to see them off.

As Ian climbed into the truck, Fezz turned back to Christa and Lucy. "Give my thanks to Gwyn, too, will you?"

"Okay." Christa waved. From inside the cab, Ian waved back.

Fezz got in and the two pulled away.

"Buckle up," Fezz said.

"I know," Ian said, already pulling the seatbelt across his chest and lap. "Oh, wait. I forgot the swan I made for my mom."

Fezz felt a lump in his throat. He swallowed hard. "You can make another one."

Ian didn't respond. His logical little brain probably found practicality in the statement.

At the post office, Fezz turned left onto North Road.

"Where are we going?" Ian asked. "Our house is the other way."

"I know, bud."

For the next couple of miles, Ian didn't speak. He just looked out the window at the marsh and the herd of cattle grazing near the old Dutch windmill at Windmist farm. For the moment, Ian seemed to take no answer as an answer. But it wouldn't last long.

Fezz turned onto the ramp for Route 138. As they crossed the Jamestown Verrazzano bridge, Fezz glanced back at the small island that claimed to be their home. It would be home no longer.

Ian's face scrunched and his eyes squinted. "Are we going to see my mom?"

"Ian," Fezz said. "We need to talk. Man to man, okay?"

"Okay. Man to man."

In the hours to come, he would lay it all out there. Every detail. Well into the night.

Ian wasn't okay. But he would be.

And so would Fezz.

Somewhere out there, in a destination unknown, a new life waited for them both.

# CHAPTER 53

KHAT CANTED the pint glass and pulled the tap handle.

Blake, Griff, Kook, and Haeli waited patiently at their regular table.

"Take your time, Khat," Blake razzed. "No one's thirsty over here."

"Hey, I'm just fillin' in," Khat said. "Fezz is the one who's supposed to play Artie in this joint. Where the hell is he?"

"He went to pick up Ian," Blake said.

Haeli's temples wrinkled. "He did? I thought Christa was bringing him here."

"She was. Actually, she was supposed to be here an hour ago. When I called her, she said Fezz had already picked Ian up. Two hours ago."

"Two hours?" Griff yawned. "Did he get lost?"

"He's telling Ian himself, isn't he?" Haeli said.

"I'd say that's a good bet. We know he wanted it to come from him. Let them have their heart-to-heart."

"That's the way it should be anyway," Kook said. "Fezz is the only one who knows how to talk to the kid."

"Ain't that the truth." Khat struggled to carry five pint glasses at once. He copied Fezz's technique, pinning them against his abdomen, but what he was missing were Fezz's baseball-mitt-sized hands. He managed to drop the lot onto the table without spilling more than ten percent of the liquid. "You know you can all get your own beers, right?"

"Wouldn't be the same," Blake said.

Haeli was first to pick a glass. She held it into the air. "To Ima."

"To Ima," the group repeated.

They drank to another fallen friend.

"It's about time we had a proper debrief," Kook said.

Griff slid Khat's pint across the table. "In that case, Khat can't partake. He was off playing Jimmy Olsen while we were putting our lives on the line."

"Hey. I'll have you know, my role was the most important of all." Khat snatched the beer back and held it with two hands. "It took a lot of convincing to get that guy to run with the story. He was scared. I mean, *scared*. Wanted nothing to do with it."

"What changed his mind?" Haeli asked.

"My powers of persuasion."

"So you threatened him." Blake said.

Khat laughed. "No. I showed him the pictures you took in that warehouse, or barn. After he stopped dry heaving into his wastebasket, he came around. In all seriousness, how can you see what happened to those guys and not want to tell the world?"

Haeli's gaze was fixed on her glass. "It *was* sickening."

"I have to agree with Khat. Without that story being published, Phillips wouldn't have been arrested and Moore wouldn't have resigned. That's a fact."

"Thank God," Griff said. "Oakley is so much better for this country."

"And how about Novak, eh?" Kook gave an approving nod. "Secretary of Defense."

"Good for him," Haeli said. "If I were him, I'd probably want to crawl into a hole."

"Na. Not Novak. That's a tough dude right there." Kook pointed as if Novak were standing nearby.

"You talk to him, Mick?" Khat asked.

Blake took a long swig from his glass. "I did. He gave a quick call after the ceremony. In case I hadn't seen the news."

"What did he say?"

"Just wanted to thank us again. Oh, and he said the investigation is

# DETACHMENT

uncovering a lot more. Apparently, Phillips was taking bribes from all over. They think he was the one who tipped off Maduro that our boys were coming for him."

Kook slammed the table with the meaty part of his fist. "That snake. They never had a chance."

"Not to be a killjoy," Griff said. "But what are we gonna do about the Novak thing?"

"I'm not following," Blake said.

"He knows about this place. He knows your name. And now he's the Secretary of Defense. It's only a matter of time before he makes the connection between us and Switzerland. Shouldn't we be going underground?"

"Maybe Fezz was right." Khat said. "Maybe it's a good time to think about hangin' it up. Trying to get on with a normal life. We could head out to middle America. Get a few little houses in a nice quiet neighborhood. White picket fences. Church on Sundays."

A dead quiet fell over the room. Four stunned faces froze. Then, they burst into laughter.

"You had me goin'," Kook laughed.

"Ass." Blake picked up a cardboard coaster and flung it at Khat. "Buck assured me we'd have nothing to worry about. Honestly, I think he already put two and two together. But he promises he'll never mention anything about us to anyone. And I believe him."

"I believe him too," Haeli said.

"You know," Khat said. "With Novak in the top job at the Pentagon, I don't think we'll need much in the way of advertising. We can be his 'go to,' like Piper's team was to Phillips."

"There's an awful thought," Kook said.

"No. I mean, for the forces of good."

Griff filled his cheeks and blew out the puff of air. "I'm pretty sure Khat still thinks he's in a comic book. 'Forces of Good.' What are we, the Justice League?"

Blake chuckled. Griff wasn't wrong. Khat did tend to have a simplified perspective on the world. But Khat wasn't wrong, either. "As crazy as it sounds, that's not far off. That's pretty much how I left it with Buck."

"Wait." Haeli leaned on her elbows. "What did you say, exactly?"

"I said if he ever found himself in need of back-channel support, not to hesitate to call."

"And?"

"And he said he would."

"He would, like the polite 'sure, I'll keep that in mind,' or he would, like he *will*?"

"I don't know, Haeli. He said he would. What else do you want me to tell you? We'll have to wait and see."

"What I want to know," Khat said through a forced grin, "is who's getting up to grab the next round?"

"I'll do it." Griff stood up and collected the empty glasses. All except for Haeli's, which was still a quarter full.

"I'd be okay if Novak didn't call for six months or so," Kook said. "I don't know what y'all are gonna do, but I'm heading out to Santa Cruz to catch me a couple waves."

"I think we've all earned a little rest and recuperation time," Blake said.

"Nice," Griff said. "I'm gonna work on my explosive ordinance retrieval robot. I'm calling him Shawty."

Blake shook his head. Most people would have thought, *Caribbean* or *Europe*. Not Griff. He was content by himself in the basement, playing with nerdy, albeit useful, toys.

Haeli put her arm around Blake. "You know what that means. We have time to visit your parents, like you said."

"You have parents?" Khat asked.

"Yes! Why does everyone find that so hard to believe?"

"You should call them," Haeli said.

"I have. Twice. They won't answer my calls."

Khat laughed. "I wouldn't answer your calls either if you were my son."

"Maybe when we show up in person, they'll come around." Haeli tapped her feet, the way she always did when she thought she was being cute.

"Yeah. Maybe." Blake wasn't sure it would be that easy. But he was

# DETACHMENT

serious about making the effort. If it meant showing up on their doorstep, then so be it. Anyway, what was the worst that could happen?

Griff came back with the round, in half the time as Khat and with three times the dexterity. "Should someone call Fezz?"

"I have," Khat said. "Two hundred times. He won't pick up."

"Maybe it's just you." Kook jabbed.

"Damn." Khat laughed. "Fezz is givin' me the Mick's parents' treatment."

Haeli pushed her unfinished beer away. "What if he really meant all that stuff about this being no life for Ian and all of that? What if he's not coming back?"

"Preposterous," Blake wanted to say. But was it? Around the table, the sudden glum mood was a good indication no one was quite so sure.

Fezz was working through something. Everyone knew it. But would he abandon them, without so much as a goodbye?

The more Blake thought about it, the more possible it seemed. When he reached into his memory, he couldn't ever recall a time when Fezz wasn't sitting at that table, or one like it. Not only as part of the team, but as its anchor. In the aftermath of the chaos, it was their cleansing ritual.

A strange, sinking feeling surged in his gut. They had been losing him all along. They just didn't want to admit it.

Blake picked up the heavy glass and touched his brow to the rim. Although he hadn't intended to speak the ominous premonition out loud, it snuck its way past his lips and into the silent room.

"And then there were five."

---

Blake's story continues soon. *Pre-order now:*
https://www.amazon.com/dp/B0B1P8NPNN

Join the LT Ryan reader family & receive a free copy of the Jack Noble story, *The Recruit*. Click the link below to get started:
https://ltryan.com/jack-noble-newsletter-signup-1

# THE BLAKE BRIER SERIES

**Blake Brier Series**

*Unmasked*
*Unleashed*
*Uncharted*
*Drawpoint*
*Contrail*
*Detachment*
*Untitled (coming soon)*

# ALSO BY L.T. RYAN

Visit https://ltryan.com/pb for paperback purchasing information.

### The Jack Noble Series

*The Recruit (Short Story)*

*The First Deception (Prequel 1)*

*Noble Beginnings (Jack Noble #1)*

*A Deadly Distance (Jack Noble #2)*

*Thin Line (Jack Noble #3)*

*Noble Intentions (Jack Noble #4)*

*When Dead in Greece (Jack Noble #5)*

*Noble Retribution (Jack Noble #6)*

*Noble Betrayal (Jack Noble #7)*

*Never Go Home (Jack Noble #8)*

*Beyond Betrayal (Clarissa Abbot)*

*Noble Judgment (Jack Noble #9)*

*Never Cry Mercy (Jack Noble #10)*

*Deadline (Jack Noble #11)*

*End Game (Jack Noble #12)*

*Noble Ultimatum (Jack Noble #13)*

*Noble Legend (Jack Noble #14)*

*Noble Revenge (Jack Noble #15) - coming soon*

### Bear Logan Series

*Ripple Effect*

*Blowback*

*Take Down*

*Deep State*

## Rachel Hatch Series

*Drift*

*Downburst*

*Fever Burn*

*Smoke Signal*

*Firewalk - December 2020*

*Whitewater - March 2021*

## Mitch Tanner Series

*The Depth of Darkness*

*Into The Darkness*

*Deliver Us From Darkness - coming Summer 2021*

## Cassie Quinn Series

*Path of Bones*

*Untitled - February, 2021*

## Blake Brier Series

*Unmasked*

*Unleashed - January, 2021*

*Untitled - April, 2021*

## Affliction Z Series

*Affliction Z: Patient Zero*

*Affliction Z: Abandoned Hope*

*Affliction Z: Descended in Blood*

*Affliction Z: Fractured (Part 1)*

*Affliction Z: Fractured (Part 2) - October, 2021*